A Dive

Darkness

Paul Franks

'Every day, society is replenished by millions of people diving into darkness.'
Dan Harmon, Story Structure 102: Pure,
Boring Theory.

Day One

Monday, March 29th, 2027

Chapter One

By seven-thirty, when the apartment buzzer sounded, her ache was so intense she had started to feel sick. Her desperate hope was that the person pressing the buzzer would again wave her magic wand and make her problem, and her ache, disappear.

'Béatrice? Hi! Come up.'

Without saying a word, Béatrice opened the faded, green velvet, lounge curtains and the window behind them. 'That's better! Now I can see you and now you can see the sparkling Seine. And breathe in some of that refreshing Parisian air.'

Béatrice looked at the frozen TV screen.

'What are you watching?

'*Killer in the Village.*'

'Which is?'

'A documentary about the search for the cause of AIDS, made in 1983. It was either that or the Presidential election. I chose AIDS.'

'I very much doubt anyone has ever said that before.'

'No, I suppose not.'

Béatrice sat down at the kitchen table and looked at her friend. 'It's taken you forty years but, finally, you're interested in mine and your father's world. You do know the killer was apprehended over forty years ago, by scientists from L'Académie, obviously.'

'Of course, I knew about AIDS and HIV, but I didn't know L'Académie was involved in its discovery. That gives me another reason to find out more about them. Anyway, what's the big deal, it's hardly a hanging offence, is it?'

'True. Oh, I almost forgot, happy birthday, Anne-Sophie!'

'Happy birthday to us!'

After a hug, Anne-Sophie was handed an envelope and a blue Tiffany's gift bag, inside which was a blue Tiffany's box adorned with the famous white satin bow. Béatrice helped herself to a cup of coffee and a slice of toast whilst her friend stared at the box.

'Can I open it now, or do you want me to wait until this evening?'

'Open it now! Live dangerously, for once.'

Anne-Sophie took a gorgeous silver pendant and matching earrings out of the box. 'Oh, wow! Thank you!' She glanced at Béatrice, 'I'm guessing you got these in Geneva last month, at the same time you bought yourself that fabulous watch.'

'No flies on you. They're *Elsa Peretti Open Heart*.'

Anne-Sophie had no idea who Elsa Peretti was, but that lady had come up trumps with the beautiful pendant and earrings. Béatrice, having swallowed the final crumb of toast and drained the last drop of coffee, looked closely at her friend, and asked her if she was OK.

'Why?'

'You seem distracted, anxious. You've got that look that tells me you've done something you shouldn't, or, more accurately, arranged something you shouldn't.'

'No flies on you either. Yes, I've arranged something I shouldn't.'

Béatrice filled up her cup and took another piece of toast. 'Let me take a wild guess. You've got a date, it's happening this lunchtime, and you're desperately trying to think of a way to back out of it. How am I doing so far?'

'Uncannily well.'

'And, having failed to come up with your own plausible excuse, you're hoping good old pushover Béatrice will, as usual, wave her magic wand and make the bad stuff go away.'

'Something like that, yes.'

'Tell me something, how many times has this happened?'

2

'Too many.'

'Who is it you're expecting me to wave my wand at this time?'

'His name's Michael.'

'And Michael is?'

'An accountant I met at a bereavement support group last month.'

'And his backstory?'

'His wife died of leukaemia two years ago.'

'And two years on he's still going to bereavement support?'

'Yes.'

'So, not only is he, I'm guessing, a decent bloke, but you and he have something in common in terms of trauma, which means you can empathise with each other to your heart's content.'

'Yes.'

'And you want me to conspire with you to do the dirty on this decent, bereaved, traumatised, still suffering, empathetic bloke?'

'Please don't put it like that.'

'How would you like me to put it? This is a bloke who will suffer more trauma by being left standing, if not at the altar, then at least at the restaurant, or wherever it is you are due to be meeting him.'

'That's a bit of an exaggeration.'

'Is it? Really? Come on, please tell me you're joking.'

This was not the reaction Anne-Sophie wanted or expected. She had certainly not received it on the many previous occasions she had asked Béatrice to bail her out. So unexpected was it that, at first, she did not know how to respond. Finally, she said, 'No, I'm not joking.'

'And I'm not helping you. This is your mess. Clean it up.'

'Please, Béatrice.'

'Not this time. Not anytime. Not anymore. I'm not your mother. You're on your own.'

'Béatrice.'

'I have to go. Unlike the rest of France, my work doesn't stop on a public holiday. I'm due in the lab in ten minutes and Stonehouse will kill me if I'm late.' She looked again at Anne-Sophie. 'And even if I did have the time, I still wouldn't help you.'

3

'Béatrice, please.'

'For goodness' sake, you're forty. Don't you think it's way past the time you started digging yourself out of these holes?'

Anne-Sophie looked down at her coffee.

'Even better, isn't it way past the time you stopped digging these holes for yourself in the first place?'

'Of course, I do, it's just...'

'Just what? Come on, quickly, I need to go.'

'It's just today. Meeting him today, of all days. The anniversary. It seems like such a big step.'

'So, why arrange it for today in the first place? Why not tomorrow? Why not Wednesday? Thursday, or Friday? I'm assuming you haven't got anything special lined up. Why don't you arrange to meet him later this week?'

'You're right, I could do that.'

'Anne-Sophie, look at me. How many blokes have you hurt pulling this same build 'em up, knock 'em down' routine?'

'I can't remember.'

'Very convenient. However, I do, and it's at least a dozen.'

'Really?'

'Yes, really. And you do know the definition of insanity, don't you?'

'Yes.'

Béatrice breathed deeply. 'OK, when are you meeting him, or, rather, due to be meeting him?'

'At one.'

'Where?'

'The Café Palais Royal.'

'And you really can't face him.'

'No.'

Béatrice took a sip of her coffee. 'OK, well at least this time show some decency and rearrange the date, yourself. Then if you must deliver a knock-out blow later, do it to his face.'

'I will do. Thank you.'

'You're very welcome. As always.'

Béatrice licked her fingers clean of toast and butter. 'What time's dinner?'

'Any time after five. It's all ready, just needs heating up.'

'Let me guess; lasagne?'

4

'As always. Good old tried and tested.'

'Many times, but delicious every time.'

'I'm sorry I'm so boringly predictable.'

'Now you're exaggerating. I would call you reliable.'

'Like your Swiss watch?'

'Exactly. A bloody expensive one, at that.'

'I'm sure it was.'

'Also as always, I'll bring wine and dessert.'

'Thank you. I'll give you your present tonight. I'm afraid I can't promise you anything as beautiful, or as expensive, as *Elsa Peretti.*'

'That's OK, I'll survive.' Béatrice took hold of Anne-Sophie's hands, 'Hope it goes well at the cemetery this morning. I know how difficult it's going to be for you and I'm sorry I can't be with you.'

'Thank you, I understand. I'll be fine. You go to work and save some lives.'

'I'll try. Don't you go breaking Michael's heart. Not today, anyway.'

With Béatrice departed, Anne-Sophie washed up the dishes then looked at the clock. Just after eight. She glanced up at the sky through the window. It had clouded over rapidly, and it looked very much like rain. The forecast looked like it was going to be accurate, as it usually was when it was a bad one. Just her luck.

She returned to the bathroom and, as her mother had drummed into her since she first picked up a toothbrush, followed her usual, thorough, oral hygiene routine. She thought about what Béatrice had said and could not deny her friend's response to her problem had hurt her. Some oldest and best friend. However, she reluctantly conceded Béatrice was absolutely right. Anne-Sophie was now forty years old. It was beyond time she grew up. Sadly, Béatrice was right about something else. After today, Anne-Sophie did not have anything special lined up that holiday week. Nothing, in fact. She knew she had to get herself a life, but for now nice and quiet was how it had to be. It was the only way she was going to recover.

After applying the faintest trace of red lipstick and putting on the gold cross necklace she always wore on her birthday, she walked to the apartment door. She collected her black umbrella and the keys to her Clio, then put on her black boots and red raincoat, her mother's last birthday present to her, and took a deep breath. She missed her wonderful mother so much that at times it was physically painful. Thérèse had done all in her power to ensure her only child did not miss out on anything when she was growing up but, although Anne-Sophie owed her everything, she also knew her mother was the reason she was reluctant to change things. When would she rip the heart out of her crumbling apartment, start a relationship, get a life, grow up? Probably never, because for Anne-Sophie that all meant moving on from her mother's death and moving on meant moving away from her mother. That was something she could not bear to do.

Her father, however, was a different story. Anne-Sophie rarely, if ever, gave him a thought. After all, his only contributions to her life had been her conception, the room she slept in and her premature birth, the latter a rapid consequence of his typically selfish, final act.

Chapter Two

When she set off in her Clio, it had just begun to rain. By the time she had parked up at the Institut Giacometti on Rue Victor Schoelcher, it was teeming down. The downpour reflected her situation and her mood. This was the first year she had visited Montparnasse cemetery alone and the first year she had two graves to look at. Her anxiety levels had steadily increased over the previous week as she fretted about how she would react when she saw her mother's grave for the first time since the funeral on January 15th. However, she was feeling surprisingly calm as she passed through the cemetery gates and walked past the Alfred Dreyfus tomb located ten yards from her destination. At that moment, her main concern was the increasingly heavy rain; thank goodness she had come prepared.

Standing in front of her parents' graves, she manoeuvred the umbrella and took out of her shoulder bag some thoughts she had jotted down in bed the previous night. Thoughts she wanted to share with her mother. How much she missed her. How she was slowly coming to terms with her absence. How the so-called police investigation into the hit-and-run had come up with absolutely nothing.

'Mum, I'm so sorry. They got away with it.'

Anne-Sophie had also wanted to tell her mother it was high time she renovated the bathroom, the kitchen, in fact the entire apartment. High time the whole wreck was dragged kicking and screaming into the twenty-first century but, when it came to the crunch, she lost her nerve.

'You see, Mother, even in death, I am in thrall to you.'

She put her notes back into her bag, laid down her spray of freesias against her mother's slab, knelt down and kissed it. As she had not written anything for her father, she ignored his headstone and instead did a one-hundred-and-eighty-degree sweep around the cemetery. Every year, she was struck that, although this was the second largest cemetery in Paris, covering forty-seven acres with thirty-five thousand plots, she hardly ever saw any other mourners. Perhaps it was due to the early hour, or perhaps because it was a holiday, or perhaps both, but once again, apart from one, elderly, shortish man, dressed head-to-toe in black, who was peering closely at the Dreyfus tomb, there was no-one else in sight.

Anne-Sophie took a photo of her mother's headstone and then checked the time, nine o'clock. She had at least eight hours until Béatrice's arrival. How was she going to kill those hours? Normally, she loved to visit the exquisite Art Nouveau Institut, but it was closed on Mondays, so this year that wasn't an option.

Before she decided her next move, she thought about how she had begun her holiday two days ago by remaining in bed, in an attempt to sleep off the physical and mental exhaustion she felt after returning to work a fortnight earlier. An exhaustion that had gone up several notches after she had single-handedly blocked a cyberattack at seven o'clock on the Friday evening, just as she was all set to leave the office.

Yesterday, she had ventured as far as the lounge sofa and checked out what Netflix had to offer. Flicking through the channels her final choice boiled down to *The Godfather* or *Killer in the Village*. She had watched the film many times, not least because her mother had told her many times that her father had been obsessed with anything to do with New York and that *The Godfather* was by far his favourite movie. Such a favourite she would have been named in honour of the film's protagonist if her father had not died four hours before she was born. Michaela Montreau! Imagine. Thank goodness her father had not, on top of everything else, left her that particular legacy. Instead, her mother had named Anne-Sophie after her grandmother, which sounded so much nicer.

Anne-Sophie knew *The Godfather* inside out, but apart from the fact it was deadly, she shamefully, embarrassingly, knew very little about AIDS. She did not really know what it was, but she did know it was vitally important not to catch HIV. Not that there was much chance of that. Béatrice constantly reminded Anne-Sophie that she could never love anyone as much as she loved her mother, and she readily conceded the obvious truth of that. Still, she was a healthy woman, with normal physical needs, but she also had high standards, and the IT suite at Banque Nord did not represent a buyer's market when it came to attractive, eligible, dating material.

Anyway, Anne-Sophie had reasoned that a holiday Sunday with nothing much else to do was as good a time as any to start building upon her barely baseline knowledge about AIDS. However, she had not got beyond the documentary's opening titles when her exhaustion reasserted itself and she nodded off. Waking up just after five o'clock, she panicked about preparing the lasagne and the salad, and *Killer in the Village* had been put on the back burner.

Now, as it was still raining, she decided she would go back to the apartment, calling at *Pastry Sébastien Degardin* en-route to buy a couple of baguettes and delicious tartes, and resume watching the documentary. In the afternoon she would walk down to Square René Viviani and buy Béatrice's birthday present. Although her budget would not stretch anywhere close to *Elsa Peretti*, she should be able to find her friend something artisanal and sparkly.

For a brief, blissful moment all was well with her mind and body, then she had a sudden, unpleasant thought and her ache returned. 'Damn, Michael.'

It was less than four hours until she was due to meet him. Time was running out to find a valid excuse and it looked very much as if she would have to go back to her default 'sore throat, possible flu, don't want to pass it on to anyone' cop-out. Tried, tested, timeless and, most importantly, impossible to disprove without a face-to-face meeting.

Heading back to her Clio, she nodded at the old man dressed in black, still intently studying the Dreyfus tomb. She noticed he was carrying three bunches of flowers and wondered what he was and who he was. A History Professor? Perhaps a descendant of the great man? Imagine! Béatrice would not have hesitated to ask him these questions. However, she wasn't Béatrice, didn't have anything like her confidence, so she didn't. She reached the cemetery gates fully intending to continue walking to her Clio, but something made her turn around. The old man was now standing in front of her parents' graves. He had placed one bunch by each headstone and was now standing in front of them with his head bowed. This was strange. It had never happened before.

9

She had never seen any other flowers at her father's grave. What was going on?

She decided to linger, hoping that, because the rain was getting even heavier, the strange man would not spend as much time with her parents as he had staring at Dreyfus's grave. Fortunately, she only had to wait another five minutes before he started walking towards her. Unfortunately, he walked very slowly, but at least this allowed her plenty of time to study him. He was grey-haired, bespectacled, short, and portly, but he was elegantly dressed in a long black coat and black bowler hat. The man walked so painfully slowly that by the time he was ten yards away the rain had gone up yet another level in terms of ferocity.

Watching the man inch his way towards her, she had too much time to think. The closer he got, the more anxious she became. However, despite her rising panic and the torrential rain, she could make out that his eyes were red. Had he been crying?

Now, the man was almost within touching distance. Anne-Sophie was in full-scale fight-or-flight mode. She had a very bad feeling about this man. Who was he? Why had he stood at her parents' graves? What did he want? Now, he was right in front of her. It was too late for flight, and she was no fighter. She was trapped.

Chapter Three

The stranger very slowly took off his hat, bowed and presented her with the third bunch of flowers.

'Happy fortieth birthday, Anne-Sophie.'

The stunned recipient of the flowers now had a choice: get soaked walking fifty yards to her Clio and never see this man again; get soaked walking fifty yards to the Chez Papa on Rue Gassendi and find out who this complete stranger, who had lain flowers at her parents' graves, and knew it was her fortieth birthday, was.

'Are you hungry?'

'I am rather peckish, yes.'

Chez Papa it was.

The fifty yards seemed to take forever but eventually she steered her companion to a window seat in the brasserie. Anne-Sophie gave her flowers and the man's sopping overcoat and hat to an attentive waiter. She hoped the coat and hat would dry sufficiently during the thirty minutes she intended their visit to Chez Papa to last. At the end of that half hour, she would have found out who he was and why he had visited her parents' graves. Then, as she could not imagine he had driven to the cemetery, she would walk him to whichever of the three close-by Métro stations was his preferred choice. At the station she would thank him for coming to the cemetery, and for her beautiful flowers, wish him well and he would make his return journey to wherever it was he lived. That would be that. No further communication would be required. That would take the time to ten o'clock, then she could decide what to do about her date. Apart from fobbing off Michael, she was now concerned that, after her soaking, an actual dose of 'flu was not out of the question, which, as Béatrice would not fail to point out that evening, would be no less than Anne-Sophie deserved.

After she ordered two Crêpes Suzette and café cremes, she broke the ice, 'Thank you for the flowers, Monsieur...'

'Oh, you must forgive me for my appalling manners. With all the excitement of meeting you, I completely forgot to introduce myself.'

Because it arrived quickly their order paradoxically produced a further delay in the proceedings as the still unknown Monsieur ate his 'delicious' crêpe almost as slowly as he walked. After he had at last finished, she tried once again, 'Did you enjoy that, Monsieur...'

'I am so sorry, I forgot again! I am not usually so lax in my manners. My name is Simon, Philippe Simon, a journalist. As you can see.'

Philippe Simon
'Crime Correspondent'
Le Parisien
10, Boulevard de Grenelle
75738 Paris Cedex 15
Tél : 01 87 39 71 00

She looked at the clock, nine-forty-five. She was already halfway through the thirty minutes she had allotted for this conversation. After ordering two more café cremes she decided to crack on, 'I couldn't help noticing you seemed to be upset at the cemetery. You obviously knew my parents.'

'I first met your father in January 1977.'

'Wow, really.'

'Yes. Fortuitously, I joined *Le Parisien* at precisely the same moment your father started working at L'Académie. As I discovered at a Rotary Club meeting, he had returned to France only a month earlier.'

'Returned? From where?'

'Twelve months in the United States.'

'I knew he loved New York but I didn't know he'd spent a year in the States.'

'Jean-Marie adored America, so much so that he went back there several times during the decade I knew him. However, to get back to my narrative, he had not let the grass grow under his feet during that first month. He was elected on to the Rotary

12

Club's Executive Committee, after what appears to have been an unusually heated contest.'

'Heated in what way?'

'The loser was very bitter, telling all and sundry he had been robbed. So bitter, he walked out of the Club and never came back.'

'Who was the bitter loser?'

'I have no idea. I do know the whole episode summed up one aspect of your father's character; his determination.'

'A trait he did not pass on to me.'

'Perhaps. What I can say is that we were best friends. In fact, I was best man at his wedding to Thérèse, your wonderful mother. May God rest her soul.'

'You knew she was killed, on Christmas Eve?'

'Of course; I came to her funeral.'

'I don't remember seeing you.'

'I slipped in at the back as the Mass was beginning. I slipped away again as it ended. A terrible business. A tragic loss. For you. For everyone connected with her.'

She sipped her café crème and studied him. If he had not cried before in the cemetery, he was certainly on the verge of tears now.

'If you were my father's best friend and best man at his wedding, why didn't you visit us after he died? I don't recall ever seeing you, in forty years.'

'Your mother did not want to see me.'

'That can't be true.'

'I am not lying.'

'Why didn't she want to see you?'

'She blamed me for your father's death.'

'Why?'

'She said I let him down.'

'And did you?'

'Yes, but not deliberately. I would never have let your father down on purpose.'

She looked at him, saw tears welling up in his eyes again and took his hands in hers. 'I believe you.'

His tears then flowed freely. 'I loved your father. I could never have done anything to hurt him, or your mother.'

13

She was suddenly pleased the lighting was low and that she had chosen a window seat, well away from the other patrons.

'How did you know today is my birthday?'

'How could I not know it? Less than two hours after your father's body was discovered on that hideous Sunday, your mother was rushed to Salpêtrière. Afterwards, even though Thérèse said she did not want anything to do with me, for your father's sake I kept my eyes on you both. More practically, the very day after your birth, I set up a small savings account in your name with Banque Est.' He slowly reached down and fumbled around inside his briefcase. 'Today, I give the savings book to its rightful owner.'

Anne-Sophie took hold of the open book and almost spat out her café crème. 'Fifty-thousand euros!'

'Enough perhaps to start up your own cybersecurity consultancy business? I hear from my more up-to-date colleagues it is a growing industry.'

'My God, this is too much. I really don't deserve this. I cannot accept it.'

'Of course, you can. You must! It is in your name; legally, it is yours. Besides you would not wish to make a sad old man, without children of his own, your own godfather, even sadder.'

'My godfather?'

'Yes, Jean-Marie and Thérèse, jointly and wholeheartedly, agreed to grant me that honour. However, I could not attend your christening because of the anger your mother felt towards me.'

She ran her finger around the plate. 'Did she never forgive you?'

'No. Thérèse was strong-willed. Of course, she was very angry, and said I had as good as killed your father. I do not blame her for her anger but the pain of earthly separation from you both, as well as the eternal separation from your father, nearly killed me too.' His head dropped and he started weeping again. 'I was in a bad way for a long, long time.'

'What can I say? I feel desperately sorry for you, and...' she paused for a second, closed her eyes, took a breath, 'and I feel anger towards my mother.'

14

He looked up. 'Do not, please! You must not. She lost her husband in dreadful circumstances. The stress and trauma for her were immense and she went into premature labour as a result.'

He took Anne-Sophie's hand. 'Thérèse was an incredible woman who did a wonderful job of protecting and raising you by herself. Don't be angry with her. Anger is a wasted human emotion and time, as I know all too well, is too precious to waste.'

It was already ten-fifteen and, having decided that her immediate curiosity had been satisfied, she stood up and reached for his coat and hat.

'Thank you, Monsieur Simon for coming to the cemetery. Thank you for mine and my parents' delightful flowers, and for an incredible amount of money I don't deserve, but for which I'm very grateful. I have your card and I promise to call you very soon. Now, would you like me to walk you to your Métro station?'

After waiting for thirty seconds, during which time he showed not the slightest sign of moving, she sat back down. He looked at her.

'The flowers and money are important, but they are not the main reason I came to the cemetery.'

'Oh? What then?'

Chapter Four

'I came because time is running out.'

When she asked him what he meant, he broke down. Because of his physical and emotional exhaustion, she felt she had no choice but to brave the rain, run to the Clio and park it directly outside the brasserie. It took five minutes for her and the waiter to help her godfather to the exit and into the car. From there, apart from the detour to *Pastry Sébastien Degardin*, she drove directly to her Saint-Victor apartment. It was a very good job the block had recently installed a lift, as, without it, Anne-Sophie was certain Philippe would not have managed the stairs to her first-floor apartment.

She sat him down in the lounge, made a pot of coffee and again asked him to explain his words. He broke down again. Eventually, after ten minutes, several sips of coffee, and a tarte, he recovered. 'I'm sorry. You must think I am a silly old man.'

She sat down beside him and clasped his hands. 'You're a silly old man for thinking it.'

'You are being very kind to me considering I am a stranger.'

'You're my godfather.' She looked at him. 'How old are you?'

'Seventy-six. The …'

'Exact same age my father would have been if he hadn't been so selfish. You were his best friend, best man and, best of all, unlike him, you have many good years yet left in front of you.'

His tears welled up again. 'If only that were true. However, in many ways, I am glad the opposite is the case.'

'What do you mean?'

'If I had not been told my news, I would not have come here today.'

She held his hands tighter. 'What news?'

'Twelve months ago, my doctor told me I had two years to live, possibly three. Seventy-two hours ago, the same doctor told me I only have weeks left.'

'What's wrong with you?'

16

'Cancer. My lungs. Riddled.'

'I'm so sorry.'

'Don't be. As a very wise woman once said to me, be glad we said hello, not sad we say goodbye.'

'Wise woman?'

'Your mother. A very wise woman.'

'Oh.'

He sat back and released his hands from hers. 'In some ways my diagnosis is a blessing.'

'How's that possible?'

'Simple cause and effect. If I had not been informed that my time was almost up, I would not be here now. For a year I have known my condition was terminal. Until Friday I did not know how terminal. Knowing the end was much closer than I thought, and necessity being the mother of invention, I made up my mind.'

'To do what?'

'To visit the cemetery much earlier in the day than in previous years.'

She sat back. 'You've been there before?'

'Every year, for forty years.'

'I had no idea.'

'Today, to my extreme sorrow, for the first time I, like you, had two graves to visit.'

'Before today, what time of day did you visit?'

'Always after lunch. After observing you both from afar, I knew you and your dear mother went there after breakfast. I had no reason to think you would break that tradition this year.'

'Never. Not now my mother is buried there too.'

'Of course. So, having reasoned you would be there early this morning I made sure I was there at the same time. Now, for the first time in forty years, I am sitting inside this lounge. It's as if I have never been away. Remarkable.'

'You've been here before? Sorry, stupid question. Of course, you have.'

'Every Wednesday I came here for supper; marvellous meals prepared by your mother. What a wonderful cook she was! Magnifique! And every course washed down with a delicious wine chosen by Jean-Marie who was a veritable sommelier.'

His face had lit up and he looked years younger. 'Staying overnight was obligatory. In that room over there in fact, even whilst your father was creating the nursery for the baby who was coming ever closer. The baby that would complete his and Thérèse's happiness.'

'Is that what he told you?'

'Yes.'

'So, on top of everything else he was a liar.'

'Sorry?'

She stood up and walked to the window. The rain was lashing down. She looked at the clock, ten past eleven. Two hours until her date. 'Has the lounge changed much?'

'Not really. The only difference I have noticed is that there are no photos of your father. There used to be many.'

'I took them down after mother died.'

'Why?'

'He let mother and me down, badly. Except for anger, I have no feelings towards my father.'

'Anne-Sophie…'

'That's all I want to say about him.'

'Your father was a good man, the best.'

'Such a good man he put himself and his work before everything else, including his pregnant wife and his unborn child.'

'No. Never. He was devoted to Thérèse from the first day he met her, just before Christmas 1980. I remember him telling me all about her the next evening at the Rotary Club. He told me he had met the woman he was going to marry. I am sure you know she worked at Banque Nord on the other side of the Garden. The same place you work now.'

'You know where I work?'

'As your godfather, even an absentee one, I've followed your every step these past forty years.'

'Oh.'

'Jean-Marie told me your mother worked behind the counter, was very proficient and that she had a lovely smile. He was absolutely smitten. So smitten, he was accused of robbery.'

'Again! Who by, this time?'

18

'By Thérèse's then boyfriend who was understandably very angry at your father, the thief who stole his girlfriend! Ha, ha. Imagine.'

'What about later? After the honeymoon period? Didn't he spend all his time at work?'

'Naturally, he worked hard, to make Thérèse even more proud of him and to help pay the mortgage on this apartment. However, his routine was to go in very early and leave at five. He did not work evenings or weekends, as those were his times with Thérèse. They were to be his times with you too. When the doctor confirmed she was pregnant he was ecstatic. They'd been trying for a couple of years and now, success! The cherry on top of the icing on the cake. He could not wait to be a father. Your father.'

She took a long drink of coffee. 'Was there another reason why you came to the cemetery this morning?'

'Ah, you are very perceptive, like both your parents.'

'Tell me.'

'I want to ask your help. However, after what you have just told me, I am not sure it is a good idea.'

'Why?'

'The reason I want your help concerns your father.'

'What about my father?'

'I want to obtain justice for Jean-Marie.'

'Justice?'

Chapter Five

'I want to find out who killed him, and why.'

She made a fresh pot of coffee and sat down opposite Philippe. 'I'm sorry, I don't understand you. What do you mean?'

'I want to find out who was responsible for your father's death.'

'I heard what you said, I just don't get it. He was responsible for his own death. Nobody else had anything to do with it.'

'Now I do not understand you. What do *you* mean, Jean-Marie was responsible for his own death?'

'You told me he was your best friend, surely you know?'

'What do you believe happened?'

'Father killed himself. Committed suicide.'

Philippe took a sip of coffee and looked at her. 'Ah, that explains the hidden from view framed photographs, your feelings towards your father and your comment earlier about his selfishness. Who told you this?'

'Mother of course. Who else?'

He took her hands and looked her directly in the eyes. 'Believe me, Jean-Marie did not kill himself.'

She shook off his hands stood up. 'What are you talking about? When I was growing up, every time I asked Mother why Father wasn't with us, she told me he'd killed himself. This was the final, fatal manifestation of his selfishness, with its main result being my mother giving birth to me a month premature.'

'Anne-Sophie...'

She started pacing around the lounge. 'You know we meant so little to him he couldn't even be bothered to write a note?'

'Perhaps....'

'So, what right have you to come here, my mother's apartment, and accuse her of lying? No wonder she cut you out of our lives. You're asking me to disbelieve everything my mother told me about my father. That's impossible. I would like you to finish your coffee and go.'

'Anne-Sophie...'

'Drink up, leave and make your own way to the Métro.'

He reached into his briefcase and produced some sheets of paper. 'Please look at these.'

'Why? What are they?'

'Photocopies of newspaper cuttings. Please sit down and read them. Once you have read them, I will go.'

After a minute's further pacing, she sat down, took the copied sheets, and started reading. *They* were two *Le Parisien* articles both written by Philippe. The first, dated March 31st, 1987, reported that,

'The tragic death of a leading L'Académie scientist is being treated as non-suspicious by the authorities. According to sources inside the Palais de Justice, the explanation for Jean-Marie Montreau's death is a straightforward one, suicide.'

She took a gulp of coffee. The second article had been tucked away on page twenty-two, near the bottom. It contained a two-line summary of the inquest carried out into the death of her father.

'The verdict was, as has been widely trailed by the Palais de Justice, suicide.'

'I must apologize for the inquest report article but there was virtually nothing left once my editor finished with it.'

'You wrote more?'

'Much more, but ninety-nine per cent of the draft ended up in his wastepaper basket.'

'Oh.'

She stood up again. 'Anyway, I've done what you asked of me; I've read the articles. Verdict suicide, an open and shut case. Your beloved Jean-Marie could not face up to the responsibility of being a father, my father, and took the coward's way out.'

'Anne-Sophie...'

Now she was verging on tears. 'Can you just leave me alone and let me enjoy the rest of my birthday in peace.'

'Hear me out first. Sit down, please.'

21

She looked at the clock, eleven-thirty; she couldn't believe it had only been four hours since Béatrice opened the curtains. It felt more like four months. She sat down and took a deep breath. 'What?'

'Do you notice anything strange about the date of the second article?'

She looked again. 'No.'

'My inquest article appeared in *Le Parisien* on April 1st, 1987. The inquest took place on March 31st, the day before the report was printed. This was only two days after March 29th, when your father had, so the Palais said, committed suicide.'

She tried to process what he was telling her. 'I still don't get it.'

'Please read it again.'

She re-read the inquest article more carefully, then looked at him. 'The only thing I can think of is that it usually takes longer than two days to organize an inquest. I mean, it took a decade to sort out Princess Diana's. Obviously, I'm no expert but, presumably, at the very least, there would have been an autopsy, a post-mortem. What about witness statements? The police must have interviewed Mother and Father's colleagues. Surely, they should have been interested in hearing what people who knew my father had to say, even if only to confirm their theory it was suicide.'

She looked at him. 'I admit the timings don't add up. It's a real shame your editor binned the draft.'

'Yes, fortunately I kept my original notes in a box.' He produced another, much larger, sheaf of papers. 'Here they are.'

Anne-Sophie felt more than a tingle of curiosity as she read through the notes. It quickly became apparent Philippe had questioned not only the haste of the inquest but the speed of the entire investigation. He quoted her mother saying the police were already inside her apartment when she returned after visiting a friend.

'You spoke to Mother?'

'Briefly. I received a tip-off and got here just before your mother was taken to hospital. As you can imagine there was a great deal going on. Police, Ambulance, Rubberneckers. People going in and out of the block. Thérèse was obviously in a bad way. She had pains in her stomach. I feared the worst for her, and you. Thank God you were both ok. She was so strong that she was able to return to the apartment the next afternoon, by which time it was immaculate, spotless.'

'Did she bring me home with her?'

'No, you were in hospital for a week after you were born.'

'Really? Why?'

'There was a problem with your lungs. Bronchiolitis. It was touch and go a couple of times.'

'Touch and go?'

'You were in the neonatal ICU for three days.'

'How do you know?'

'I rang the hospital each day until you came home.'

She hugged him. 'Thank you.' Then she looked down at her hands. 'I'm sorry I shouted at you.'

'Not a problem. I understand. It has all been a shock, on today of all days.'

'That's an understatement.' She sat down and resumed her scrutiny of the notes. 'Did mother go to the inquest?'

'Yes, but I only spoke to her very briefly after. She left very quickly. She was extremely angry and upset. It was the last time we spoke before she cut me out of her life, and yours.'

'Angry with whom? What?'

'At the process or lack of. No testimonies, no post-mortem. No Malherbe. No-one from L'Académie, or anywhere else for that matter. There were no police or psychiatric reports. Thérèse was not called to give a witness statement, no one was. I think she shouted the word 'whitewash' several times, very loudly.'

'Wow!'

'Your mother felt due procedure had not been followed, as indeed it had not.'

She leaned forward and looked at him directly. 'Why hadn't it?'

'Someone wanted this done and dusted in double quick time.'

'Who? Why?'

'That's why I came here, after forty very long years, to appeal for your assistance to help me try to finally work it all out and piece it all together before it was too late.'

'Why didn't you follow your suspicions up at the time?'

'My editor blocked me from writing any more about it; blocked anybody from writing about your father's death. In fact, every crime journalist in Paris was blocked by every newspaper editor in the city from writing about it. I know, they all told me.'

She stood up. 'Why? Why would they do that?'

Chapter Six

Before Philippe could reply, Anne-Sophie's phone buzzed.

'Damn.'

'Happy birthday! Hope you're still ok for one o'clock. Really looking forward to it. See you there. Michael.'

'Everything alright?'

'Yes, fine.'

'What is it?'

'Sorry, I just need to reply. It'll only take a second.'

'Hi. Thank you. So sorry, I'm going to have to cancel. Something unexpected has come up. Speak soon. A-S.'

Now she felt relief, not anxiety, surging through her. The out-of-nowhere arrival of her godfather had been a godsend. She had extricated herself from her date with Michael without having to lie and incur a guilty conscience, a double win. That crisis now resolved she could give Philippe all her attention. After another half an hour, he would be gone, and her life could return to its normal equilibrium. Suddenly, she was looking forward even more to that evening's joint birthday meal with Béatrice and popped a bottle of Crémant de Loire into the fridge.

'All sorted. Now, where had we got to?'

'I was just explaining there had been a de facto ban on press reporting of your father's death.'

She checked the time, eleven forty-five. Now her anxiety about meeting Michael had disappeared, she felt ravenous.

'Would you like some lunch?'

'Please, that would be lovely, thank you.'

She stood up and looked out of the window. It was still raining. If anything, it was even heavier than when they had left Chez Papa. She went into the kitchen and rooted around in the fridge. Ten minutes later they were sitting down and tucking into a ham salad which Philippe described as 'delicious.'

She looked at him. 'Well! This has been a morning of surprises and no mistake. Turns out neither of my parents were the people I thought they were. I thought my mother was perfect and I thought my father wasn't fit to lace her shoes. Turns out I was wrong on both counts. Mother lied to me. She made me believe Father was interested only in his career and, not being able to cope with the pressure of that *and* becoming a father, took the easy way out.' She took a sip of water. 'You know, at first, I merely resented him. Then resentment turned to anger, which morphed into hate. Why did she do it? How could she do it?'

'Protection. Love.'

'What, she lied to me because she wanted to protect me, because she loved me? Come on, I'm not Harry Potter and you're no Dumbledore, you'll have to do better than that.'

'Thérèse knew that what happened to your father was no suicide. Jean-Marie loved her, and he could not wait to love you. Your nursery was the personification of that love. I notice, despite all your professed hatred towards Jean-Marie, you still sleep in the room he made for you and still wear the cross he gave your mother as a Christmas present that very first December they met. The cross you touch whenever you are thinking about something.'

'Get to your point.'

'So, if suicide is ruled out, what is left? It could hardly have been a tragic accident.'

She stared at him. 'My God.'

'Precisely. Thérèse knew your father had been killed.'

'It doesn't make any sense. Who would want to kill him? He was a scientist for god's sake, someone making a positive contribution to society. Not someone doing the opposite, like a rapist or a murderer.'

'As I said, this is why I came to you; to help me fill in the gaps.'

'Why me? I'm not a detective, I've never investigated anything in my life.'

'Remind me, what is your job?'

'Bank cybersecurity analyst.'

'But you have never investigated anything? Really?'

Anne-Sophie acknowledged Philippe had a point. Of course, she had investigated many cases of suspicious cyber activity at Banque Nord, the one she had dealt with last Friday evening being just the latest episode in a long-running series. She had also researched many more actual cases, including the Morris Worm, Levin Hack and Melissa Virus, for her online qualifications.

'Investigating cybercrime is one thing, evidence in these investigations is mostly, by definition, digital in nature. Investigating a possible murder, a forty-year-old murder, is a completely different kettle of fish.'

'I agree but digital or not, the basic principles are the same. Finding and looking at evidence, evaluating it and presenting your case to the authorities.'

'But-'

'I know that your cyber-skills will be very useful in all manner of ways if you agree to help me. However, it will not be without risk.'

'Meaning?'

'You may have to get very close to, perhaps even cross, the boundaries of legality. Are you comfortable with that?'

'No, I'm not! I've never knowingly broken the law. Well, apart from taking a puff of a joint once at university. Oh, and a couple of speeding fines, but I didn't speed deliberately.'

'Of course not. However, as I explained, time is running out, so I must know, will you help me or not?'

She stood up and walked around the lounge all the while touching her cross. After a minute's pacing, she sat down again. 'I have to say no. This is crazy. What makes you think I can help you? I'm certainly not the best person to ask. I'm probably not in the top one million people in this city. I'm not a detective, I'm a computer geek. A not very successful one at that. Seriously, you would be much better off asking the police or a private detective to help you.'

'I doubt the police would entertain me for a second. They barely have the resources to deal with the here and now, never mind re-open a forty-year-old case. As for a private detective, my salary does not cover such an expense.'

'I could pay for it. Out of the fifty-thousand euros I did not possess until an hour ago.'

'It is your assistance, expertise and commitment I seek, not your money.'

'Another thing, despite what Mother said at the time, I've no idea if my father was killed. For all I know it could just have been the ramblings of an upset and angry widow, a traumatised new mother whose hormones were flying all over the place. I'm going to have to see and hear more convincing evidence than, with all due respect, your very brief newspaper articles before I commit to anything.'

'However, you are not saying no?'

'I'm not, but to spend my precious annual leave pursuing this I need to be convinced it's more than a wild goose chase.'

'This is no wild goose chase I can assure you and whilst you may not be a detective, you have a motivation no one else shares.'

'Really? What?'

'You need to find out what happened to your father. No one else, not even I, can share that motivation.'

'As you've said twice already, your time is running out. You have more than enough motivation to discover what really happened.'

'Agreed, but you have more; the kind of motivation that will give you the moral licence to use your technological skills to cross lines if required.'

'If I was caught doing something illegal, I'd lose my job. I can't afford that.'

He stood up. 'I understand. You would rather stay here, in your cave.'

'What does that mean?'

'Have you read Plato?'

'No, I prefer Dan Brown.'

'In Plato's *Allegory of the Cave*, people leave the cave in order to find fulfilment. To find out the truth of what happened to your father and why it happened, you will have to leave your cave, this apartment.' He took a sip of coffee and looked at her. 'I think today it would be called 'Plato's Safe Space.''

'I'm sure it would.'

'Anyhow, you would be doing a reverse Plato.'

'Now you've really lost me.'

'The cave was a dark place and when people left it, they went out into the light. To find out the truth you will have to cross the line and enter a dark place, perhaps a very dark place.'

'You're no salesman.'

'I am sorry. Colleagues have told me numerous times that I over complicate matters.'

'If your cave analogy is anything to go by, they're right.'

'There is something else you have to consider very carefully.'

'Go on.'

'Your mother was right to want to protect you.'

'Of course, she was. She was my mother.'

'I refer to something more than a mother's natural instinct. As we have both mentioned several times, my time is running out, so let me place my cards on the table. I think dark forces killed your father.'

'Ah, you read Dan Brown too.'

'This is no joke.'

'Which of the 'dark forces' in particular are you referring to?'

'The ones that could kill a man and remove him from history in the space of three days.'

'What?'

'Tell me, have you ever entered Jean-Marie Montreau into a search engine?'

'No.'

'Do not waste your time; nothing comes up. As far as the internet is concerned, your father does not exist. Never existed.'

'Oh.'

'Those same dark forces have been shadowing my every step for the past forty years.'

'What?'

'My phone has been tapped, emails hacked, apartment broken into. I could go on.'

'It sounds exactly like Dan Brown.'

'It does.'

'You said before that I needed to find out what happened to my father. Need is a strong word. What did you mean by it?'

'For two reasons you no longer have a choice.'

'What happened to free will?'

'Ah, you do know something of philosophy.'

'I attended a talk once at university, mainly because of the free wine and cheese. Why do I no longer have a choice?'

'First, you need to establish a psychological connection with your father. It's clear to me that your mother, for all the right reasons, cut you off emotionally from your father. I'm no psychologist but helping me in my quest could be an excellent way of helping you to learn about, and connect with, your father. And, you must not forget, this could be your last chance to do so.'

'As you astutely commented, you're no psychologist. Reason number two?'

'You are in mortal danger.'

She sat forward. 'Me! In danger?'

'Thanks to me coming to the cemetery, and now to the apartment, the dark forces will be shadowing you too. If they were not already.'

'What?'

'You are a marked woman, may have been since you were born. Like me, the dark forces probably know everything about you. They will hunt you down like they hunted down Jean-Marie.'

'I haven't done anything wrong.'

'Neither had your father. Neither have I.'

She took another, bigger, drink of water. 'Bloody hell.'

'That's what I meant by your mother protecting you. She was so aware of, and frightened by, these dark forces, that she tried to shut out everything, and everybody, connected to your father's world, including me. That's why she lied to you about Jean-Marie, to protect you. It was the only way to save you. This is your safe space. Like Plato's cave, it is a prison, but it is safe, or it was, up until this morning, and I greeted you at Montparnasse.'

'God Almighty' She stood up, paced around, and then looked at him. 'And you agreed with her keeping me imprisoned?'

'Whilst she was alive, albeit reluctantly, yes. Now she is dead, no. That is why, for the first time in forty years, I arrived at the cemetery at the same time as you. I believed you deserved to know the truth about your father and your mother. I believed I was the person best qualified to tell you the truth, in fact, the only person. I knew this was my last opportunity to do so because....'

'Time is running out.'

'Correct.'

She sat down. He took her hands and looked at her. 'I meant it when I said you have unique levels of motivation, emotional and physical. Also, if you want to live, you do not have a choice.'

'What?'

'It is a matter of life and death, literally, your life, your death. Like your father, the dark forces will not hesitate to remove you, all trace of you.'

'My god.' She looked at him, 'What can I do about it? If anything?'

'The only way you can save your life is to find out who took your father's. To do that, you must leave your safe space. You must leave your cave.'

'And go where?'

'Into the darkness.'

Chapter Seven

Anne-Sophie was again moved to touch her cross when Philippe asked her after lunch whether or not she had made up her mind to help him.

'Not yet, I'm still coming to terms with your callousness.'

'What do you mean?'

'You've put my life in danger, deliberately.'

'Are you telling me you would have preferred not to know the truth? That it had died with me instead?'

'At this precise moment, yes. It's not pleasant thinking I should avoid standing in front of the window of my own apartment, just in case the dark forces are watching me, waiting for their moment to pull the trigger.'

'I think with all due respect you are being rather over-dramatic. This is not *The Godfather*.'

'That's easy for you to say. Very easy.'

'You need to decide quickly. If I have to do this alone, I would much rather know sooner than later.'

'With all due respect, you've had forty years to make your decision. You expect me to make mine in,' she checked the clock, 'forty minutes.'

'Another, with even more respect, exaggeration.'

'Apart from your diagnosis, is there any other reason why you're rushing me into making a decision?'

'An event is happening this Friday which represents a very big opportunity.'

'Tell me more.'

'I will but only if you agree to help me.'

Their eyes locked for ten seconds, then she poured them both some coffee. 'What else do you remember about my father's inquest?'

'Mainly, the speed of it. I was expecting a long, drawn-out affair: Start; Adjourn; Reconvene at a later date. That kind of thing.'

'And the other journalists? What were they expecting?'

'There were no other journalists there, I was the only one.'

'Really?'

'Unfortunately, yes. There is no question this was an important story, full of public interest and a certain amount of voyeurism.'

'Voyeurism?'

'L'Académie was one of the two most important laboratories in the world at that time. Its former Deputy Director of Virology had just been found dead in his own apartment, by his pregnant wife. Obviously, many people were curious to know what had happened but...'

'But?'

'But there were other events happening in the world of great significance that same day. Many journalists were out of town, out of the country, on a different continent. It did not help that the press release announcing the inquest somehow was mislaid, lost, perhaps never created, I do not know. I only got wind of it because my contact in the Palais called me half an hour before it started to let me know it was happening.'

She was pacing up and down the kitchen, touching her cross. 'Do you remember the name of the inquest judge? Or the names of any of the police officers who investigated the case? I'm sure they'd clear up the confusion very quickly if we could just speak to them.'

'The lady who presided over the hearing was Madame Roulet.'

'I've heard that name before.'

'She is now France's Chief Justice.'

'That's why; she's done well.'

'Very.'

'What about the police?'

He took a sip of coffee. 'The officer in charge of the investigation was Detective Inspector Eric Mules.'

She could not help but notice Philippe's lip curled slightly when he mentioned the Detective Inspector's name. 'What is it? You don't like him?'

'I do not! I dealt with him for nearly forty years, and he was never anything other than sarcastic and rude. From the very first to the very last, we rubbed each other up the wrong way. He often

33

accused me of poking my nose into police business and writing codswallop. The dislike was mutual. Over time it became intense and evolved into loathing.'

'You speak of him in the past tense? He isn't dead, is he?'

'No, thank goodness for you he is alive and kicking. Thank goodness for me he retired six months ago and is now, in time-honoured, stereotypical fashion, drinking himself to an early grave. His successor is a breath of fresh, non-alcoholic air.'

'Can we speak to the judge and the detective?'

'Of course. We should also speak to a couple of journalist colleagues of mine who might have even more information.'

'How do we speak to Roulet and Mules?'

'We call them. I have their numbers in my phone.'

'Simple really. Where do they live?'

'She is in Saint-Cloud. He is in Montreuil.'

'One west, one east.' She looked at him over her cup. 'And you live where?

'The Marais, very close to the Musée Carnavalet.'

'Halfway between the two.'

Her phone buzzed again.

'Hi, birthday girl! Hope things weren't too difficult for you this morning. Really looking forward to this evening. B x.'

'Hi, fellow birthday girl. Yes thanks, all ok at the cem. Things have taken an interesting turn since. Me too. A-S x'

'Oooh! Interesting sounds…interesting…very. Looking forward even more to this eve now x. ps did you do the right thing by M?'

'Sorry about that.'

He gave her his phone. 'No problem. Now, call Madame Roulet.'

'Me? No way! I don't know her. You do, I presume?'

'I do, but you have the element of surprise. A most useful weapon. It will put her completely onto the back foot.'

There was only one problem, Anne-Sophie had spent one of her university summer vacations contacting businesses, asking them to buy advertising space. She found the whole 'reading from a script' experience gut-wrenchingly awful and had quickly discovered it was not the job for someone who lacked a below-average level of self-confidence, someone who took each 'no' as a very personal hammer blow. Her supervisor told her it would get easier, it never did. Now Philippe was expecting her to make an out-of-the-blue, extremely cold call, to the highest-ranking judicial officer in France. Her insides had started to melt. She needed the toilet.

'I feel sick.'

'Come on, speaking to her will help you make your decision. Consider it a tentative first step towards at least taking a peek outside of your cave.'

She thought about how Béatrice would react to a similar challenge and, taking a deep breath, she dialled the number. 'Hello! May I speak to Madame Roulet please?'

'Speaking. Who is this?'

'Anne-Sophie Montreau.'

'How can I assist you?'

'A long time ago, forty-years ago, to be precise, you were in charge of an inquest into the death of my father, Jean-Marie Montreau.'

'I agree, forty years is a long time. There have been many inquests since. I am now seventy-six-years old, so my memory is not what it was I'm afraid.'

'This particular inquest had several unusual aspects.'

'Really? How so?'

'My father died on Sunday, March 29th,1987. The inquest took place just two days later.'

'Ms Montreau, I am extremely busy. What is it you want from me, specifically?'

'Specifically, I would like to meet you. Even more specifically, in an hour.'

'Out of the question.'

'I need to talk to you about the inquest.'

'If it's been forty years, one more day can't hurt.'

'But-'

'Tomorrow.'

'Whereabouts in Saint-Cloud are you, specifically?'

'Parc de Montretout. The house is called *L'Haut*. Goodbye, Ms Montreau.'

Anne-Sophie gave the phone back to Philippe, who smiled, 'Well done on making the call. Do not worry, tomorrow will be fine.'

'You're joking. We're going there right now.'

'What?'

'Never mind element of surprise and putting her on the back foot, seeing us standing there at her front door will have her reeling.' She took his hand and led him to the door.

Philippe was beaming as they left the apartment block, got into Anne-Sophie's Clio and set off to Saint-Cloud.

'What are you grinning about?'

'Like father, like daughter.'

Chapter Eight

As they entered Saint-Cloud she asked him what would happen when they got to Madame Roulet's.

'What do you think?'

'Surely, it's what you think that's important. After all, I haven't interviewed anyone connected to a possible murder inquiry before; you must have done.'

'You are right, many times. However, the fact that the victim was your father means that your questions will carry greater weight. Madame Roulet will find it harder to refuse to speak to you and more difficult to lie.'

'In other words, I'm your useful idiot.'

'That's rather a crude way of putting it. I think in this instance I prefer Plato.'

'Your favourite. Was he less crude than me?'

'He was of his time, as you are of yours. As we all are of ours.'

'I'll take that as a yes, then.'

'As he said, each of us is always seeking the half that matches him or her.'

'They or them.'

'Sorry?'

'They or them. Some people don't like to be pigeon-holed by he/she, him/her. It's very much of my time.'

'I see. Well, the concept of 'matched opposites' applies just as well in life, friendships, and work, as it does in love. I have some of the skills we need to succeed in our quest and some of the passion. You have different skills and even more of the passion. We are good foils, therefore, according to Plato, we should make an excellent team.'

'If it's good enough for Plato, it's good enough for me.'

'Excellent, Dan Brown would agree I am sure of that. After all, Robert Langdon does not solve his myriad of mysteries by himself. Fortuitously, he always seems to find himself paired with the person most able to supply the skill sets he lacks. Even more fortuitously for the heterosexual Robert, this is usually a very attractive, intelligent person of the opposite gender; very him and her.'

'Ah-ha! So, you do read Dan Brown.'

'Guilty as charged.'

'Béatrice would like you.'

'Béatrice?'

'Oh, so, you don't know everything about me after all?'

'I do not remember making any such claim. Who is she?'

'Béatrice Lapain is my oldest friend and Deputy Director of Virology at L'Académie.'

'The current incumbent of your father's erstwhile role.'

'Yes.'

'She is a follower of Plato?'

'She may well be. She knows a lot about a lot. She's certainly very keen I should find my other half as quickly as possible. I'll ask her about Plato later on; she's coming round after five for our birthday dinner.'

'That is a tight deadline if we are going to speak to Roulet, Mules *and* my two colleagues.'

She glanced across. 'You'll make yourself even more ill if you stress about deadlines. Rome wasn't built in a day and a forty-year mystery isn't going to be solved in one either.'

'I am sorry, I have waited a long time for this moment, and, despite my illness, I am feeling very energized.'

'So, how would Plato suggest we tackle the Chief Justice?'

'He would suggest you lead, and I chip in, as and when required. I am paraphrasing obviously.'

'I gathered that. I don't know if that makes me your useful idiot, or your human shield.'

'When it comes to our second interviewee, retired Inspector Mules, a human shield would be extremely apposite. Anyway, we have arrived, and it is too late to discuss the finer details of your position vis à vis 'idiots' and 'shields', except to say you are neither.'

She looked at her dashboard. 'We made excellent time.'

'Thanks to the speed you were driving at.'

En-route, Anne-Sophie had taken perverse pleasure from Philippe's obvious discomfort at her driving. His beam had totally disappeared. She felt it was deserved payback for what she considered his underhand presentation of a fait accompli.

'Meaning?'

'You are a fast driver.'

'I'm a decisive driver. I drive to the limit, not beyond it. I'm not bad considering it took me six attempts to pass.'

'Six?'

'Technically, five; I ducked out of one because of a panic attack.'

'I see.'

'Cheer up, despite the rain and my driving, we're here and still in one piece. So, fill me in on Madame Roulet.'

'There are many things I could tell you about her, but the most important one at this moment is that she is a very tough cookie.'

'Great.'

'I am positive you will be a match for her.'

'Thanks for the vote of confidence.'

'You are very welcome.'

Anne-Sophie got out of her car and looked around her. She knew Saint-Cloud's reputation as one of the wealthiest places in France, never mind Paris, and the exclusive Parc de Montretout estate seemed to be home to the wealthiest of the wealthy. Anne-Sophie's ten years old, very the worse-for-wear Clio, looked extremely out of place.

They pressed *L'Haut*'s security buzzer for five minutes before they got a response.

'Yes?'

'Hello Madame Roulet. Its Anne-Sophie Montreau.'

'I told you, tomorrow.'

'We just happened to be passing and thought, you know, as you sounded so friendly on the phone it would be rude not to call in and say hello.'

'Horse manure.'

'Ten minutes and we'll leave.'

'Five minutes. Take it or leave it.'

They walked through the opened gates and were greeted by a very stylishly attired, arms-folded, grim-faced Madame Roulet. She was clearly taken aback to see Philippe walking behind Anne-Sophie.

'You never mentioned you were bringing a crutch. You must be desperate if you need him to hold your hand.'

'What happened to all your bonhomie?'

'Come in, ask what you want to ask, then go. My family is arriving soon.'

As they sat down in the inquest judge's sumptuous lounge, Anne-Sophie, encouraged by Philippe, took the lead. 'It must be lovely to have a family. I don't have any, apart from my godfather here.'

Her host looked over Anne-Sophie's left shoulder. 'The clock is ticking. Four minutes.'

'I came here because I thought you might be able to clarify the confusion that surrounds my father's inquest.'

'What confusion?'

'I suggested during our phone call the inquest appeared to have been a rushed job.'

'You did.'

'The inquest itself was over and done with in less than half an hour.'

Madame Roulet took a sip of her coffee. 'Really?'

'Really.'

'Who told you that?' She looked at Philippe, 'Oh, your crutch.'

'That can't be normal.'

'If you say so. Three minutes. The clock is ticking. I would get on with it if I were you.'

'How are inquests allocated?'

'The judge receives notification.'

'Where from?'

'The Procureur's office.'

'The Procurer. What was his or her name in 1987, please?'

'I cannot recall.'

'Really?'

'Really.'

'What did you make of the post-mortem report?'

'I did not see one.'

Anne-Sophie forced herself to stay seated. 'Surely, there must have been a post-mortem. In the circumstances...a hanging...suicide...'

'You need to improve your listening skills. That isn't what I said. There may well have been a post-mortem, I said I did not see it. Two minutes.'

'Wasn't that unusual?'

'Perhaps. However, as this was my very first inquest, I may not have been fully up to speed.'

'Really? Your first inquest?'

'Really.'

'Would you mind taking us through the events of the morning, such as they were.'

'I was at home in Saint-Denis, having breakfast, wondering what I was going to do that day.'

'From Saint-Denis to Saint-Cloud; you've come a long way. *L'Haut* indeed.'

'Due reward for years of service to the people of Paris and France.'

'You were telling us that you were at something of a loose end.'

'I got a call at breakfast saying I must go to the court immediately.'

'Who called you?'

'I presume someone from the Procureur's office. Anyhow, I had to dash to get myself ready, iron my blouse, do my hair, makeup, brush my shoes, all those things. You understand?'

'Totally.'

'When I arrived, there was someone from the press. Was that you, Simon?'

'Yes.'

'I also remember a woman getting very angry and shouting at me.'

'That would have been my newly widowed, just-given-birth, mother.'

'Shouting at me wasn't going to bring her husband, your father, back.'

'Did you know anything about my father?'

'Nothing.' Madame Roulet looked at her clock. 'One minute.'

Anne-Sophie leant forward. 'What happened after my mother shouted at you?'

41

'I was taken into a side room, a small office.'

'And then what?'

'I read the case file.'

'What was in it?'

'The name of the deceased, Jean-Marie Montreau; his address- Rue Rollin, Saint-Victor - and the manner of his death.'

'What did it say about that?'

'Death by hanging; the most likely explanation, suicide.'

'What? You're telling me the verdict was written as a kind of script? You had no say in the matter?'

'It is not a script, Ms Montreau, it is guidance. If anything comes up during the proceedings that diverges from the guidance, the judge is duty bound to take it into account.'

'Sounds like you were more puppet than judge.'

'May I remind you, this is my house, not a witness box.'

'Pity. Speaking of which, what about witness statements?'

'I did not see any.'

'You mean the police hadn't interviewed my mother, my father's colleagues, or any of his many friends?'

'Again, that's not what I said. If they did, I did not see anything in writing, but that's a question for the police, not me.'

'So, there was nothing that was going to make you diverge from the guidance, was there?'

'Time's up Ms Montreau.'

'When it was over, how did you feel?

'Satisfied. Relieved.'

'And then my mother started shouting again?'

'Yes.'

'She was right, wasn't she?'

'About what?'

'The inquest being a whitewash.'

'I said, your time is up.'

'You literally had no clue, did you, about what constituted a proper inquest? What happened after the farce ended?'

'I went home.'

'Taken, no doubt, by your on-expenses taxi back to Saint-Denis?'

'Time for you and your crutch to go, Ms Montreau.'

'Did you ever attempt to find out anything about my father? Who he was? Where did he work? Why he might have killed himself?'

'No.'

Anne-Sophie stood up. 'So, in short, despite this inquest being an absolute sham, you never voiced any concerns. You kept your tight, Saint-Denis trap shut. Talk about a useful idiot, how the hell did you become Chief Justice? Who was your crutch? The Procureur? It won't take long to find out who that was, you unhelpful bitch.'

It was Roulet's turn to stand up. 'Leave. Immediately.'

For some reason, Anne-Sophie thought about the moment in *The Godfather* when Michael Corleone discovered a rival family had tried for a second time to assassinate his father. She felt chills sweep through her body and stepped towards an immobile, emotionless Madame Roulet.

'And now here you are, forty years on, in perfect Saint-Cloud, wearing your perfect clothes, sitting in your perfect house, waiting for your perfect family, looking forward to having a perfect afternoon. Well, lucky you. I'll start doing the job you should have done four decades ago; finding out the truth about my father's death, who murdered him and why.'

'Get out!'

Sitting in the Clio, she responded to Philippe's amazed look.

'What? That stuck-up old hag had it coming.'

'She did.'

'Before you ask…'

'Yes?'

'I'm in, one hundred per cent in. It's time.'

'Time?'

'Time, I dived into the darkness.'

Chapter Nine

'Juliette, my darling.'

'I'm sorry to intrude. I know every minute is precious right now.'

'You wouldn't do it unless you thought it important.'

'Correct.'

'You have some news you wish to share?'

'I have just had a visitor. Two, actually.'

'Yes?'

'Anne-Sophie Montreau and Philippe Simon.'

'Well, well, at last, after forty years; bound to happen eventually. What did she, they, want?'

'Information about the inquest.'

'What did you give them?'

'A few crumbs, nothing significant. Nothing they did not know already or couldn't work out between them. What is important is that she has finally got around to asking questions. I thought you should know, immediately.'

'You thought right. Thank you. You have done well, as always.'

'My pleasure.'

'I'm intrigued by the girl. What is she like?'

'Feisty, full of fight. I doubt she will back down.'

'Like father, like daughter.'

'Exactly.'

Chapter Ten

Anne-Sophie had entered *L'Haut* convinced that her father's death had *not* been the result of foul play. She believed Madame Roulet would clear up the mystery and then she would take Philippe to Le Marais, drop him off and resume her holiday. No harm done; no more time wasted.

She left *L'Haut* certain her father *had* been killed. The inquest proceedings had been a farce, she had heard it directly from the unrepentant, borderline hostile, horse's mouth. The paradigm had shifted. She had to find out what had happened to her father. Who had done it? Why had it been done? She now had no choice, not because of what the dark forces might do to her, but because of what they had done to her father.

As soon as they got back into the Clio, she asked for Mules' number. The detective's wife answered. No, Anne-Sophie could not speak to her husband as he was sleeping off his lunch. When would he wake up? Not long, in thirty minutes perhaps. Anne-Sophie, worried about being back in time for Béatrice but, determined to keep the momentum rolling, assured Mules' wife she would be there in an hour.

She looked at Philippe. 'Do you want to come?'

'Of course, I would not miss this for the world. Not that you should be building your hopes up. Something tells me Mules is still off the wagon.'

Driving to Montreuil, it took all Anne-Sophie's mental capacity to maintain her concentration on the wet road. She had never seen spray like it and her driving required one hundred per cent focus. However, she was fuming about what she had heard from the judge. Haughty was the least of it, such incompetence and insouciance! The old cow obviously hadn't given a single thought to her father then and wasn't wasting any brain cells on him now. How did so many incompetent people like Roulet make it to the top?

Precisely an hour after they had left Roulet, the Clio pulled up in front of Mules' house, which, from the outside, was a much more modest affair than *L'Haut*. Anne-Sophie was worried. Unless the detective had woken up the journey would have turned out to be a waste of time.

Mules' wife, Céline, was less elegantly dressed than Madame Roulet, but much more importantly she had a warm smile and Anne-Sophie took an immediate liking to her. After telling them that Eric was just rousing himself, she poured them coffee and then returned to her household chores. Five minutes later, Mules walked in looking like the proverbial death warmed up.

'Who have we here? Simon! What the hell?'

Céline spun round instantly. 'Eric!'

Anne-Sophie stepped forward and introduced herself. She extended her right hand, a gesture which Mules ignored.

'Oh yes. And why have you barged your way into my house on a Monday afternoon?'

Again, Céline responded quickly. 'Eric!'

'It's a fair question.'

'We haven't barged in anywhere but, to answer your question, my father died forty years ago. I'm told you were in charge of the so-called investigation.'

'I was in charge of many investigations, young lady. You'll have to give me more than that.'

'My…'

'I need coffee. Céline?' He took a gulp. 'That's better. You were saying, Ms…'

'For the second time, Montreau. My father, Jean-Marie Montreau, died forty years ago in his apartment in Saint-Victor. He was found hanging from his bedroom ceiling. Verdict suicide. Ring any bells?'

'The only thing ringing right now is my head. Céline, give me some tablets.'

Anne-Sophie was beginning to feel dismayed. Although Mules was awake, her dash to Montreuil looked like it was going to be a waste of time. The guy was a mess, glassy-eyed and stinking of booze. What a loser, a clichéd loser at that. She only kept her thoughts to herself because she did not wish to offend Céline who, as well as possessing a warm smile and excellent manners, obviously had the patience of a saint.

46

Philippe felt no such qualms. 'I told Anne-Sophie you were an arrogant, alcoholic no-hoper. I was right. Look at yourself. Have you lost all your self-respect?'

'Go screw yourself, you interfering old fool. What's this got to do with you anyway?'

For the third time Céline remonstrated with her husband. 'Eric, please!'

Anne-Sophie moved closer to Mules. 'He's my godfather, and he's…'

'He's what?'

Philippe stepped in between them. 'Nothing. We should leave. We are wasting valuable time here.'

'First sensible thing you've said today, Simon. First sensible thing ever, I don't doubt.'

Anne-Sophie waited ten minutes to see if Mules showed any signs of improvement. He did not. If anything, he deteriorated. It looked like he could be sick at any minute.

Finally, at three-thirty, her patience ran out and she stood up. 'I'm sorry Céline, I must go. Thank you for the coffee. Inspector Mules, I can't tell you how I feel about you because I do not wish to offend your lovely wife. Here is my card. If you sober up and the bells start ringing about Father's case, please contact me. I won't hold my breath. I've been doing enough of that for the past thirty minutes.'

Philippe could not resist chipping in. 'You are right, let us go. Perhaps the reason Mules is keeping schtum is because he was in it up to his neck. Perhaps that bad smell is not the booze, it is the stench of corruption.'

Mules' reaction was remarkably swift for someone nursing a serious hangover. He was in Philippe's face in a flash. 'Say that again you old…'

'Eric, no!'

'Get out.'

Back in the car, Philippe spoke first. 'Being asked to leave one house in an afternoon may be regarded as a misfortune, to be asked to leave two in less than two hours looks like carelessness."

'Plato?'

'Oscar Wilde. I'm paraphrasing, again.'

'Of course.' She slapped her hand on the steering wheel. 'What a waste of time. I'm sorry to drag you here in this awful weather. In some ways, he was worse than Roulet.'

'No problem and, for what it is worth, I do not think it has been a waste of time.'

'Tell me more, I could do with cheering up.'

'I think Inspector Mules was putting on an act, playing for time.'

'What makes you say that?'

'I've known him for forty years. His default position is the negative, the defensive. He usually comes round.'

'But in there you said…'

'I did not mind kicking him where it hurts, metaphorically. It was a golden opportunity. One that few people could resist, certainly not me. A little revenge for decades banging my head against his thick brick wall of a head.'

'You don't think he was in it up to his neck then?'

'Never say never, but I doubt it. The bottom line is I would not be surprised if he contacts you tonight.'

She took a deep breath. 'Thanks, that has cheered me up.' She looked at the time on her phone and saw there was a text.

'Sorry to hear that. Hope it gets resolved. Very happy to rearrange for later this week. Michael.'

'I'll run you back home, OK?'

'Perfect, thank you.'

On the way back to Philippe's apartment on the Rue de Sévigné, she popped into the Montreuil Carrefour Hypermarché. There she stocked up with groceries, wine, toiletries, towels and, she had no idea why, a pair of men's pyjamas.

His apartment, located very close as he had said to the Musée Carnavalet, was quite basic, with a single bedroom, a lounge and a kitchen. Whilst he made a pot of coffee, she surveyed the lounge/diner. One thing above all else struck her, its sparseness. There were no ornaments, no family photos, no suggestion that Philippe had ever been in any kind of relationship. The thought choked her up and she was relieved it took him five minutes to emerge with the coffee.

He sat down beside her and took her hands in his. 'It is none of my business of course but you seem worried about something.

Or someone, perhaps? Something or someone, separate from our investigation.'

At first, as she usually did when anyone apart from Béatrice enquired about her private life, she was going to say everything was fine. However, Philippe's gentle enquiring manner changed her habit of a lifetime. 'I was supposed to meet a guy for lunch. Because of what happened this morning, I cancelled it.'

'I am sorry if I messed up your plans. You will make a new arrangement?'

'Don't worry, you didn't mess up anything. I may rearrange it. I may not. Perhaps.'

She finished her coffee and stood up. She fully intended to say goodbye, thank him once again for his incredible generosity and promise she would see him tomorrow. Something in his eyes changed her mind.

'OK, Godfather, it's time to make you an offer I don't think you will refuse. Come and share mine and Béatrice's joint birthday meal. It will be just like the good old days; you can stay the night and I'll bring you back here in the morning.'

Unable to speak, he squeezed her hands, and they exited the apartment. Before they got into the Clio, her phone buzzed again.

'Oh, for goodness sake.'

Chapter Eleven

It was four o'clock. He hadn't moved since they'd left. Again and again, he looked at her card.

Anne-Sophie Montreau
Cybersecurity Analyst
'Banque Nord'
21 Rue de Vaugirard,
75006 Paris
+33 1 53 63 86 60
asm@BanqueNord.orange.fr

She'd been sitting in the chair opposite him. At last. She'd him asked if her father's case rang any bells. He'd almost laughed when she said it. The bells hadn't stopped ringing for forty-years. Nor had the feelings of guilt.

Chapter Twelve

Anne-Sophie had much to ponder on her drive back to Saint-Victor. At the forefront of her thoughts was Béatrice. They had known each other since their joint first day at nursery school and as Béatrice was three hours older and had always been the first to do, well, everything, Anne-Sophie often thought of her as her big sister. Recently, Béatrice's behaviour had been anything but sisterly, so it was no great surprise when, just as they were leaving Philippe's apartment, Anne-Sophie received a message saying she'd been held up and wouldn't arrive before seven. This was by no means the first time since her promotion four years ago that Béatrice had been 'held up', 'delayed', 'caught up', or 'stuck at work looking through sample results'.

Although she had no direct experience of either of these things, Anne-Sophie understood that with promotion came extra responsibility. She also knew that her friend was a workaholic, but surely, she couldn't work all day, every day, could she? Anne-Sophie often wondered what Béatrice did outside of work but, no matter how subtly she tried to tease snippets out of her, Béatrice never gave away anything concrete about her extra-curricular life. It was incredible how she managed to fend off Anne-Sophie's enquiries with a combination of feeble jokes, generalisations, smokescreens, throwaway lines, or blatant diversions.

However, the shoe was on the other foot when it came to Anne-Sophie's life. There was not a single thing she had done or was doing, that Béatrice did not know about, or want to know about. It had really started to grate with Anne-Sophie that, whilst Béatrice literally knew everything about her, she, deep down, hardly knew anything about her friend. What made the situation even harder to cope with was the dawning realisation that her friend's questioning had become even more intrusive after her mother's death. In the last three months, Béatrice's appetite for her latest news had been insatiable and, at times, claustrophobic.

Even more galling and perplexing to Anne-Sophie was that, up until today, she really hadn't had anything interesting to share.

Despite all these negative thoughts, she remained hopeful the birthday meal would be a cheerful, relaxing finale to what had been an unexpectedly exhausting, sometimes shocking day. So much for a peaceful, restorative break! After ensuring Philippe was comfortably ensconced on the sofa, she turned on the heating. By seven o'clock, when the buzzer sounded, the apartment was very warm, and her godfather was snoring.

'Hello! Come up.'

Armed with bottles and a delicious-looking lemon flan, Béatrice's eyes immediately rested on a just stirring Philippe.

'Béatrice, meet my godfather, Philippe Simon. Phillipe, this is Béatrice, my oldest and dearest friend.'

'Hi! What a wonderful birthday surprise for your goddaughter.'

He kissed her hand. 'Enchanted. Very happy birthday, Béatrice.'

After apologising for not managing to buy her friend a birthday present, Anne-Sophie left her two guests to introduce themselves to each other over Crémant de Loire, whilst she slipped the lasagne into the oven, sorted out the salad and garlic baguettes and put on her favourite album, *Voulez-Vous,* as background music. Forty-five minutes later, the three of them were sitting around the kitchen-diner table tucking into the food and washing it down with the first of Béatrice's two bottles of vin rouge. The hot oven had warmed the apartment up even further and Anne-Sophie studied her friend.

'Aren't you roasting in that cardigan?'

'I'm fine.'

'I've got loads of t-shirts. Some of them might even be clean, ha ha.'

'Honestly, I'm fine.'

'Are you sure? It's no problem to…'

'I'm OK! Drop it, please.'

Philippe looked at the pair of them. 'I must say this is delicious wine, Béatrice; to match Anne-Sophie's delicious lasagne.'

'It's good to know all those wine-tasting holidays weren't wasted.'

'So, what have you two been talking about whilst I've been busy in the kitchen?'

'Your godfather has been telling me about his career as a crime reporter which has been extremely fascinating.'

'Has he told you about why he appeared, out of the blue, at Montparnasse cemetery today? Why he's decided to enter my life after forty years?'

'No, you hadn't reached that point yet, had you, Philippe?'

'No, not yet.'

Anne-Sophie could see that Philippe, like every other man Béatrice came into contact with, had fallen under her spell. For some reason, this raised her already high level of irritation with her friend another couple of notches. She could feel a repeat of her Saint-Cloud tirade brewing. She decided to employ what her trauma therapist, Valerie, called a displacement tactic and launched into her narrative of the day's events.

To Béatrice's frequently open-mouthed astonishment, Anne-Sophie filled her in on what had occurred during the previous twelve hours. As a result of her friend pumping her for every single, minute detail, the telling of the tale took almost two hours. By that time, they had nearly finished their second bottle of red, of which Anne-Sophie had drunk well over half.

'So! How's about that?'

'I'm stunned. So, your father was …'

'Killed. Whether deliberately or accidentally we don't know. We obviously need to do a lot more digging. I'm banking on the drunken Detective Inspector sobering up by tomorrow.'

Béatrice looked at Philippe, then turned back to Anne-Sophie. 'And did you do the honourable thing about Michael?'

'I told him the truth. Something unexpected had cropped up and I had to cancel.'

'What do you think Philippe?'

'About?'

'Your goddaughter's love life. Or lack of.'

'This has nothing to do with Philippe. I've told him very little about Michael.'

'Don't you think it's a waste of a gorgeous, intelligent, sexy woman?'

'Béatrice!'

'How would you have felt, Philippe, if someone like Anne-Sophie had led you on and then knocked you down?'

'I haven't led anyone on.'

'Really?'

'Yes, really. Now, as you would say, drop it.'

Béatrice looked at her phone. 'My god! It's way past ten already. I have a very early start tomorrow, with loads to do. I had best be off. Philippe, it's been a pleasure. I hope to see you again very soon. And Anne-Sophie! What an exciting birthday!'

'Let me walk you down to the exit. I could do with a blast of fresh, cool air.'

When they reached the street, she asked Béatrice how things were.

'Me? Just the same, you know.'

Usually Anne-Sophie would have accepted this response without demur, but this time, whether as a consequence of too much red wine, her irritation levels, her exhaustion, Béatrice's baiting about her disastrous dating, or an amalgamation of all the above, for the second time that day Anne-Sophie decided to break the habit of a lifetime.

'That's the trouble, you see, I don't know. You never actually tell me what you're up to these days. Or who you're up to it with. I, on the other hand, gladly tell you everything that's going on, even though it is, in the general order of things, about as interesting as drying paint, and you know why I do that?'

'No, but I'm sure you're going to tell me.'

'Because you're my oldest friend, and that's what friends, especially ones who've known each other since they were knee-high, do, tell each other things. You don't do that. You tell me nothing. Worse than that, you use my secrets as a conversation piece with a complete stranger and as a way to have a dig at me.'

'Hardly a stranger, he's your godfather.'

'Whom I did not even know existed until twelve hours ago. Friendship isn't a one-way street. I've just about had enough.'

'I'm sorry you think I am such a bad friend. I can't help it if I keep my cards close to my chest, can I?'

'Would it hurt you to reveal some of your hand occasionally? Just to tip the see-saw fractionally back towards me?'

Béatrice studied her finger nails which Anne-Sophie noticed were bitten to the quick. 'You're right. It wouldn't. I'm sorry.'

When her friend glanced at her phone, Anne-Sophie was shocked to see a hint of fear momentarily in her eyes.

'What is it? What's wrong?'

'Nothing.'

'Béatrice?'

'I really have to go. I'll be in touch very soon.

As she watched Béatrice head off in the direction of the Luxembourg Garden, she heard 'Voulez-Vous' coming from her jeans pocket.

'Aha.'

Chapter Thirteen

Because Philippe had already cleared the kitchen table it didn't take long to complete the tidying and washing up, after which Anne-Sophie sat down next to him and took his hands in hers. 'Thank you for all your help.'

'You are very welcome. It was, as you predicted, just like the old times. Thank you for a delicious dinner.'

'I have some news for you.'

'Good, I hope?'

'Mules.'

'He has contacted you?'

'Yes, you were right. He wants to meet.'

'Perfect.'

'I need to decide when and where.'

'You are in charge. Your father's murder, your decision.'

'How about Le Marais tomorrow morning, at eight? I'll run you there first thing.'

'Excellent.'

'Is there a brasserie close to your apartment where we can get breakfast?'

'Yes, La Cidrerie du Marais, at the end of my street.'

'Great. I'll call Mules back before he changes his mind, or has a nightcap.'

Five minutes later the meeting had been arranged.

'That's a good job. Now, how about some hot chocolate?'

'Thank you. That would be a wonderful end to a very productive day. A productive birthday to boot.'

'I'm sorry Béatrice put you in an awkward position.'

'About?'

'My love life. Or rather, the mess I'm making of it.'

'It's none of my business. I'm here to help you resolve your past, not involve myself in your future.'

'That's a bit like the chicken and the egg, as Plato probably didn't say.'

'As Dan Brown absolutely never said!'

'No!'

Whilst she waited for the aged kettle to come to the boil, she called Béatrice. 'Hi.'

'What's wrong?'

'Nothing, except I feel guilty.'

'About what?'

'I'm sorry I nagged you about your cardigan.'

'Oh that. Not a problem. I'd forgotten about it to be honest.'

'Good.'

Suddenly, Anne-Sophie could hear the climax of the Prélude to Bach's 'Cello Suite No. 1 in G Major'. Just as suddenly, it stopped.

'Yet another thing I didn't know about you.'

'What?'

'You're into classical music.'

'I'm...'

'I'll leave you to it. Bye.'

Instead of, as usual, dwelling upon her hurt feelings, Anne-Sophie walked into her mother's bedroom and started getting it ship-shape for her godfather's sleepover. She thought about what he had said to her before the brief conversation with Béatrice. Never mind her birthday being productive, unprecedented would be a more apt description; her first birthday without her mother for one thing. The mother, whose jewellery boxes she was about to put inside the safe inbuilt into her bedroom floor. This was new territory for her, the one part of the apartment she had never been allowed to investigate. Locating the key inside her mother's underwear drawer, she opened the heavy door and propped it on the hook. Exposed, the safe was a much bigger space than she had imagined from the outside. She found bank statements and utility bills dating from 1987 strewn along the length of the safe. Then, tucked underneath the documents, hidden from sight, she found a dozen shoeboxes.

'Hello?'

She took the boxes into the lounge and placed them on the table in front of a suddenly wide-awake, curious, veteran journalist. She returned to the bedroom and made up his bed. Then, she prepared the hot chocolate, and sat down opposite him. For five minutes she eyed the boxes, uncertain whether she should look inside them. Eventually, she thought that if she did not have the right to do it then no one had. Her father had some family in Artois, but they had not been in touch for years. Forty years, in fact.

'In for a cent as they say.'

She opened each of the boxes and was amazed to discover diaries, notebooks, newspaper and magazine cuttings, letters, postcards and photos. Her father's diaries, notebooks, letters, postcards and photos. He had been a stranger to her materially, as well as physically and emotionally and, apart from her cross, and the photos she had thrown into an empty drawer, she had no physical evidence of her father's existence. Now, at last, she had that physical evidence. Lots of it.

It was too late and there was too much of it to look at now, but she quickly perceived that what she had found was mainly connected to her father's position at L'Académie des Médecine et Sciences on the Rue du Dr Roux, where he had worked for a decade. For that reason, she had a thought that Béatrice might be interested in looking through this treasure trove too. At least it would be something the two of them could do together and bond over, not argue about.

She looked quickly through the boxes and found in the final one a notebook titled '1987'. This appeared to contain the last entry of all, dated Friday, 27th March. She handed the book open at that page to Philippe, who had been studying her and the boxes very carefully. He murmured, 'His last working day.'

'The final entry is intriguing: *At last! I have it.*'

What 'it' was, there was no clue. She only knew her father had been killed two days after he'd written it.

Anne-Sophie wondered if her mother had deliberately concealed these boxes from her. She had not been allowed into her mother's bedroom unsupervised even as an adult. That had always irked her but now it made complete sense when she thought about what Philippe had told her today. Her mother must have been worried that the more she learned about her father's life and the more questions she asked about his death, the more she would want to seek the truth and the more she would put herself in danger. If her mother was still alive, Anne-Sophie would thank her very much for her protection but tell her she was now a grown-up woman and she had made up her mind to uncover the truth, whatever the consequences. Let the chips fall where they may.

If her mother was still alive.

'Philippe!'

'What is it?'

'I've just thought. My mother. What if she was murdered too?'

'I am listening.'

'After all, the police did not locate the driver of the white van which hit her at eighty kilometres an hour. How hard did they try to track down the culprit? Perhaps they made no effort at all, or they conveniently forgot to chase up leads during the holiday period. Then it was a new year and, well, you know, there are many other crimes to investigate. What if- what if the dark forces got to Mother as well?'

'It's a horrible thing to say but if Thérèse was murdered, it would certainly fit my hypothesis very neatly.'

She sat still for a minute then looked at the time, ten o'clock. 'It's too late tonight to open another line of enquiry.'

'I agree.'

'However, you did say that if I agreed to help you, you'd tell me more about the event happening on Friday. The event you said represented a very big opportunity.'

'I did.'

'I've agreed. So?'

'This Friday night there is a gathering of the great and good at the Ritz.'

'In four days?'

'Time is indeed running out, in several ways.'

'It sounds important. What's the occasion?'

'A fortieth anniversary.'

'There seem to be a lot of special fortieths at the moment. Who's attending?'

'Executives from Big Pharma; Public Health officials, Scientists, Medics.'

'Why this week?'

'Forty years ago, an agreement was signed which settled a long-running dispute.'

59

'Between?'

'The French and American governments.'

She again looked at the clock, ten-fifteen. She was done for. 'OK, quickly, tell me in one sentence why this Ritz event concerns me, us, my father.'

Day Two – Tuesday, March 30th, 2027

Chapter Fourteen

'I don't remember asking for an early wake-up call.'

He had been woken by his buzzing mobile phone, followed by the sound of a distorted voice he had not heard in forty years.

'She is asking questions. Making waves.'

'I know.'

'How?'

'For forty years her every step has been watched.'

'Right.'

'How do you know.'

'I realise it's been a long time but surely you have not forgotten the golden rule?'

'Remind me'

'Don't ask me any questions.'

'Ah, yes.'

'Tell me what you know.'

'Apparently, the girl's behaviour was rather, shall we say, assertive. She knows the inquest was a sham.'

'She's a bright girl.'

'Bright enough to connect the dots.'

'She visited a retired police inspector, Mules.'

'Mule by name, mule by nature.'

'Stupid?'

'Stubborn. Unorthodox. Incorruptible.'

'A threat?'

'Obviously.'

'At what point do you respond?'

'You mean we, don't you?'

'You seem to have forgotten the second golden rule.'

'Which is?'

'I don't exist.'

Chapter Fifteen

'Because whoever was responsible for your father's murder will be there.'

Philippe's late-night bombshell about the Ritz kept Anne-Sophie awake long after she'd gone to bed. No sooner had she finally drifted off than she immediately woke up again with a start. Something had happened during the previous evening which did not make sense. What that something was, she couldn't work out. However, as far as her sleep was concerned, this time it was terminal. At four o'clock, she gave up the ghost.

Two hours later, Philippe walked into the lounge and noticed Jean-Marie's photos restored to the mantlepiece.

'Someone's been busy.'

Whilst Anne-Sophie made scrambled eggs and toast, Philippe turned on the TV news. She looked up and saw a tall, thin, tight-lipped man, with almost white hair and a long nose, smoking a cigarette.

'Who's that?'

'Hervé Parcelle.'

'Who?'

'I take it you're not following the presidential election campaign?'

'No but I take it you are.'

'Avidly, until four days ago.'

'So, who is he?'

'The Minister of Justice and hot favourite to be our next President.'

She walked over and turned off the television, 'I see. Anyway, breakfast is ready, so let's sit down and eat mindfully, rather than mindlessly. I'm guessing you eat in front of the TV in Le Marais?'

'Guilty as charged.'

She poured out the coffee. 'What are you expecting from Mules this morning?'

'A much better performance than yesterday that is for sure.'

63

'Let's hope so. It could hardly be any worse. Unlike the rain.'
'Indeed.'

Just over an hour later, as the rain continued to pour down, she dropped Philippe off at La Cidrerie before parking outside his apartment. Fearing he and Mules would already be at loggerheads when she arrived, she sprinted down the street and into the entrance but, even so, some of her fears had already been realized. A red-faced Philippe was seated at a ninety-degree angle facing away from a grinning detective.

To her relief and his credit, Mules was unrecognizable from the hungover wreck of yesterday. Clean-shaven, wearing a jacket and tie, she took it as a promising sign he meant business. However, if she expected him to apologize for yesterday's behaviour, she was soon put right. He didn't behave in a way which suggested he had done anything wrong. Quite the opposite; he greeted her warmly and announced he had ordered two pots of fresh coffee,

'Just to get us going.'

'Could we have some toast too, please.'

She looked at Philippe who responded with a faint smile, as if he'd known all along that Mules would be like this. She did not mind Philippe's frostiness; she was just relieved to see them not engaging in fisticuffs. Whilst Mules was at the counter ordering the toast, she whispered, 'Cheer up. Like him or not, he can help us. We need him.'

After Mules poured out the coffees, and the toast had arrived, the three got down to the matter in hand.

'Are you in a more communicative mood this morning?'

'I'm here, Simon, that's all you need to know.'

'Tell us what you remember about the evening my father died.'

'The station got the call round about five-forty.'

'Who from?'

'I don't know.'

'Then?'

'We took a couple of cars to the apartment, only to find we'd been beaten to the punch.'

'What does that mean?'

'By the time we'd got to Saint-Victor, at five-fifty-five pm, *Brigade Criminelle* officers were already on, or rather inside, the scene.'

'*Brigade Criminelle*?'

'That's what their warrant cards said.'

'Inside the apartment block?'

'Yes, according to their team leader. The same team leader who told me in no uncertain terms to go away and mind my own business.'

'Could he do that?'

'Technically, yes.'

'What was his name?'

'I didn't get it.'

'What was your, and your team's, actual involvement in the crime scene investigation?'

'None. The boys from the *Brigade* were busy doing their thing.'

'What was their thing? Mother told Philippe the apartment was immaculate when she returned the next day.'

'That's what they do; arrive, investigate, sweep, clean and leave.'

'Sounds very similar to what happened in the Alma Tunnel in August '97.'

'It does.'

'And no-one else got a look in?'

'No. Not my boys at least.'

She took a sip of coffee. 'Apart from the generic, what else do you think the *Brigade* did inside my parents' apartment?'

'That's a great question. Unfortunately, I do not have an answer.'

'What did you think when you saw the *Brigade* there?'

Mules swallowed a large volume of coffee. 'I was intrigued.'

'Why?'

'Because the *Brigade* does not in general get involved with, or investigate, straight-forward deaths. They investigate unusual cases, often involving famous or important people.'

'Father wasn't a famous person.'

'No, but the fact these guys were there at all told me there was something different about this case.'

She looked at Mules. 'Why would my father's case be unusual?'

'That's another very good question. I don't have an answer to that either.'

'Did you not do any research into my father, about his career for example? I would have thought that would have been a minimum requirement in a suicide case. Or have I read too many crime thrillers?'

'My direct involvement with the case ended after my visit to Rue Rollin. I watched what happened after that from the outside.'

'Meaning?'

'There was a ring of steel thrown around the case. No-one could get close. Not even you, Simon, or the rest of the rat pack.'

'True.'

'What did you see happening, from the outside?'

'A hastily arranged but efficiently executed inquest, followed by the locking down of the case.'

'And your verdict on the investigation was?'

Mules took another gulp of his coffee, then shrugged.

'What does that mean?'

'To be frank, I had, have, my suspicions.'

'Tell me, please.'

'I felt very uncomfortable with the whole affair: the *Brigade*, the inquest, the context. It's not every day a high-ranking virologist, who is happily married and an imminent father to boot, kills himself without warning on a sunny, Sunday afternoon.'

'Ah, so you did do some digging?'

'Yes. Whatever Simon has said to you about me, and I admit I am far from perfect, I never gave less than one hundred per cent to a case. Go on Simon, tell me I'm wrong.'

'You are not wrong.'

'Thank you. So, to be honest, the case stank to high heaven. Certain rare cases nag away at you and never leave you. This was definitely one of those.'

'Mother called the investigation a whitewash.'

'Your mother, rest in peace, was absolutely correct.'

'A lot of people seem to have picked up on the fact that she died.'

'Montreau is a name I have carried around with me for four decades. Of course, I saw the newspapers last Christmas. I'm very sorry for your loss. Both of your losses.'

'Thank you. Do you have any suspicions about her death?'

'Until foul play is ruled out, never say never.'

'Did you see my mother at all on that Sunday?'

'She arrived outside the block at about six-fifteen.'

'Did you speak to her?'

'Briefly. She asked me what was going on. I asked her where she had been. She told me she had been to see a friend. Almost immediately the *Brigade*'s team leader came across and whisked her away. The only time I saw her after that was when the ambulance arrived to take her, and you, to hospital.'

'I see. Before we came to Montreuil, we visited Madame Roulet.'

'Lucky you. An interesting conversation I bet. Stuck up old hag.'

Even Simon allowed himself a smile at that.

'I think she knows more than she told me.'

'I'm sure she does.

Philippe asked Mules another question. 'How do you think the *Brigade* got to the apartment before you?'

'A tip-off.'

'Who from?'

'Best guess? *The Direction de la Surveillance du Territoire*, the *DST*, as was.'

'*DST*?'

'The *DST* was a domestic intelligence agency.'

'No longer?'

'It is now the *Direction Générale de la Sécurité intérieure*. *DGSI* for short.'

'Why would an intelligence agency be involved with Anne-Sophie's father? He was a scientist.'

'Stranger things have happened. It wouldn't be the first time.'

Anne-Sophie asked Mules why the *DST* would tip off the *Brigade*.

'To keep people like me and Simon from sniffing around.'

'But, as I keep on asking, why?'

'I have theories obviously, nothing concrete.'

'How can I find out something concrete? Is there any way I can discover more about Father's death and the investigation?'

'There should be a police dossier, a written record of the investigation. There must be a dossier. Somewhere.'

'Where?'

'My best guess is that, if it's anywhere, it will be buried deep inside the Palais de Justice. Very deep.'

She turned to Philippe. 'Perhaps we should ask Hervé Parcelle if he would mind us having a look for it?'

She looked at her phone, eight-thirty. Probably due to her lack of sleep and the early start, she was still feeling sluggish, so she ordered more coffee.

'What do you suggest we do next?'

'If I was in charge, I'd treat it as a cold case.'

Anne-Sophie leaned forward and looked at Mules closely. 'Go on.'

'There are certain questions that a detective reopening a cold case asks.'

'Such as?'

'First of all, are there any unresolved questions?'

'Plenty. Who? Why? What? How? That's just for starters.'

'Are there additional interviews that need to be completed?'

'There were none done at the time.'

'Are there documents or evidence that need to be located?'

'The police dossier you referred to earlier, for one.'

'Was a motive identified?

'None identified, because none was sought.'

'Was the crime scene organized or disorganized?'

'The apartment was very organized by the time the *Brigade* finished their tidying up operation.'

'If a suspect was identified during the original investigation, what has he or she been doing since the incident?'

'Officially there was no crime and therefore, no suspect or suspects.'

'Is there a weak link suspect?'

'There might well be, but we haven't come across one yet because of what I said in my previous answer.'

'Lastly, has the crime scene been revisited for additional evidence or information?'

'I doubt it. No, wait! Yes, yes it has!'
'What is it? Tell me.'

Chapter Sixteen

'How many boxes?'

'A dozen.'

'Sounds like top quality primary evidence, a potential goldmine. They should certainly be worth looking through. I'm sure Simon is already licking his lips.'

Philippe put down his knife and fork with a clatter. 'What does that mean?'

'I bet you're thinking there's money in those books.'

'That is low, even by your reptilian standards.'

'Boys! Can we focus on the task at hand, please?'

Mules held up his hands. Anne-Sophie looked at Philippe. 'As you keep telling me, time is running out.'

'I do apologise, forgive me.'

She turned back to a grinning Mules. 'And you can wipe that smirk off your face and tell us what our next step should be.'

'As you know, in any murder investigation, and I think we can all agree that this is a murder investigation, it's all about means, motive and opportunity. If it was me, I would be piecing together what your father was doing during his last week, focusing especially on his final weekend. If there are any big clues to be found in respect of means and opportunity, you'll find them there; perhaps motive too.'

'How can we find any of this out? This is an ice-cold case. It happened forty-years ago.'

'I'm not saying it's going to be easy but there are avenues we can explore. They may turn into cul-de-sacs but that does not mean we should not drive down them. For starters, we now have the notebooks. Then, sitting here right in front of us is Simon. Surely, you must know something about Monsieur Montreau's movements that last week?'

'Am I wrong Mules in thinking you're enjoying this?'

'No, Simon, you're not wrong. Once a cop always a cop.'

'I thought you might say that but is there also an element of guilt involved?'

'What does that mean?'

'Knowing you did not do your job properly back in the day?'

'And you did?'

'You are confident you can do this sober?'

'I'm confident I have the method that can help Anne-Sophie get closer to the truth; a tried and trusted method developed over forty-plus years of police work.'

'And that method is?'

'Hard work! Leave no stone unturned. There are no short cuts, no magic bullets, there never are in any walk of life, agreed, Simon?'

'Agreed, Mules, and please stop calling me Simon. My name is Philippe.'

'In that case, you'd better start calling me Eric.'

'Thank you, Eric, I will.'

'And yes, Philippe, I can do this sober. I only drink when I'm bored and, right now, I'm not. Far from it.'

'We're glad to hear it. Aren't we, Philippe?'

'Absolutely.'

Mules produced a notepad and a pen from his coat inside pocket. 'OK. Let's do a recap. What do we know? What can we prove? What do we need to find out?'

'You're the very experienced, retired detective, so please start.'

'As I said earlier, the *Brigade* knew about your father's death before anyone else, certainly your mother.'

'We know this because…?'

'The *Brigade* boys got there before I arrived with my team. We didn't exactly hang around, but they were already inside the apartment block. Working back from five-fifty-five, the *Brigade* must have been contacted almost immediately after your father died. Possibly by the *DST*.'

'I see.'

Mules raised his cup to his lips where it hovered. 'Christ.'

'What is it?'

'Whoever called the Brigade must have been responsible for your father's death and if the caller was from the *DST* then the *DST*, or rogue elements thereof, killed your father.'

Anne-Sophie felt her insides turn to ice. 'What?'

'Think about it. First of all, if your father's death was a genuine suicide there would have been no urgent phone call to the Brigade.'

'OK.'

'If it was an ordinary break-in gone wrong, then the criminal would have not called the *Brigade Criminelle*. He, or she...'

'They or them...'

'Would have got out of there as fast as lightning and run like hell. So, what are we left with? An intelligence operation, which means the *DST*.'

'The case just got a hundred times bigger.'

'Yes, Si...Philippe, I agree. OK, so, for some, as yet unknown, reason, the *DST* kills your father, then they tip off the *Brigade* who arrive more or less at the same time as someone contacts my station. The *Brigade*, having gotten your father and mother away from the apartment, conduct a sweep and clean job. If they're looking for something, they try, possibly unsuccessfully, to locate it. Finally, they remove anything which incriminates the perpetrators.'

'Looking for what?'

'Boxes of notebooks, perhaps?'

'Of course! I thought Mother had hidden them away from me. Perhaps they'd been located in the safe all the time, even before father's death.'

'You know what? It may not have been a genuine *Brigade* unit. It may have been a *DST* sub-unit in *Brigade* gear.'

'Those rogue elements you mentioned?'

'Yes! I would bet my mortgage on it; what's left of it.'

'Right.'

'Meaning there was no need for a tip-off after all. It was all planned in advance, to the second.'

'I can't believe what I'm hearing.'

'Unfortunately, I can. Then, the inquest is handed to a novice, who says she had no time to prepare, who also says she was too nervous to notice, until yesterday, that she was being used to present basically a drama script after being schooled by God knows who. In short, it's a classic intelligence services operation.'

'It's more than that, Eric.'

'Philippe?'

'It's a conspiracy.'

'Thank goodness, at last something I can relate to. Dan Brown territory. Explain please.'

'Look at who's been implicated so far. The intelligence services, the judiciary, the police, and the press bosses who told us hacks to steer well clear. Even you got warned off, Eric, by those self-same dark forces.'

'Absolutely. Now, I've just remembered something else.'

'Go on.'

'The *Brigade* leader, he had a scar under his right eye socket.'

'You've never seen him since?'

'Never. Not in forty years. Unsurprising, as spooks tend to keep their heads down. Finding him would be a massive leap forward in terms of unravelling Philippe's conspiracy.' Mules leaned back. 'So, as I said, our top priority is to find out exactly what happened during the week, and the weekend, leading up to your father's death.'

'How do we do that, exactly?'

'We ask someone for information.'

'Of course, but who?'

'The apartment block's security manager; if anyone will know anything about the comings and goings that weekend, it will be him.'

'No disrespect, but how do we track down a security manager from forty-years ago?'

'I've already done it.'

'How?'

'I went back to my 1987 cases' notebook.'

'First Philippe, then my father, and now you, all keeping notebooks. Incredible, I thought women were the organized gender.'

'And what is the name of this block security manager?'

'Henri Hérault.'

Mules stood up, drained his coffee and looked at Anne-Sophie. 'Do you fancy a run up to Montmartre? Rue Cortot to be exact.'

'Sure, why?'

'To speak to Monsieur Hérault, of course.'

She stood up, put her coat on and turned to Philippe. 'Are you OK with this?'

'I wanted you to meet my two colleagues today.'

'As I said to you enroute to Saint-Cloud, stop stressing. We can still see them later. Give them a call, arrange something for late this afternoon. Come on Eric, let's go.'

Chapter Seventeen

Thirty minutes after leaving Philippe to rest, de-stress and, possibly, sulk, in his dry, warm apartment, Anne-Sophie and Eric were standing in the seemingly endless torrential rain, ringing Monsieur Hérault's security gates' buzzer.

'Nice house.'

'Nicer location, right next to the Musée de Montmartre.'

A wary-sounding voice answered their buzzing, 'Yes?'

'Monsieur Hérault? My name is Anne-Sophie Montreau.'

'Yes?'

'Do you remember my father, Jean-Marie Montreau?'

'Vaguely. Can you give me more information?'

'I will, of course. Please may we come in?'

'No, I'll come to you.'

Two minutes later, Anne-Sophie was eyeing with mild disgust a short, thin figure.

'I'll keep this brief. My father died forty-years ago. You were the apartment block's security manager. The inquest verdict was suicide. We, that is Detective Inspector Mules and I, were wondering please if there was something out of the ordinary you can recall about the week leading up to my father's death; about the weekend he died?'

'Ah, yes, a tragic business. Mules? I remember you now, yes. You are still operational I see. I'm surprised, I thought you would have retired by now.' He rubbed his chin. 'I don't mean to be rude but weren't you superfluous to the investigation back then?'

'There appears to be nothing wrong with your memory, Hérault, which is excellent news as I suspect it will come in useful. I remember when I arrived at the scene you kindly informed me that officers were already inside the building. Using that same excellent memory, do you recall any other unusual comings and goings during Monsieur Montreau's final days?'

'Unfortunately, not. The first out of the ordinary thing I noticed that entire week and weekend, was the arrival of the police that sunny Sunday evening.'

'Did you know or recognize the leader of the unit?'

'Not at all, no. Why? Should I have done?'

'Did you see my father much during the course of his last week?'

'No more, no less, than normal. As a matter of routine, he was an early starter and a not-too-late finisher.'

'No signs, on those rare occasions when you did see him, that his mood or behaviour was altered in any respect?'

'Not at all. He was as charming and polite as ever.'

'What about my mother? Did you see much of her?'

'Again, not really until that Sunday evening, and then only very briefly, before she was taken to hospital.'

'So, to sum up, you cannot provide Ms Montreau or myself with any great insights into her father's behaviour and mood that week?'

'I'm very sorry but no, I cannot.'

'And there were no suspicious movements in and around the apartment block that particular Sunday?'

'Absolutely none.'

'Were you questioned by the *Brigade* or anyone else in authority?'

'No, a humble security manager is very low down on anyone's questioning list.'

Mules looked at him closely, 'Not always.'

'Is there anything else you can tell us, no matter how small or insignificant?'

'No, Ms Montreau, nothing. I'm sorry. I only wish there was, I liked your father very much.'

After saying their goodbyes, and getting into her Clio, she turned to Mules.

'You know what I think?'

'He's lying?'

'Absolutely.'

'What makes you suspicious?'

'How much do you think a humble security manager earns?'

'Nowhere near enough to buy a lovely house in a fashionable part of Paris, with high-tech security gates.'

'Correct but that's only one part.'

'What else?'

'He couldn't look at me directly. Plus, he didn't see, hear, or notice anything unusual during that last week of my dad's life, not one single thing.'

'Which makes you think what, exactly?'

'He was either a terrible security manager, or he was part of, or at least an accessory to, Philippe's conspiracy.'

'Making this an inside job?'

'Yes.'

'Bravo! We'll make a detective of you yet.'

'Detective or not, we're not much further forward. Where next?'

'We stay here.'

'What?'

'I looked you up on LinkedIn last night.'

'Why?'

'Research; tell me, what does a bank systems analyst do, precisely?'

'According to my job description, defend against security breaches, identify, investigate, and mitigate cybersecurity threats. In practice, I monitor event logs for suspicious activity. When I feel something requires further investigation, I gather as much information as I can and pass it higher up the food chain.'

'Where are you, in food chain terms?'

'At the bottom, Tier One.'

'How long have you been doing the job for?'

'Ten years.'

'Which makes me think either you're a terrible systems analyst or you prefer to hide your expert light under a very large bushel.'

'Where are you going with this?'

'If I asked you to hack into someone's data, would you know how to do it?'

'I would never do that, never. I'd be sacked immediately.'

'I didn't ask you that. I asked you if you knew how to do it.'

'I'm CISSP qualified.'

'What does CISSP stand for?'

'Certified Information Systems Security Professional.'

'Is that good?'

'One of the most sought-after credentials in the industry.'

'But it doesn't appear on your LinkedIn profile?'

'No.'

'Why?'

'Is there a point to all these questions? Because if there isn't, and if you don't mind, I'd very much like to get on with doing something much more useful and productive; like find out who killed my father, and why.'

'Are you able to hack into other people's data, yes, or no?'

'Yes!'

'Have you brought your laptop?'

'I take it with me everywhere, why?'

'I would like you to demonstrate your CISSP skills.'

'How?'

'By accessing Hérault's bank account.'

'What? You're asking me to break the law? Didn't you listen to what I just said? If it ever got out, I'd lose my job. Probably be arrested.'

'I did hear you say loud and clear that you wanted to find out who killed your father and why.'

'I also said I wouldn't break the law, ever.'

'Listen to me. Do you think that, after forty years, the people who killed your father, are going to play nice, confess to murder, put their hands out, ask to be cuffed and let themselves be taken to the nearest courthouse?'

'I'm not stupid.'

'No, but you are naïve. You have to fight fire with fire. These gangsters killed your father. May have killed your mother. They're not going to have any qualms about killing you too.'

'Philippe more or less said the same thing.'

'For once in his sad life, old Simon was right. They won't have any qualms about killing you, him, me, or anyone else who gets caught in the crossfire. Especially you.'

'I get the message.'

'I hope so because it's decision time.'

'What does that mean?'

'You have to decide who you are going to be.'

'Decide between who?'

'Mary Poppins or Michael Corleone.'

Chapter Eighteen

'OK, I'm into Hérault's Banque Nord account.'

'And?'

'Every month, from the beginning of 1983, through to December 1987, 10,000 francs goes into his account via standing order. Then it stops.'

'Presumably his regular pay.'

'Hérault also held another account.'

'Surprise, surprise.'

'This one was set up on Monday, April 30th, 1984. The payments were irregular. 50,000 francs one month, 30,000 the next, and so on but always in cash. In 1986 and 1987 sometimes two or three different payments a month were being paid in.'

'Interesting.'

'Wow!'

'What?'

'Guess how much was paid into his account on March 30th, 1987?'

'Tell me.'

'250,000 francs.'

'Cash?'

'Yes.'

'I'd like to say I'm shocked, but I'm not.'

'Then, another 250,000 francs, also in cash, went in a month later.'

'Henri Paul, the prequel.'

'As far as I can tell that's the final payment.'

'A month after your father's death.'

'Half a million francs. Enough to buy a very nice house in Montmartre.'

'Most definitely, with enough left over to quit a boring-as-hell, dead-end job.'

'What does all that cash mean?'

'Hérault was in the pay of somebody, perhaps multiple somebodies.'

'Paid for what?'

'Information, a commodity that never loses its value. In this case, the information must have been extremely valuable, half a million francs worth.'

'Anything else?'

'To give someone, let's call that someone the *DST,* access to your parents' apartment. Also, to turn a blind eye and keep his mouth shut. A combination of all of them, according to context and circumstance.'

'Where do you think all this cash came from?'

'I'm guessing the *DST.* It certainly fits our hypothesis that your father was murdered. A murder planned, orchestrated and carried out by elements of the *DST,* rogue or official, perhaps a secret sub-unit. The fact there were sometimes multiple payments into Hérault's second bank account suggests he may have been providing information to more than one agency.'

'Such as?'

'Take your pick from the other French intelligence agencies, perhaps the *CIA* and/or *MI6.* The possibilities are, as they say, endless.'

'A regular gravy-train.'

'For three years, yes.'

'I wonder why the account was set up in late April '84?'

'My educated guess is that at this point, your father was notified to the *DST* as a person of interest; someone to keep an eye on.'

'This is madness. All these spooks interested in my father. Why? It makes no sense.'

'Your father must have done something, been suspected of doing something, or threatening to do something, which put him onto the intelligence services' radar; something worth half a million francs plus to someone.'

She touched her cross and looked at Mules. 'My father, a virologist, on intelligence agencies' watch lists. It's hard to take in.'

'It would not be the first time a scientist came up on the intelligence services' radar and it ended badly. Ask the widows of Frank Olson and David Kelly.'

'Who?'

'I'll tell you later. OK, let's think about it. Somebody tells the *DST* they should stick close to your father. One way to keep tabs on a suspect is covertly, via an insider with easy access to the suspect's home.'

'Enter Monsieur Hérault.'

'Absolutely. The *DST* would want to build up a picture of your father's behaviour, and his routine. Not only him but your mother too.'

'Because?'

'In case intelligence operatives were instructed to move and act quickly, make a sudden intervention, perhaps even to physically eliminate your father.'

'Instructed by?'

'Unless they were completely rogue elements, their political masters.'

'We're back to Philippe's conspiracy.'

'Correct. The *DST* had to know everything that was going on so they could identify a moment, or moments, to strike. Hérault would have been invaluable to them, especially on the fateful weekend, providing them with live, real-time updates of your parents' movements.'

'He as good as killed my father.'

Mules turned to her. 'Let's go back. Perhaps leave the talking to me, at least at first. You won't get anywhere if you lose the plot. Don't forget to think big picture. Our goal is to find out what happened to your father. Please keep it together, for his sake.'

'I'll try.'

As she approached the gates, Anne-Sophie could see Hérault standing at the upstairs window, phone in hand, looking directly at them. When he answered the buzzer, Eric asked him if, this time, he would let them into his house. After a few seconds, Hérault opened the gates and took them through to a very plush reception room. There was a pot of coffee waiting for them.

She whispered to Eric, 'Who ever said cheats never prosper was lying.'

Hérault seemed relaxed. He asked why they had come back so quickly. Eric told him he had more questions to ask about Monsieur Montreau's death. Looking out of the window, Mules asked him again if he'd noticed anything strange about Jean-

Marie's behaviour in the days leading up to his death. He repeated he was sorry but there was nothing that sprang to mind. Eric again asked Hérault to clarify if he'd noticed anything, or anybody, unusual that week, or the weekend. Any ''out of the ordinary'' activity in the area outside the apartment block. That drew another blank.

Then Eric looked at Hérault directly. 'This is a very nice house.'

'Thank you.'

'Houses in this area don't come cheap.'

'I suppose not.'

'When did you buy it?'

'I can't remember exactly. Sometime in the early nineties perhaps. No, it was nearer the time of the bicentenary of the revolution. Maybe the year before.'

'1988?'

'If you say so.'

'Your excellent memory should tell you so. Now, Hérault, let me be frank with you. Even in 1988, you must have had to take out a big mortgage to be able to buy this lovely house, in this expensive area, on a security manager's wage.'

'There was no mortgage.'

'Really?'

'I paid cash.'

'Amazing. How come, bearing in mind, with all due respect, your job, you could lay your hands on such a large amount of cash?'

'Very simple; a relative died. Left me a lot of money.'

'Ah, very convenient for you.'

'An old aunt I hardly knew. She lived down in the south, Montpellier.'

'Even more convenient.'

Anne-Sophie looked at him, 'Lucky you.'

'Yes, Ms Montreau, lucky me. Inspector Mules, let me also be frank and ask you a couple of questions.'

'Fire away.'

'When did you retire and when were you going to tell me?'

Mules said nothing.

'Lost your tongue?'

Mules remained silent.

'Impersonating a police officer, even an old, alcoholic, police officer, and using that position to gain access to a property under false pretences are, the last time I looked, very serious offences. Or have I got that wrong? Perhaps the law has changed in the past six months, and I didn't read or hear about it.'

'As a recently retired Detective Inspector, I have six months grace before I lose my powers of access and authority.'

Hérault got to his feet. 'Bull.'

Immediately, Anne-Sophie stood up and was in Hérault's face. 'You weasel! You've got some nerve preaching to us about the law. We've got all the evidence we need to get you put away for the rest of your scumbag of a life.'

Mules stepped in between them.

Hérault stepped back, then shouted, 'Get out!'

Eric grinned, then, without Anne-Sophie noticing, threw a ball of paper at Hérault's feet. 'That's a shame. We were just beginning to dry off.'

Back in the car, seeing her worried frown, Eric raised his hands. 'No one has asked me to return my badge, yet. Until they do, I carry on. What? What's the worst he can do? Ring up my old station, who will tell him to sling his hook and then tell me to return my badge in my own good time.'

'Let's hope it doesn't come to that.'

'Anyhow, let's not worry too much about what's going to happen to me. Hérault has more immediate pressing matters to concern him.'

'Such as?'

'Instinct tells me that, after our first visit, he was so spooked he rang up his old handler from the *DST,* or whichever agency it was he was working for.'

'And?'

'He told whoever it was he contacted about our conversation. I think Henri had a very nasty shock the first time around. The second time, it seemed he was ready for us, with his pot of coffee and so on, even to the extent of having an oven-ready cliché about his conveniently deceased aunt from Montpellier to hand. All thanks to his handler.'

'So, you're thinking the *DST* will be onto us?'

'I've no doubt about it.'

'Philippe was right.'

'About?'

'I'm in a race. I need to discover who took my father's life before they get to me.'

'These are high stakes you're playing for.'

'The highest?'

'Yes.'

She opened up her laptop. 'There's one last thing I want to do before we head off.'

'Yes.'

'Give you another demonstration of my CISSP skills.'

'Go on.'

One minute later, she showed him her screen.

'Blank. Even I, a Luddite, could manage that.'

'Do you know what that is?'

'As I said, a blank screen.'

'That, according to the Préfecture of Police in Paris records, is the official police dossier of the investigation into my father's death.'

'Hell.'

'Dark forces, Eric. Dark forces.'

Chapter Nineteen

'Henri, it's been a while.'

'Yes, Jacques, forty years.'

'That long? Time flies et cetera.'

Forty years on, Jacques occupied the same seat, tucked away in the same corner of the same cellar bar, with a clear view of everyone coming in and out. Hérault placed his leather jacket on the back of the chair and was about to sit down when Jacques gave him a ten Euro note.

'Go and get yourself a coffee and a pastry. Better make it two pastries. You need feeding up. What's up? No-one looking after you, keeping you warm at night, or are you still relying on the good ladies of Pigalle for that? After giving them forty-plus years of your custom, I should think you've qualified for discounted rates by now.'

Five minutes later, after Hérault had finally sat down, Jacques sat back and looked at him. 'So, here we are again, just like the good old days. What do you want?'

Hérault had been more than spooked by Anne-Sophie and Eric turning up at his security gate, he had been horrified. Even before his visitors returned to Anne-Sophie's Clio to voice their suspicions about him and hack into his bank accounts, he had picked up his phone and called someone he had not spoken to in four decades. The phone call had settled his nerves somewhat. However, they had been jangled again when Anne-Sophie and Eric returned barely fifteen minutes later. By the time the ensuing conversation came to an abrupt halt they were shredded.

Hence the meeting, thirty minutes after his 'guests' had left for a second time, in a small brasserie in the Rue du Chevalier de la Barre. The brasserie was situated in the shadow of Sacré-Cœur Basilica, an irony not lost on Hérault. He had a very strong feeling it would take divine intervention to get him out of the hole he now found himself in. After just about managing to keep up his lies during the two interviews with the retired Detective

Inspector and the ultra-aggressive Montreau girl, he was certain he would not stand up to a third.

Sitting opposite Hérault was a dishevelled, unshaven, rain-sodden, seventy-something, white male. Henri had often wondered during the three years he had collaborated with Jacques, which reputable organization would employ such a scruffy loser. Especially one with a very visible scar under his right eye-socket, a product, he speculated, of Jacques' upbringing in the mean streets of Marseilles.

His wonderment had begun on the last Saturday in April 1984, when that same scruffy individual insistently rang the entry buzzer to the Saint-Victor apartment block. At this point, Henri had been working as the block's security manager for a year and a half. 'Apartment Block Security Manager' was a big title, but there was nothing big about his job which involved little more than replacing lost keys, arranging for damaged stairwells to be repaired and unblocking a scarcely believable number of blocked toilets. Eighteen months in, Hérault was bored, unhappy and increasingly frustrated. After paying for rent, shopping, and Saturday nights in the Pigalle, there was precious little left of his monthly salary of ten thousand francs.

So, when Jacques, as this loser called himself, asked Henri if he fancied doing something that was in the interest of national security, required very little effort but would be rewarded with large amounts of easy cash, Hérault was in a very receptive mood. This was Saturday afternoon, and, in a few hours, he would be back in the Pigalle, enjoying his one night of relaxation of the week. So, he had thought, why not? Any money was welcome. Easy cash was very welcome. Defending the honour of France came as an added, albeit, in Hérault's grand scheme of things, well down his list, bonus.

On March 29th, 1987, three serene years spent pocketing large amounts of that easy money came to a crashing halt. The shock, revulsion and guilt Henri felt when he saw Jean-Marie Montreau being carried out in a body bag and dumped into an ambulance, was not even slightly assuaged by the two-hundred-and-fifty-thousand francs he received that same evening. Hérault had known immediately he was now in an immensely vulnerable position; if they, whoever they were, could murder a well-respected, happily married, father-to-be scientist for no good reason that Hérault could fathom, they would surely have no compunction about doing him, a no-good, friendless, low life, in at any time. If he went to the police and confessed to what he knew, then he would no doubt be charged with numerous offences, including being an accessory to murder; even perhaps of the murder itself. Stranger things had happened. Even then, Jacques would still most likely arrange his early exit, stage left, in one of his white vans, before it came to a trial.

In his, until now, final meeting with his handler on April 30th, 1987, Henri had been told to buy a nice house, forget the two of them had ever met, and never, ever, contact Jacques again. However, as far as Hérault was concerned, the conversations with Anne-Sophie and Mules had changed the game totally. He had followed Anne-Sophie's life closely and knew about her job as a cybersecurity analyst at Banque Nord. It was obvious she had illegally accessed his bank accounts. He suspected that she, in trying to track down the truth of her father's death, had put two and two together very quickly. She and that grinning goon Mules must have realized immediately that his wages did not extend anywhere close to buying a gorgeous, detached property, situated in one of the most desirable spots in Montmartre. He could not complain. He had always known it had only been a matter of when, not if, he was rumbled. He might not believe in God, but he absolutely believed in karma.

So, here he was, sitting opposite Jacques, having told him what had occurred with his visitors, especially what he suspected about Anne-Sophie's hacking. Despite the wet, chilly weather, Henri was sweating profusely and hoping against hope his old handler would have some comforting words for him.

'You want me to help you out, Henri? You're having a laugh, surely? You're on your own, pal.'

'But...'

'But what? What will you do when I tell you to get lost? Who will you run to? If you're stupid enough to go to anybody, or tell anybody any of this, who would believe you? If you do run to somebody, you know very well you'll end up in the same white van as your old friend, Jean-Marie Montreau. A friend who you, in case you had forgotten, betrayed for five-hundred thousand francs. Money which you used to buy yourself a very nice house, before spending the next forty years sitting on your puny backside, sweating over porn mags and videos. Money that, may I also remind you, was handed over on strict condition you kept your mouth well and truly shut.'

Jacques took perverse pleasure in observing the look of terror on Hérault's face. 'And, if you do end up in a white van, I guarantee there will be even less of your body to perform an autopsy on than there was of Montreau's. Understood?'

'Understood.'

'Good. Now, get lost.'

Taking for granted a cowed Hérault would do as he had done four decades ago and follow instructions, a contented-looking Jacques picked up his phone and wallet. Meanwhile a stunned, but now well out of Jacques' sight, Hérault reached into his back pocket and took out a scrap of paper on which was scrawled a contact phone number. He looked up at Sacré-Cœur's beautiful white dome, crossed himself and decided, for the first time in his life, to put his faith in divine intervention.

Chapter Twenty

He put down his cigarette, 'Secure line, midday, this can't be good news.'

'It's not.'

'Spit it out.'

'Do you remember the Montreau case?'

'Remind me.'

'March 1987. L'Académie virologist, Jean-Marie Montreau, about to throw a serious spanner in the works, required an intervention.'

'OK.'

'You remember it now?'

'Vaguely. Was I involved?'

'You're a cool one. I'll give you that.'

'Well, was I?'

'My boys did the crime. You arranged the cover-up.'

'You can prove that?'

'Outrageous!'

'Well, can you?'

'I haven't called you to start an argument. Do you remember the case?'

'Why have you called?'

'A butterfly is flapping her wings.'

'Name?'

'Anne-Sophie Montreau.'

'The daughter?'

'Yes, she's emerged from her cocoon.'

'A lone butterfly?'

'No, there's a kaleidoscope.'

'Names?'

'Retired Detective Inspector Eric Mules and Philippe Simon, a journalist who is also the girl's godfather. Mules is dogged, determined and desperate to shed forty years of guilt from his shoulders. Simon is similarly guilt-ridden and itching to make amends for his cowardice before his time runs out.'

'What do you mean?'

'He's dying. Knocking on the proverbial death's door.'

'It's not all bad news then.'

'Things have escalated in the last hour.'

'Tell me.'

'The security manager of the Montreau apartment block, Hérault.'

'What about him?'

'He might turn.'

'You cut him loose?'

'In a manner of speaking, yes.'

'Let me guess. He came to you for words of comfort and protection. You told him to get lost.'

'Something like that.'

'Clever. Now he's a loose cannon, exactly what I do not need right now. Don't they teach you strategy at that school for spies of yours? Or at least get lectures from someone who has read Sun Tzu? God knows how you got to the top. Correction, I do know. Now you come to me, why? What for? Comfort? Protection? Cover? It's 1987 all over again. Remember that? You were panicking like a turkey at Christmas when you called me. 'Procureur! Help me! Help me!' What was needed in 1987 was an intervention, not an execution. Things certainly escalated after that; you in panic mode; the Montreau woman nearly giving birth on the pavement. Absolute total chaos until I arrived and took matters in hand. The ambulance, the clean-up, squaring the press, fixing the inquest, providing you with a backbone, as well as toilet paper.'

'I didn't call to hear another of your sanctimonious monologues about my apparently unlimited shortcomings. You're not Mr Perfect, not by a long chalk. If I was in your shoes, I'd be treading very carefully.'

'Is that a threat?'

'We both know we sink or swim together.'

'I sink, you sink. You sink, I swim.'

'Screw you.'

'What if I were to tell you to get lost?'

'That would be a mistake.'

'Would it?'

90

'Do I need to spell it out?'

'Spare me. So, what to do?'

'Things may spiral out of control quickly, especially if Ms Montreau keeps utilising her formidable computer skills.'

'All thanks to another of your balls ups.'

'What does that mean?'

'Do I need to spell it out?' There was a knock at the door. 'Yes.'

'Are you ready, sir?'

'Two minutes.' He took a drag on his cigarette. 'Be quick. What do you want?'

'To work on a plan.'

'Plan?'

'Of containment.'

'Call me tonight, after eight, same line.'

'OK. Have you spoken to our..?'

'Mutual friend? Yes, this morning, at three o'clock.'

'And?'

'He didn't say much except to remind me of his two golden rules.'

'Which are?'

'One, he doesn't take questions. Two, he doesn't exist.'

'I remember.'

'Another thing.'

'Yes?'

'There was one piece of unfinished business in 1987. We need to finish it, or, more accurately, find it.'

'I'd forgotten about that.'

'That's one of the many differences between us, I never forget anything.'

'Apparently not.'

'Never. Well, unlike our mutual friend, I do have to take questions. Speak later.'

Chapter Twenty-One

He was back at his house in Montreuil, parking his Saab, when the call came. He grinned.

'Mules?'

'Yes? Ah, it's you. I wondered when you'd call. It was only a matter of time.'

'I need to see you.'

'I'm sure you do. When?'

'As soon as possible.'

'Where?'

'Parc des Buttes-Chaumont. The Suicide Bridge. You know it?'

'Don't I just.'

'Half an hour.'

'What's the rush?'

'Can you be there?'

'My diary's rather full.'

'Is it hell! Do you want to help the Montreau girl?'

'Help you save your skin you mean.'

'Will you be there or not?'

'I'll be there.'

Mules ended the call. As it happened, the last thing he had expected was for Hérault to call him so soon. However, it appeared he *had* managed to turn the screw on Hérault's panicky emotional state a notch tighter. He immediately called Anne-Sophie.

'Where are you?'

'Le Marais.'

'Good. Stay there.'

'Because?'

'Hérault just called me.'

'What! Why?'

'I think he's on the verge of jumping ship.'

'Brilliant.'

'As long as I can offer him certain assurances.'

'Such as?'

'A safe house, witness protection, immunity.'

'What? Protection? He colluded in my father's murder for God's sake. He can rot in hell for all I care.'

'I agree with the sentiment but it's time for a bit of realpolitik.'

'Meaning?'

'It's all about leverage.'

'I still don't get you.'

'You're going to have to bite the bullet.'

'Stop going round in circles. Please just tell me what you mean.'

'He's worked out you've accessed his bank accounts and realized the game is up.'

'I see.'

'Plus, I'm surmising he's been abandoned by his handler. Which I must admit I didn't see coming. I didn't think he or she…'

'They or them.'

'Would be so stupid. Hérault knows he is rapidly running out of road.'

'Us, or nothing.'

'Precisely.'

'You're meeting him where and when?'

'In twenty-five minutes, at the Suicide Bridge, Parc des Buttes-Chaumont.'

'Suicide Bridge? Hardly sounds like something the Paris tourist board would be keen to publicize; definite Dan Brown territory. What is it?'

'What it says on the tin, a twelve-metre masonry bridge, twenty-two metres above the lake; perfect suicide material.'

'Right. So, in short, you're suggesting I go along with this?'

'I know it's going to stick in your throat, but the positives far outweigh the negatives. As we know, Hérault has information, a lot of information. I think it's worth swallowing your pride, as well as your anger; at least in the short-term.'

'I'm not sure I want to do deals with vermin.'

'Let me find out what he has to say, then we can work out our response. I won't say anything to him in terms of an offer, that's your call. Any delay should work in our favour; turn the screw even tighter.'

'Right.'

'And, if he is prepared to spill the beans, you're one, two, maybe multiple steps closer to finding out who killed your father and why.'

'OK, Eric, I trust you. Go ahead, meet with Hérault. Call me as soon as you're done.'

He started up his Saab and grinned again. 'Form is temporary, class is permanent. Retired or not, you've still got it, Mules. Still got it.'

Chapter Twenty-Two

I am due to land at Charles de Gaulle, Friday, four-pm.
I will see you at the Ritz at seven.
TM.

Chapter Twenty-Three

After walking up one hundred and seventy-three steps in the pouring rain, Mules decided that whatever else he'd still got, fitness was not one of them. It took him a good minute to recover from the exertion. This was obviously God's way of telling him to stay off the booze for good. As he approached the Suicide Bridge, he noticed it was now fenced with wire mesh. This meant there was one less issue to contend with, should the worst come to the worst. This felt even more relevant when he arrived at the bridge and encountered a shattered-looking, cigarette-smoking Hérault, with a holdall bag slung over his shoulder.

'You look grim.'

'Thanks. You would look the same if you were in my shoes.'

'Which shoes are they?'

'Let's go for a walk.'

Mules looked at him, 'Harder to hit a moving target, is that it?'

'Something like that, yes.'

'Wanting to dodge the bullet.'

'Yes.'

'Dead man walking?'

'Get lost.'

Mules grinned.

They walked up to the Temple de la Sybille. Even here, with its three hundred and sixty-degree panoramic views of the Parc, Hérault still looked tense.

'Pull yourself together, man. I doubt there'll be any *DGSI* operatives up here. Not yet anyway.'

'I'm not so sure.'

'You really are worried.'

'With observational skills like that you should have been a detective.'

'If this is how you talk to people you want to cut a deal with, how do you treat people whose help you don't need?'

'Who says I want to cut a deal?'

'Why else would you call me and beg for a meeting as soon as possible?'

'You're enjoying this aren't you?'

'With observational skills like that you should have been an excellent apartment block security manager. Shame they weren't so sharp between five-fifteen and five-forty-five pm on March 29th, 1987. Or in the days leading up to it, or so you claim.'

'Very funny.'

'Anne-Sophie Montreau isn't laughing. As you discovered this morning.'

'She needs to watch that temper of hers.'

'Never mind her. Cut to the chase. What do you want?'

'Witness protection. Immunity. A safe house.'

'In return for?'

'Telling you and Ms Montreau everything I know, and everything I suspect, about the lead-up to her father's death.'

'I see.'

Hérault grabbed Mules' wrist and looked at him directly. 'I'm not sure you do. Listen to me. I was outside the block the entire time. I didn't do anything inside the apartment. I didn't witness anything inside the apartment. I cannot prove or disprove anything that may, or may not, have occurred. I know only as much as you do, that Jean-Marie Montreau's dead body was brought out of the block and put inside what looked like an ambulance, but which I know was anything but. You will find it impossible to prove anything. I seriously doubt this case will get anywhere near a court, but, if it does, I will tell the judge I was simply passing on information to people who told me I was doing my patriotic duty.'

'For which you were royally rewarded to the tune of the best part of a million francs.'

'Any judge and jury will deem that due reward for protecting the national interest.'

'You kept quiet about it for forty years, why sing now?'

'It doesn't take an Einstein to work out that someone with Ms Montreau's computer skills has, albeit illegally, gotten into my bank accounts from the 1980s. It wouldn't take even an alcoholic, retired Detective Inspector long to work out where all my extra money came from, or where it went.'

'Why witness protection?'

'Cutting to the chase, don't pretend you don't know who we are dealing with here. You were there in March 1987. You were also there in the thick of the action in the early hours of August 31st in the Alma Tunnel. Don't tell me you've forgotten? You know what the intelligence services are capable of. They are animals, savages, without mercy or compunction.'

Mules was taken aback by Hérault's reference to his involvement in the Alma Tunnel investigation. He certainly remembered that. Those events involved many of the same actors involved in the Montreau case, himself included. If the truth about that night was ever taken seriously, if people actually read the evidence freely available to everyone, then the establishment roof might cave in.

'I'm guessing you contacted your old handler who told you to get lost and keep your mouth shut, or else.'

'I'm here, that's all you need to know.'

'I know you're scared. Are you going back to your wonderful, 'paid for by your conveniently dead aunt' house after this?'

'Are you crazy? What do you think this bag is for? My next stop is the *hotelF1* close to Stade de France.'

'Paying in cash?'

'Yes.'

'You're good at that.'

'Ha, ha.'

'So, you want to be put into a safe house?'

'As soon as possible.'

'Then you'll talk?'

'I'll sing, dance, whatever you want me to do.'

'How much do you know?'

'First things first; a safe house, then Ms Montreau finds out everything I know.'

'Call me in a week. I should have an answer for you by then.'

Hérault grabbed Mules' wrist again. 'A week! Are you out of your mind? You think I've got a week? Never mind a week, I may be dead in a day, by tonight, this afternoon. Then Ms Montreau will have got nothing out of me. Time is running out, Mules.'

Eric looked at his watch; almost one o'clock. 'OK, let's walk back down to the road. I'll call Ms Montreau from my car.'

For a split-second, Mules thought Hérault was going to hug him. Certainly, for the first time during the conversation, his face had brightened up.

'I'm not promising anything. It's down to Ms Montreau. She's calling the shots.'

'I know she is. Tough lady.'

'You bet.'

As they walked back across the Suicide Bridge the rain seemed to intensify but the big plus for Mules was that it was downhill all the way to his Saab.

Chapter Twenty-Four

It took only one question; until that moment, Hervé Parcelle had given a flawless display; urbane, unflappable, witty and across all the detail. After twenty-five minutes, he had the assembled media hacks eating out of his hand. Watching in Philippe's lounge, even Anne-Sophie was engaged and impressed.

'He's good.'

'Slick, I'll give him that.'

'He reminds me of Judge Roban in *Spiral*.'

'I doubt Parcelle would be enamoured by that comparison. Roban is a bad guy, is he not?'

'Not at all. Anyway, some women like a villain. The same women who might think Parcelle attractive.'

'Do you?'

'Mmm, possibly; if he wins the election, then, yes, absolutely.'

Philippe was relieved to see she was smiling as she said it.

Anne-Sophie had just commented that Parcelle would be even more of a shoo-in after this performance when the question came:

'Minister Parcelle, Paul LeBlanc, *Le Parisien*. Tell me, are there any skeletons in your cupboard that you'd like to share with the French electorate?'

'Are there any skeletons in your closet?'

Cue uproar. Anne-Sophie, who had stood up to go and make lunch, sat down again. 'What is it? What did I miss?

'Shush, please.'

LeBlanc's response was immediate, 'What do you mean by that?'

'You asked me a question. I asked you one back.'

'Why use the word closet?'

'It's a synonym of cupboard. What's your problem?'

'It's obvious, isn't it?'

'Is it?'

'Everyone here thinks so.'

'If you say so.'

'I do.'

'How old are you?'

'Twenty-nine, not that it's any of your business.'

'It's so typical of your snowflake generation, your politics, your worldview.'

'What does that mean?'

'Taking offence at every tiny comment. Here's a scoop for you all, breaking news. If I become President, I promise to dish out thicker skins to everyone under the age of thirty.' If this was a joke no-one in the room seemed to appreciate it. 'You think you can ask me any question, about any aspect of my life, hoping to expose any cracks. However, if I turn the tables, you crumble. Pathetic.' He looked around the room. 'Ah, Marie. You have a question?'

'Two, actually. Is it OK?'

'My pleasure. Fire away.'

'Thank you. First, do you consider the election to be in the bag?'

'Not at all. Fifty years ago, I lost an election which I thought I had sewn up. That memory still stings. As a result, I take nothing for granted, ever.'

'Second, can one of your election promises include sending every thin-skinned, snowflaky, twenty and thirty-something reporter, an umbrella and raincoat? Especially the female ones.'

'I'll add it to my manifesto.'

With the thinnest of smiles, a smile that friends and foes alike said barely reached his lips, the thick-skinned Minister of Justice walked out of the press conference.

Anne-Sophie stood up and resumed making lunch. 'Wow, for the first time ever, something interesting happened in politics. I'm just not sure what that something was. Why the brouhaha?'

When Philippe did not respond she looked at him. He looked upset.

'What is it?'

'Parcelle's mask slipped. I did not like what I saw underneath.'

'What did he say to the reporter that was so bad? I don't get it, sorry.'

'He used the word closet.'

'So?'

'It was a reference to the reporter's homosexuality. Open homosexuality I may add, Paul is married, with children.'

'You know him?'

'Of course, he is something of a protégé, at least I like to think so. I took him under my wing when he first started. Very smart cookie. Great potential, courageous, extremely popular with the press gang.'

'Sounds like Parcelle may have picked on the wrong guy.'

'Yes.'

'That's a shame,' she said, turning off the TV. 'Anyway, come and eat some lunch, Mules will be calling any minute. I've a feeling we'll need to be ready to get going as soon as he rings.'

However, as they attacked their chicken mayo and tomato baguettes, she resumed their conversation about what they had just witnessed. 'Will the kerfuffle do Parcelle any harm?'

'I doubt it very much, at least not with his target demographic.'

'Which is?'

'Fifty-plus, white male, conservative. Any kind of bigotry, against any kind of minority, goes down extremely well with them.'

'You think it might be a battle Parcelle wanted to fight...might enjoy fighting?'

'Yes, you may well be right. Homophobia, xenophobia, misogyny, it all comes alike to those morons. Parcelle obviously feels a culture war will not do him any harm amongst his - appropriately named – base. Quite the opposite.'

'I'll tell you one thing.'

'Go on.'

'He didn't answer the question.'

'Which one?'

'About having skeletons in his cupboard.'

'No, he didn't.'

'I bet he's got plenty of those. What do you think?'

'I would imagine so. None of us are skeleton-free, but politicians are probably worse in that respect.'

'Especially French ones.'

'Ha, yes, there is certainly a history of that.'

'What about your colleague, Paul? He'll be OK?'

'Absolutely! Knowing Paul, I think at this very moment he will have begun searching for every Parcelle-related skeleton out there.'

'Hervé's rattled the wrong cage, or closet.'

'Very good, yes. Meanwhile, as we are talking about journalists, whilst you were out with Mules, I contacted my colleagues, Françoise and Emil. I've arranged for us to meet this afternoon in their second home.'

'Which is where?'

'A bar adjacent to L'Académie.'

'I see. Well, as you keep mentioning them you obviously think they can help our cause.'

'I do.'

'Great. I look forward to meeting them. Did you arrange a specific time?'

'Four o'clock.'

She heard 'Voulez-Vous'. 'Here we go.' She put her phone onto speaker-mode. 'Hi, what's happening?'

'As I thought, he wants a deal. Information in exchange for protection.'

'And you're happy?'

'Yes, if you are. You call the shots.'

'As I said, I trust your judgment. I'm not overjoyed about it but, if you think it's a deal worth making, I'm happy to go ahead.'

'Hérault will be delighted. He's a nervous wreck.'

She looked at the clock. 'OK, so, we'll be over for one-thirty?'

'Sounds good. See you then.'

Running the water to wash the plates, she thought to herself that finally she was going to find out the truth. Forty years of secrets and lies were about to be washed away and, at last, after a lifetime of feeling nothing for him, she was able to shed tears for her father.

Chapter Twenty-Five

As she had done earlier with Philippe's phone, Anne-Sophie downloaded anti-malware software to Eric's devices.

'Is it any good?'

'The best.'

'Which company is it?'

'ASMAMS.'

'Never heard of it.'

'Hopefully, you will do, one day. It's brand new. The techie behind it is brilliant.'

Once Mules, Anne-Sophie and Philippe had refuelled on the coffee, bread and cheese provided by Céline, they were ready to get to work on Hérault.

'Ms Montreau and I are going to take you through your story. Monsieur Simon will tape. Ready?'

Hérault looked remarkably cheerful considering he was about to be grilled and had not partaken, or been asked to partake, of the coffee, bread and cheese. 'Yes, retired Detective Inspector Mules, I'm ready.'

'OK, let's go.'

Over the next thirty minutes, Hérault proceeded to freely spill the beans about his relationship with his handler, the man he knew only as Jacques. He told them how Jacques had made his initial approach at the end of April 1984 with promises of financial reward in exchange for information. Jacques had delivered that money as soon as Hérault started keeping his side of the bargain.

'You did it for the money?'

'Yes, Ms Montreau, I did it for the money. How terrible of me! I know that makes me a bad person in your eyes. If it's any consolation, which I'm guessing it won't be, my greed made me a bad person in my own eyes too.'

'I just don't understand how you could put on a show of being my parents' friend yet facilitate them being spied upon.'

'I was told it was a matter of national security, that it was my patriotic duty to allow Jacques, and whoever worked for him, to do what they needed to do. I was told I was being paid to protect the nation's interests. What's wrong with that? What's the difference between doing what I did and being in the armed forces?'

Philippe interjected. 'How much of this money earned in the name of patriotic duty and national security was declared on your tax return?'

'None of it.'

'All the more reason for you to be very straight with us now. You wouldn't want to end up in the same boat as Al Capone, would you?'

'What?'

'If you don't tell us everything, we'll report you to the tax authorities.'

Mules resumed the interrogation, 'So, you say that for two years nothing much happened, then you began giving information to other, unknown, agencies, and your payments increased accordingly?'

'I didn't speak to other agencies I only ever spoke to Jacques. He said the information was being passed on to other, unspecified, agents, who were willing to pay for it too.'

'We asked you this this morning what Jean-Marie's mood was like during that last week. Perhaps now you'll be honest with us. No BS, I can smell it a kilometre away.'

'Jean-Marie was tense, no question. Monday through to Thursday he left much earlier than usual, before six, and came back to the apartment much later, after eight. He looked terrible. Thin, pale, and unsmiling, like he had the weight of the world pressing down on him. I couldn't understand it. I thought he should be happy; a good job, a lovely wife, first child on the way.'

'You sound jealous?'

'I was. He had everything going in his direction and yet he seemed very unhappy.'

'Did you ask him what was bothering him?'

'Of course.'

'Of course, he did. The more information he obtained the more he got paid.'

'That's only partly true. Believe me or not, Ms Montreau, I liked your father, and your mother. Who couldn't like them? I had no idea it was going to end as it did.'

'My father was tense and anxious you said?'

'Yes, very. The first and only time I saw him smile the whole week was Friday evening.'

'Please tell us what you remember about that.'

'He returned about seven. It was a lovely evening, a really promising spring evening; warm, perhaps the first one that year. He had a spring in his step too.'

'Did you speak to him?'

'Yes, I said to him it was nice to see him smiling again.'

'How did he respond?'

'He told me he had spent a very pleasant half-hour in the Luxembourg Garden on the way home. I knew then something good must have happened, something that had put him in a more cheerful frame of mind, made him want to go to the Garden.'

'How did you know?'

'That was his go-to place when he was in a happy mood or had something to celebrate.'

'Any thoughts what that something was?'

'None.'

'Did you tell Jacques?'

'No, I was busy that night. New people were moving into an apartment. It was non-stop all evening.'

'What happened next?'

'Very early the next morning, I'm talking six o'clock, Jacques was on the phone telling me to be on my mettle that day and Sunday. Telling me that if I saw Jean-Marie, or spoke to him, I was to contact Jacques immediately. He told me to forego my usual Saturday night's activities and get an early night.'

'What activities?'

'The Pigalle.'

'And your reaction to the call?'

'I knew I had to be on the ball Saturday and Sunday. That meant not going out but getting that early night and eight hours sleep.'

'Were you curious about what was going on?'

'Of course.'

'But you didn't ask too many questions?'

'Not of Jacques, no.'

'To anyone else?'

'Just myself.'

'Yourself?'

'I had a bad feeling.'

'Bad enough to refuse the money, or warn my father?'

Hérault's head dropped. 'No.'

'Were you ever married?'

'No.'

'In a relationship?'

'In high school, just for a few weeks. Apart from that, no.'

'So, you've only ever had to worry or think about yourself?'

'Yes.'

'You say you didn't ask Jacques any questions?'

'No.'

'Did you ask about the money?'

'I never asked about the money. I did something, I got paid. Sometimes I did nothing and got paid.'

'That must have been nice for you?'

'Free money. Who doesn't like that?'

Mules snarled. 'No one, as long as it's not blood money, scumbag.'

Anne-Sophie stroked her cross and leaned forward in her chair. 'I have a question.'

Chapter Twenty-Six

Yes?'

'What did Jacques look like please?'

'Short, squat, greasy hair.'

'Anything else?'

'What do you mean?'

'Any identifying features.'

'He has a scar under his right eye, if that's what you mean.'

He noticed his three inquisitors exchange looks, first of amazement and then satisfaction. Bullseye! At last, something good had happened and the words 'divine intervention' flashed through his head. They said it was never too late to go back to the church and, if only he could get out of this mess in one piece, he vowed he would be banging on the door of Sacré-Cœur Basilica early next Sunday morning.

'Parisian?'

'No, the South. Judging by his accent, Marseilles.'

'Not far from that conveniently rich, conveniently dead, aunt of yours.'

'Hysterical, Mules. You should have taken to the stage when you retired, it's never too late.'

The rain was lashing down again. It was so loud on the roof, that Anne-Sophie had to move her chair closer to Hérault to hear him properly. 'Now, that Saturday.'

'Yes?'

'Did you see much of Father?'

'He was in and out a lot that morning.'

'Any idea where he was going?'

'L'Académie. He came back to the apartment twice and both times he went back there.'

'How did he seem to you? What was his mood?'

'Anxious, stressed, tense; he virtually ran in and out of the block each time.'

'Did he tell you what he was doing at L'Académie?'

'All he told me was that he was meeting a colleague.'

'And you kept Jacques up to speed?'

'Yes.'

'And the afternoon? Was that just as frenetic?'

'No.'

'Why?'

'Your father went to Le Vésinet. He left after lunch, about two o'clock.'

'Le Vésinet?'

'Yes, to the west, Saint-Germain, Versailles, that way.'

'I know where it is, I got a speeding ticket there in 2019.'

'Did Monsieur Montreau give you any information, any insight, as to why he was going there?'

'No Mules, none at all.'

'How long was my father away from the apartment?'

'Let me think; a good three hours. It's forty-five minutes each way, even when the traffic is flowing, never mind on a Saturday afternoon.'

'So, he must have returned between four and five o'clock.'

'Definitely nearer to five. The light was just beginning to fade a touch, and I was starting to feel hungry. Speaking of which…'

'Did he say anything when he returned?'

'Nothing. However, he looked- I'm sorry, it's difficult to put into words.'

'Try.'

'Red-eyed, shaken up, and pale.'

'Did you see him again on Saturday night?'

'No, I did not see him until Sunday morning. Can I ask something please?'

'You can ask.'

'I know I don't deserve anything but I'm just about all in. Please may I have a little piece of bread and a small chunk of cheese?'

Despite Eric's disapproving look, Anne-Sophie gave Hérault the food, and poured him some coffee too.

'Thank you.'

Mules took over the questioning, 'What time did you first see Jean-Marie on Sunday morning?'

'Approximately eight o'clock.'

'In what context?'

'He said he was having to go to L'Académie, in his word, *again*.'

'Did he say why he was going?'

'No, but he was in a hurry.'

'You were curious obviously.'

'Obviously, but I did not want to press him too hard.'

'Didn't want to put him on his guard? Is that it?'

'Yes, partly. Plus, he did not look well. Again, you won't believe me, but I was genuinely concerned for him.'

'What time did he return to the apartment?'

'About eleven.'

'And his mood?'

'Down in the mouth; he seemed fragile. I remember his eyes were red again.'

'Like he'd been crying?'

'Yes, he must have been very stressed.'

'Did you see him again after that?'

'I did, in the afternoon. He and Thérèse left the apartment at about one o'clock to go for their regular Sunday afternoon walk to the Garden.'

'The Luxembourg?'

'Of course. They always went there on a Sunday, rain or shine.'

Anne-Sophie asked, 'How long were they out for?'

'They were gone for two hours. Your father looked much calmer when he returned. He was...'

'He was what?'

'Stroking your mother's tummy and saying ''Not long now, my darling.'''

Philippe took hold of his goddaughter's hand.

'And after that?'

'After that what?'

'Did you see either of my parents again?'

'Your mother left the apartment at five, as she also did every Sunday, even when she was heavily pregnant.'

'Where did she go?'

'Jardin des Plantes, to see her friend.'

'The friend's name?'

'Marguerite.'

'You really did know everything about them, didn't you?'

Mules curled his lip, 'That's what he was getting paid for.'

'What happened next?'

'Your father went out almost straight after your mother.'

'Where to?'

'L'Académie, once again. Said he had work to do, important work. I called Jacques straight away to let him know what was going on.'

'And then?'

'Almost immediately a white van drew up. Two men in council employee gear got out. I let them into the block.'

Anne-Sophie felt herself beginning to tremble. 'Did they say anything to you?'

'No.'

'Did you know them?'

'Not at all, I'd never seen them before. I haven't seen them since.'

'Would you recognize them if you saw them again?'

'I doubt it. They were wearing baseball caps pulled down tight over their heads. They were carrying rucksacks. That's all I can tell you. One was white, the other black.'

'The rucksacks?'

'No, the guys.'

'How long were they in the block?'

'I would say ten, fifteen minutes maximum, before…'

'Before what?'

'Your father came back. He was running. Told me he'd forgotten something.'

'Forgotten what?'

'He didn't elaborate.'

'And then?'

'I tried to stop him from going inside but he was insistent. He virtually pushed me out of his way.'

'And then what happened?'

Hérault took a sip of coffee, politely asked Anne-Sophie for a top-up and took a deep breath. His hands were gripping his knees. 'After ten minutes, the two council guys left in their van. And then, well, all hell broke loose. Police vehicles, an ambulance, a white van; as Mules and Simon know only too well.'

'Do you remember any more details? Did you recognize anyone?'

'No, only Jacques. It all happened so quickly.'

'What happened later? After the hullabaloo had died down.'

'I saw Jacques that night, at ten o'clock.'

'And?'

'He gave me a bag full of cash.'

'A big bag?'

'Yes.'

'Half a million francs big?'

'Yes, plus another fifty thousand.'

'What did you do with that little bonus?'

'What he told me to do. I kept it in my flat and spent it over the course of the next few months, in small amounts.'

'Did he say anything else to you?'

'That I would do well to keep my trap shut and to pay the half a million francs into my account in two lots. He would see to it that no questions were asked. As cash buyers could strike very good deals, he said I should use the money to buy myself a house. No-one would ask where the money had come from but if they did, I was to tell them it was a legacy from a dead aunt in Montpellier. He was right about the house; the one I liked was on sale for 750,000 francs. I got a quarter of a million knocked off for cash. The seller asked me no questions whatsoever about my background, nor where the money came from.'

'Lucky you.'

'Lucky me.'

Anne-Sophie's shaking right hand was touching her cross.

Mules asked another question, 'How was Jacques when you saw him this morning?'

'What do you think?'

'That's why you rang me?'

'Yes.'

'You'd run out of road?'

'There was no road left to run out of.'

'And, to reiterate, you want…?'

'Protection.'

'From the same fate as befell Anne-Sophie's father?'

'Yes.'

112

'Have you got anything else to add?'

'No, Retired Detective Inspector, I haven't. Except…'

'Except?'

'Something I've only just remembered.'

'Go on.'

'There was a guy who went inside with the *Brigade,* tall, thin, black hair, wearing a black hat, trench coat and smoking a cigarette. Long, thin nose.'

'Who was he?'

'I don't know his name.'

'OK.'

'But I do know he was the Procureur. I heard Jacques mention it to a colleague.'

Anne-Sophie stood up and said, 'Nobody seems to know this guy's name. Roulet didn't, or so she said.'

Mules approached Hérault, 'Anything else to add?'

'No, that's everything.'

'Get up.'

'What for?'

'Get up!'

'What do you mean?'

'What I say, get up off your disgusting backside.'

'What for?'

'Time's up.'

'Where am I going?'

'No idea. The *hotelF1* perhaps? I'm not interested.'

'But…'

'But nothing. We might not be able to prove it in a court of law, but we all know you allowed Anne-Sophie's father to be killed, that you were an accessory to his murder.'

'But…'

'You're on your own, scumbag.'

'You can't! Out there, I'm a dead man walking. I told you this. You know it. You said so yourself at the Suicide Bridge.'

'Good riddance to bad rubbish.'

'You promised me protection.'

'Did I? Sorry, I don't recall that. Must be losing it, my age.'

'You'll be responsible for my death.'

Mules had already turned his back on him and switched on the TV news channel. 'Shame. Goodbye.'

'Who the hell is that?' Hérault had stood up and was staring at the TV.

Anne-Sophie looked at him. 'What? You look like you've seen a ghost.'

'I have, a forty-year-old ghost. Who is that?'

'Don't you follow politics?'

'No.'

'That's one thing we have in common then, the only thing.'

'Who is he?'

Mules was walking towards Hérault. 'Still here, scumbag? I told you to get out.'

Hérault pointed at the TV screen. 'For God's sake, who is he?'

Now it was Philippe's turn to look at Hérault. 'What is it?'

'It's him.'

'Who?'

'The Procureur.'

Anne-Sophie spun around and looked at the TV. Her legs almost gave way. 'Lying bitch.'

'Will someone tell me who the hell he is?'

'Monsieur Hervé Parcelle.'

'Why is he on the telly?'

'He's the odds-on favourite to be France's next President.'

Hérault's legs did give way. Fortunately, Mules caught him and propped him up on his chair.

'Lucky bastard's just gotten himself a reprieve, as well as some more bread and cheese, even a glass of wine, perhaps.'

'And Philippe's conspiracy just got even bigger.'

Hérault was whispering.

'What's he saying?'

Philippe bent down and listened, 'There is a God. There is a God.'

Chapter Twenty-Seven

Amidst the maelstrom amongst his campaign team initiated by the climactic ending of the press conference, only one person was keeping calm, the person apparently with most to lose if the ensuing fall-out was not contained. The man at the eye of the storm, Hervé Parcelle.

His sang-froid even in the most extreme circumstances was legendary. Colleagues recalled him being the only minister who kept his head during the nightmare of the Friday 13th attacks in November 2015, when everyone else, including the Prime Minister and the President, were losing theirs. His political opponents had long since given up trying to rattle him. His rivals for the Presidency had not even tried.

One explanation for his calmness was that, of course, Parcelle knew why his team was concerned but did not care. What if he had upset a homosexual reporter? What if the gay rights activists were up in arms? These people were not, as the modern terminology would have it, his base. Woke lefties were not his target demographic, were never going to vote for him, so why waste time talking, thinking, and worrying about them?

He decided to let his team get their anger at what they believed was a tactical faux pas out of their systems and meanwhile carry on as if nothing had happened. His campaign motto, 'Business as Usual' might not win any prizes for originality, but it played very well with the fifty-plus, heterosexual, male conservatives, who made up the overwhelming majority of his support. As his strategists kept telling him, more than half the country's eligible voters were above the age of fifty and he was very happy to focus all his time, effort, marketing and advertising revenues on them. The wokeocracy could go hang themselves. He smiled thinly at his own, this time, inadvertent slip of the tongue.

His office having emptied he was sitting back in his chair with his feet up on the mahogany desk. His next interview with Radio France was fifteen minutes away and he saw an opportunity to take a rare breather. He should call his wife and tell her not to worry about the manufactured sound and fury coming from liberal politicians and the even more liberal media. The Radio France interview was not likely to produce similar levels of outrage, manufactured or otherwise. It was being conducted by an old friend who owed him a few favours, so he was unlikely to face many, if any, curveballs.

Instead, he mused on Paul LeBlanc. Parcelle did not know him and what he had said to him had been business, not personal. Far from being a faux pas, the comment was the product of astute political calculation. The greater the fuss from the left, the greater the support from the right. Yin and Yang. Culture wars they called it. He did not care two hoots about any of that. All that mattered was making it into the Élysée on April 25th. He was seventy-six years old. One term would be sufficient to fulfil his, as Shakespeare described it, vaulting ambition. Never mind hanging themselves, once he was safely ensconced in the Élysée, the left and right could hang each other. He always had been, always was, and always would be, a non-conviction politician, a political centrist, an opportunist like his mentor Chirac. Like his idol, he would govern from the centre. Business As Usual.

His rêverie about walking up the steps of the Élysée hand-in-hand with his wife, waving triumphantly to the excited, adoring crowds on a gloriously sunny, April Monday morning, was rudely interrupted by a call to his secure line.

'Hello?'

'It's me.'

'You cannot have forgotten I said call after eight.'

'You have a problem.'

'Let me correct you. It's never 'you have a problem', it's always 'I have a problem.' Never forget, if I go down, you go down with me, but not vice-versa. Understood?'

'Yes.'

'Start again.'

'I have a problem.'

'Better; continue.'

'They know *you* went into the apartment immediately after Montreau was strung up.'

Parcelle's legs came off the desk and sat up straight, but his voice remained calm. 'Explain.'

'Hérault recognized your face on TV.'

Parcelle reached for a glass and the permanently filled bottle of brandy which had been a fixture on his desk since he had first occupied the ministerial chair in 2013. He poured out a finger. 'Who do you mean by they?'

'The Montreau girl, Simon and Mules.'

'Hérault is with them?'

'Yes.'

'Where?'

'At Mules' house in Montreuil. Hérault has told them everything he knows about Montreau's death. He expected to be kept safe at Mules's house as a reward. Mules was having none of it and was about to kick him out when he turned on the TV and your face appeared. Hardly surprising as you are currently the leading news story across all media platforms. Hérault asked who you were. It appears he never forgot your distinctive visage over these past forty years but, as he has no interest in politics, he never put two and two together.'

'Until the day you tell him to get lost and cut him loose.'

'I made a mistake.'

'Yet another in a long, long line.'

'A mistake almost as big as the one you made this afternoon, getting the liberal media up in arms, thus ensuring your face has been a permanent fixture on every news channel in the country, probably the world, for the past two hours.'

'I'm also on the radio in ten minutes. How do you know all this?'

'I planted a device inside Hérault's jacket pocket when I met him in Montmartre.

'How did the others react to his revelation?'

'Disbelief, followed by outrage, followed by delight. Not a good afternoon for you so far. After the last couple of hours, your red-hot favouritism to be the next President has surely been downgraded to warm, at best. That is if you even make it to election day.'

Parcelle gulped the brandy down in one go and poured himself another finger. 'This is your screw-up! You better have something good up your sleeve.'

'I'm not a magician.'

117

'Don't I know it!'

'As the situation has reached a tipping point, I have no choice.'

'Meaning?'

'Desperate times equal desperate measures. Unless I do something very quickly, we will all go down. I have oven-ready plans in place to take them all out.'

'Plans?'

'Capture, transportation, elimination.'

'And the cover story?'

'This is why I called, that's your bit.'

'Finally, we get round to the reason for the call. What is my bit?'

'Squaring, or silencing, the media.'

'Don't worry your thick, clueless head. I'll make sure there isn't any undue sniffing around. The editors know what I am capable of should they refuse to toe the line. Unless someone digs very deep, the four will never be connected but if someone does pick up a shovel, they'll go the same way as the not-so-fab four.'

'Especially Paul LeBlanc?'

'Especially him.'

'I thought so.'

'When does your plan kick in?'

'They're now under twenty-four-seven surveillance. As soon as one of them slips up, they'll be snapped up and carted off to the forest. Once one goes, the rest will follow.'

'The domino effect.'

'Precisely. Simon is the likely first domino.'

'Death's door?'

'Falling off its hinges.'

'Good. It all sounds in hand, for once. As you say time is of the essence. It only takes one call from them to the wrong person in the media and we are screwed.'

'We have one immediate problem.'

'Go on.'

'Their devices, we cannot access them.'

'Surely that's impossible.'

'They have anti-malware software our techie guys haven't seen before and haven't managed to break down, yet.'

'Tell them to pull their feckless fingers out, and fast, otherwise, they'll be taking a one-way trip into the forest too.'

'There is another, less immediate, problem.'

'What?'

'The third member of our triumvirate, how do we let him know?'

'We don't, we can't. As ever, we must wait for him to contact us.'

'Right.'

'One of these days our mutual friend will discover mistrust and lack of openness have consequences. You cannot be half-in a conspiracy. He cannot blame us if we act without his knowledge or say so.'

'Precisely.'

'OK, you have done well, I suppose, eventually. Now I should call my wife. Not something you have to worry about.' He put his legs back on the table and poured another finger of brandy. 'Why did you never marry?'

'I was in love once.'

'The one and only love of your life?'

'Something like that.'

'What happened?'

'That love was stolen from me.'

'I see. OK, back to the present, call me after eight, and stick to it this time. Unless, God forbid, something else major crops up.'

'Will do.'

Parcelle ran his hands through his grey-white hair, drained his third brandy in one gulp and poured himself a fourth. There was just time to regain his sang-froid before Radio France came-a-calling. Enough time to make a quick phone call. However, he did not call his wife.

Chapter Twenty-Eight

Before setting off to meet Françoise and Emil at the Au Jean Bart opposite L'Académie, Anne-Sophie texted Béatrice:

'Hi! Incredible news. Hervé Parcelle was involved in my father's death! Can you believe it? More later... P and I are on our way to the Au Jean Bart. Can you join us? A-S x'

For most of the journey, she was silent. Eventually Phillipe asked, 'Penny for them.'

'Knowledge is power.'

'As Francis Bacon wrote, or to be pedantic: Knowledge itself is power.'

'Whatever he wrote, Hérault just gave us incredible knowledge and huge power.'

'He did. A lot of people would give their eye-teeth to have that information. We could derail Parcelle's campaign in a heartbeat. The big question is...'

'Do we do that?'

'Precisely. What do you think?'

'We know at least one journalist who would be very happy if we shared our knowledge with him.'

'Paul LeBlanc?'

'Absolutely. OK, we're almost there. Let's put Parcelle on the backburner until after we've spoken to your colleagues.'

As she parked her Clio in front of Au Jean Bart, Philippe said, 'I give you advance notice. They are quite the couple, in every respect.'

'Meaning?

'They're always together.'

'Meaning?'

'They've been journalist colleagues for forty-five years; husband and wife for forty.'

Even the very short distance from the street to the bar left them soaked but Anne-Sophie forgot about the rain when she saw the husband-and-wife journalistic duo sitting side by side in the downstairs dining area. She did a double take; talk about look-alike couples; grey-haired, bespectacled and plump, they were even wearing matching red sweaters and black trousers. She swallowed her amusement, put on what she hoped was her game face and thanked them for agreeing to meet at such short notice.

'My pleasure.'

'Mine too.'

'Did either of you ever meet my father?'

'Straight down to business! I like it. Tragically only the once.'

'Same.'

'What do you remember about him, please?'

'Ladies first, Françoise.'

'Well, as I say, I only met him once.'

'Where did you meet him?'

'Right here. It was a first, Jean-Marie had never come to the bar for a drink anytime I had been here.'

'Which has basically been opening hours for almost five decades.'

'Thank you for the interruption, Emil. And he had not come for a drink this time either. He sat down beside me at the bar and told me he was meeting a friend. He waited for ten minutes, and then, as his friend did not turn up, he left.'

'Did he say who this friend was?'

'No.'

'When was this? Did you talk about anything specific? What was his mood? His behaviour?'

'Oh, it would have been 1987, March. Perhaps the Wednesday of the last week in March.'

'Just before he died?'

'Sadly, yes.'

'And can you remember how he acted?'

'He seemed nervous, agitated, on edge.'

'Do you remember any of the conversation?'

'It was hardly that.'

'Emil, what about you? Where and when did you meet my father?'

'Coincidentally, here, at more or less the same time as Françoise, end of March 1987. I am guessing it must have been the same week, in fact. Thursday or Friday; I'll say Thursday. I had seen your father at conferences before, but never here.'

'Did he say why he'd come?'

'Just as he told Françoise, to meet a friend. A friend, who, again as Françoise said, did not turn up.'

'And you've no idea who this friend was?'

'None at all, sorry.'

'And his state of mind?'

'I am going to sound like a broken record, but again it was very similar to how he appeared to Françoise, edgy, distracted, tense.'

'OK, thank you. Philippe suggested to me en-route that L'Académie was not a happy camp in the 80s. What do you say to that, please?'

'Your turn to go first, Emil.'

'Thank you, Françoise. There were arguments and disagreements of course. I would suggest most institutions and organizations suffer from friction at one point or another.'

'Was L'Académie better or worse in this respect?'

'No doubt at times it was bad.'

'How bad?'

'Toxic. There was a lot of ill feeling between different sections; within different sections also.'

'Ill feeling about what?'

'Many things. Even back then L'Académie was a big institution.'

'Anything specific?'

'Well, there were the virologists, people like your father, who specialised in traditional DNA viruses. Then there were the Submariners.'

'And they were?'

'Retrovirologists.'

'Why Submariners?'

'Their P3 lab was designed to prevent deadly pathogens from escaping or entering; it was so airtight it was compared to a submarine.'

'I see. Françoise, what do you recall about these divisions?'

'Perhaps the virologists thought that all the publicity the retrovirologists were getting was going to their heads.'

'Publicity about what?'

'Discovering their version of the AIDS virus.'

'Their version?'

'LAV. The Americans had their own, which they named HTLV-IIIB on April 23rd, 1984.'

'I see. Emil, did you hear anything about the discord?'

'I heard your father was in the bad books with his boss, Louis Malherbe, the former Director of Retrovirology, now enjoying his retirement in leafy Le Vésinet.'

'Who told you this? The virologists?'

'It came from both sides. It was common knowledge in L'Académie.'

'And therefore, in this bar.'

'Was there anything in particular which caused Malherbe to be annoyed with my father?'

Emil and Françoise looked at each other, and at Philippe.

'What?'

Françoise answered first, 'The gossip was that your father was a challenging colleague.'

'What do you mean?'

'That was all I heard.'

'Emil?'

'I heard the same.'

'And you didn't ask my father if the gossip was true?'

'No, as I said, your father very rarely ventured into the bar. On the one occasion he did, he was gone again within ten minutes.'

'I'm surprised you didn't go and ask him in his lab or office. You were journalists, surely any disharmony in such a famous institution was food and drink to you?'

'If I'd asked it might have meant me being barred from this bar, ha, ha. That would have been professional suicide. Oh, I'm sorry Ms Montreau; forgive my lack of tact.'

'No problem. Please continue.'

'To be honest, and I mean no disrespect to him, or his memory, but your father was something of a bit-part player by the time he died, a scientific sideshow. L'Académie was replete with brilliantly talented men and women, rising like cream to the top. Unfortunately, your father was going in the opposite direction, milk that had gone sour.'

'That's a polite way of saying he was yesterday's man?'

123

'Well, yes. I suppose he was. It happens, I'm afraid. Careers often resemble snakes and ladders don't they. In science, if you don't play the game, you don't climb the ladder.'

'Sometimes you fall back down the ladder.'

'Yes, Emil, I'm sure Ms Montreau completely understands the metaphor.'

'You're right, I completely do. My father did not play the game.'

'No.'

'Is there anything else you can tell me about him?'

'Nothing. As I say, I only talked to him that one time. Tragic.'

'Is there anyone else at L'Académie, anyone who was there in the '80s, who is still there now and might be able to help me?'

'That's an excellent question. Emil, can you think of anyone?'

'Malberbe's successor, Stephen Stonehouse, I'm sure he was there in the early 80s.'

'Do either of you know Béatrice Lapain by any chance?'

'Oh, Béatrice! Lovely girl. Bright, funny, charming.'

'Stonehouse is her boss.'

'Now there's someone who does know how to play the career game.'

'She knows exactly which, and more importantly, whose, lever to pull, which ladder to climb.'

'Absolutely no chance of her falling back down the L'Académie ladder.'

'None whatsoever.'

'Not unless she gets pushed off.'

Anne-Sophie looked at Emil. 'That's rather cryptic, and sinister. What do you mean?'

'Oh, nothing.'

Emil's twinkling eyes told Anne-Sophie a different story.

Chapter Twenty-Nine

Sitting in her Clio, Anne-Sophie reflected on what she had just heard at the brasserie. 'As you said, quite the double act.'

'After working the same beat together for forty-five years, they are twin-like, identical twins at that. They can read each other's thoughts and complete each other's sentences.'

'Platonic?'

'In many ways, yes.'

'It was interesting hearing them talk about the two camps. I had no idea turf wars existed in science.'

'It is human nature. Wherever there are people, there are divisions, there are conflicts. It is Darwinian.'

'Béatrice has never mentioned any rifts.'

'Perhaps what goes on in L'Académie stays in L'Académie.'

'What do you think Emil meant about Béatrice being pushed off her career ladder? That was a weird thing to say.'

'Man proposes but God disposes, neither is the way of man in his own hands.'

'Another Plato-ism?'

'Thomas à Kempis.'

'How do we get from Thomas's wise words to Béatrice's game of career snakes and ladders?'

'None of us knows what is around the corner. One minute you are up, the next minute you are...'

She squeezed his hand and kissed it. 'Keep going, brave soldier.'

'I will, for as long as I can.'

'Now, speaking of Béatrice, let me see if she's replied.'

'Hi. Wow! How? Busy this afternoon/evening. Will try to call later. Keep in touch! B x'

'No problem. Will do. I need to ask a favour please. A-S x'

'OK, done. Now, I know who I want to contact next.'

'Malherbe?'

'The very same. You can read my mind. Perhaps we are going to turn out to be the next Françoise and Emil, ha ha.'

Philippe looked at the windscreen. Moisture had returned to his eyes. 'I only wish we had the time.'

This time she took both his hands. 'I know, but remember what my mother said, let's make the most of this time.'

'I am cherishing each moment we have together.'

'Good. Now, if you give me Malherbe's number, it's my turn to make a call. I'm presuming you've got it?'

'I have.'

Anne-Sophie dialled and put the phone on speaker. 'Hello. Can I speak to Monsieur Malherbe, please?'

'May I ask who is calling?'

'Anne-Sophie Montreau.'

'Is Monsieur expecting your call?'

'No.'

'Let me speak to the Monsieur. Please hold for me.'

'I will do, thanks.'

She rolled her eyes at Philippe, mouthed 'the Monsieur', smiled and started stroking her cross.

'Hello. Miss Montreau?'

'Monsieur Malherbe?'

'Louis, please.'

'Anne-Sophie, please.'

'You asked to speak to me?'

'Do you remember my father? Jean-Marie Montreau.'

'Ah yes, a fine fellow. A tragic loss. A good man to work with, a better man to know.'

'I never knew my father. And since my mother died on Christmas Eve, I can no longer ask her about him.'

'I read that news.'

'Where?'

'Her obituary was in L'Académie's January newsletter. A second tragic loss for you.'

'Yes, everyone keeps telling me how tragic my losses are. Fewer people are able to offer practical assistance. However, that is very kind, thank you.'

'You're most welcome. You were enquiring about your father?'

126

'Yes, I have been pondering whether to write a biography of my father as a memorial, a tribute. There is so little about him on the internet; nothing, actually. I think his life, and death, deserve a wider audience, don't you?'

'Oh, I see. Well, yes, of course. As I said, he was a fine fellow.'

'In light of my ambition, I was wondering if you could tell me about your relationship with my father; give me a sense of the type of man he was, what he was like to work with and so on.'

'OK. Well, let me see. Unfortunately, it is thirty years or more since we worked together.'

'Forty, to be precise.'

'Is it really? My goodness. Time does fly. Well, I would say Jean-Marie was a hard-working man, a talented virologist and respected by all his colleagues.'

'That sounds like the obituary he should have received after his death but didn't. With all due respect, Louis, this hardly gives me an insight into Father's character, or his personality. What was he like as a colleague? What were your relations with him? You were his boss. You worked with him for ten years.'

'Yes, it was a decade. A long time! I am sorry not to give you more. I am an old man, and this is an unexpected call.'

'Of course. I'm sorry to be so abrupt.'

'I would say he was a pleasure to work with. We all got on very well together at L'Académie.'

'Really? All of you? All of the time?'

'Well, not everybody, not all the time, no. That is impossible, of course. There are bound to be moments of tension, that is only the natural order of things.'

'Can you describe any of these moments of tension, please?'

'Well, we had discussions about budgets and resources of course. He was a virologist, and I a retrovirologist, so we had different priorities for the best way forward for L'Académie. There are only so many ways you can cut up a pie.'

'And, naturally, you made sure you and the rest of your submariners got the most pieces of that pie, and the biggest.'

Malherbe paused before responding, 'It hardly seems that you need any input from me. You seem very well informed already.'

'Can you please give me any specific examples of these discussions about the pie?'

'Not really, no. Who got what in terms of the budget was an ongoing struggle. There was nothing unusual in that. That is the nature of progress, whether in the jungle or the scientific institution. It's Darwinian.'

'I'm certainly beginning to gain that impression. Apart from sorting out who got the most pieces of pie, were there any other areas where you and my father had tense moments?'

'Not that I can recall. There were no big disagreements between us. No dramas. Things may have got heated occasionally, but, as I said, this is only natural in a big institution, filled with big egos. My own included, I might add.'

'My father was at one stage Deputy Director of Virology at L'Académie. Can you tell me anything about his demotion? After all, you say he was talented, hard-working, a "fine fellow", hardly a recipe for punishment I would have thought?'

'No, I had no knowledge about that.'

'Really? You were his boss, the Director of Virology. You expect me to believe you had no idea? Seriously?'

'Yes, seriously. I can assure you it was a decision taken by people way above my paltry pay grade.'

'How far above?'

'The top floor.'

'But you agreed with the decision?'

'Those are your words, not mine.'

'Did you complain about it?'

'It did not pay to question the powers that be. It never does.'

'You obeyed orders. I get it. Who was in overall charge of L'Académie in the mid-80s?'

'The Director-General at that time was Deraingeur. A great man.'

'Still alive?'

'Barely.'

'You've had forty years to ponder what happened to my father. Do you have any theories as to why he killed himself?'

'I thought long and hard about Jean-Marie's death. I was deeply affected by it; we all were.'

'And?'

'Unfortunately, I cannot bring any new information to light. He was dedicated, and a hard worker. Often, he worked too hard. Apart from your late mother, his work was his life.'

'In the week before Father died, did you meet him outside of work?'

'No, we never met outside of work.'

'Never?'

'Never.'

'Did you see my father during work hours in the week before he died?'

'Once or twice during the first part of the working week, as normal.'

'Were there any hints he was unusually depressed or anxious?'

'None at all.'

'And the end of the working week?'

'I was busy packing for a trip.'

'Oh. Where to?'

'America.'

'Lucky you. What about his final weekend?'

'What about it?'

'Did you see him then?'

'I repeat, we never met away from L'Académie. I never saw him at the weekend.'

'Is there anybody in L'Académie who was around in the eighties that you would recommend I talk to about my father, please? Anyone you can recall who had strong opinions about him, either way.'

'No, Anne-Sophie, I would say not. I reiterate, Jean-Marie was universally held in high esteem, well-liked, well regarded and well respected.'

'So well-liked, well regarded and well respected he got shoved back down the career ladder.'

'That was nothing to do with me.'

'Did the police interview you after his death?'

'No.'

'Was anyone at L'Académie interviewed?

'No one, no.'

'Did you not think that was strange?'

'Why would it be strange, Anne-Sophie?'

'In suicide cases, surely the police speak to anyone closely connected with the victim. You and several others worked with my father for many years.'

'We did.'

'Yet the police did not feel it necessary to speak to you about his state of mind?'

'Perhaps you need to ask the police this question, not me.'

'I will, thank you. Do you recall anything about the inquest?'

'No, but I was told it was a very quick event.'

'It was. You weren't there?'

'No, as I told you, I was in America when all this occurred.'

Stroking the cross, Anne-Sophie remembered something Philippe had told her. 'Please may I ask you another question?'

'Of course.'

Chapter Thirty

'Will you be at the Ritz this Friday?'

'My goodness, you are *extremely* well informed. I congratulate you; your sources are impeccable.'

She smiled at Philippe. 'The best. Well, are you going?'

'I am.'

'One last question.'

'Yes?'

'Can you remember who told you about the fake-inquest?'

'No, I am sorry, I cannot recall that. I may have read about it in a newspaper, perhaps. Such a long time ago, my memory, you know, old age.'

'Well, thank you so much, Louis. I'm sorry I interrupted your day. You've been most helpful and informative.'

'My pleasure. Now, Anne-Sophie, you must come and visit me here in Le Vésinet one day and soon. I live at *Le Sous-Marin*, 38, Avenue de la Prise d'Eau. Telephones are all well and good, but they are no substitute for face-to-face.'

'I would like that, yes, very much. Would you be agreeable to a face-to-face meeting if my research for Father's biography requires it, please?'

'Yes! By all means. An hour in your company would I am sure brighten up any old man's day. I am no exception.'

'Marvellous. Thank you, Louis. You've been very helpful, Goodbye.'

'Thank you, Anne-Sophie. Have a good evening. Good luck with your research.'

Anne-Sophie slapped her left hand on the steering wheel. 'Talk about dead end.'

Her phone buzzed.

'Sure. Anything. Ask away. B x'

'Can please you arrange for the two of us to meet your boss tonight or tomorrow? To do with my father of course! A-S x'

After five minutes of sitting in the Clio and showing no sign of going anywhere, Philippe turned to look at his goddaughter.

Once again, she had the cross between her first and second fingers. He wondered what she was trying to work out.

Again, her left hand hit the steering wheel. 'Got it! You lying old devil!'

'Sorry?'

For the full five minutes, she had been infected by a brain worm. Malherbe had said she must come to visit her in Le Vésinet. Anne-Sophie had heard someone else mention Le Vésinet recently, but she could not for the life of her think who, or when. There had been so many conversations and phone calls in the past thirty hours that everything had melded into a blur. It had annoyed her to distraction. She had to remember. It was something important, very important. Telling her brain to slow down, she retraced every movement and every conversation from the past few hours.

At last, it came to her. Hérault had stated her father had gone to Le Vésinet on the Saturday afternoon but he had no idea why. Françoise and Emil had mentioned Malherbe was spending his retirement in Le Vésinet. He had more or less just invited her to visit him, in Le Vésinet.

'Buckle up!'

'Where are we going? What is it?'

Forty-five minutes later, they were driving into Le Vésinet. She had heard it described as one of Paris's hidden gems. Certainly, the houses looked to be on a par with Saint-Cloud. Better in fact, classier, less showy, more old money than new. Soon she was pressing the doorbell to *Le Sous-Marin*, a very desirable, white wedding cake of a residence.

A severe-looking gentleman answered.

'We've come to see Monsieur Malherbe.'

'Do you have an appointment?'

'Just tell him Anne-Sophie Montreau couldn't wait for that face-to-face meeting he mooted an hour ago.'

The severe man returned after five minutes and offered to relieve them of their soaking-wet coats. Then he escorted them into a high-ceilinged lounge with Art Nouveau features, where they found Malherbe sitting in a very comfortable red velvet armchair, nursing a glass of Calvados.

'Thank you for seeing us, Louis.'

'Did I have a choice?'

'You always have a choice.'

'Really?'

'You have a choice now. You had a choice in 1987.'

'Did I?'

'Of course you did! For example, how to deal with difficult colleagues, the ones who wouldn't toe the line, the awkward squad, independent-minded thinkers, the ones who are perhaps a little jealous of colleagues' successes, always challenging the party line; those ones.'

'Ah, yes.'

'Did you come across many of that ilk when you were in charge of L'Académie?'

'A lot of the jealous guys, I'm sure of that. We were very successful in the Submarine. Many colleagues did not like it.'

'How did you deal with the awkward squad?'

'I tried to accommodate them within the team. Of course, a certain amount of creative tension is required to drive the team forward.'

'Sounds Darwinian.'

'Ha, yes. I suppose it does.'

'What if you couldn't accommodate them, couldn't adapt, or refused to be accommodated? Were too challenging, too creative, caused too much tension?'

'Then they were moved on.'

'Where to?'

'Lille for example. Vietnam. Senegal. There was no lack of opportunity at L'Académie, or elsewhere. Science has no limits, no boundaries, the world was their scientific oyster.'

'Was my father independent-minded?'

'Of course, I explained that to you during our phone call.'

'Explain how that independence manifested itself.'

'He had a mind of his own about many matters.'

'You've said that; give me examples, please.'

'Scientific issues related to virology. Complex, complicated matters.'

'Too complicated for a non-scientist like me?'

'Well, it would take a long time to discuss them, and it is, after all, nearly my supper time.'

'Expecting something tasty?'

'Indeed, sea bass, fresh from Nouvelle Poissonnerie this morning.'

'Sounds delicious. Let's hope it's well filleted, you can't be too careful at your age.'

'It will be.'

'What was the tone of your disagreements with my father? Were the exchanges friendly?'

'Often, yes.'

'Sometimes, no?'

'Sometimes, no. It happens.'

'What was your discussion with Father like on the afternoon of Saturday, March 28th, 1987? In this lounge, the day before he died?'

'You are not the police, and I am not on trial.'

'Do not overreact, Louis. As any loving daughter would, Anne-Sophie wishes only to establish her father's movements during his last hours on earth.'

She locked her eyes on Malherbe's. 'I'll start again. Did you meet my father in this room the day before his death?'

'I did. I won't deny it.'

'You denied it earlier, several times. Why did you lie to me?'

'I'd forgotten about it. Tiredness and hunger do terrible things to the mind. As does dementia.'

'And alcohol?'

'That too.'

'What did you and father talk about?'

'Matters relating to laboratory politics, I suspect.'

'Suspect?'

'I do not remember exactly. It was such a long time ago, I'm sorry.'

'So, you cannot recall the contents of a two-hour conversation between yourself and a colleague who, twenty-four hours later, was found dead in his apartment?'

'No, I'm sorry, I cannot. I was in the middle of a very busy, stressful period, I'm sorry.'

'Do you remember why it was you and my father fell out originally?'

'No.'

'I heard you and your team were rather full of yourselves after the discovery of the AIDS virus.'

'Who told you that? Ah, Françoise and Emil. They should have taken a leaf out of my book and retired a long time ago. It's sad really how they cannot let go, hanging around Au Jean Bart, like a pair of old soaks.'

'So, you weren't full of yourselves?'

'Not at all! I resent that notion. We were successful, we did amazing things, but we were never arrogant.'

'You said you were in a busy period in late March 1987. Why so busy?'

At this moment the manservant re-entered, looking more severe than ever. 'Monsieur Malherbe is extremely tired. I think you and the journalist should leave, now.'

'But-'

'Now.'

As they stood up Malherbe looked at her, 'Anne-Sophie.'

'Yes?'

'It is not me you need to speak to.'

'Who then?'

The butler stepped in between them. 'Please leave.'

She gave Malherbe a withering look, 'Watch out for bones in the sea bass, Louis.'

Getting into the car, Anne-Sophie looked at Philippe. 'Another very wet waste of time, I'm sorry.'

'There is no need to be sorry. Professor Malherbe looked extremely rattled, and I would not bet against him being on the phone right now.'

Reminded by that comment, Anne-Sophie checked her phone.

'Why? He's not involved as well, is he? Ha, ha. I'll try. B x'

'Ha. Don't think so, but never say never. Thanks. x'

She rubbed her cross. 'I wonder who Malherbe meant when he said I needed to speak to someone else.'

Chapter Thirty-One

Malherbe had an open bottle of twelve-year-old Calvados on the table in front of him and a full-to-the-brim glass at his elbow. He directed his manservant to dial the number and pass the receiver to him when the connection was made. 'Hello?'

'How are you, Louis? Is that the clink of a brandy bottle and glass, or just my imagination?'

'This is no time for your Sahara-dry wit. The Montreau girl, and that interfering hack, Simon, have just been and gone.'

'Social call?'

'Hardly. Baying for blood, mine mainly. She knows Jean-Marie came here on the Saturday afternoon.'

'No reason to hit the bottle with such force.'

'You know fine well I will be in the deepest dirt if the truth about Montreau comes out; prison is not out of the question.'

'Louis, whilst you were thirty-thousand feet up in the air, en-route to DC, a man died in suspicious circumstances. A baby girl was left fatherless. After four decades of ignoring him, hating him, she has been roused, perhaps by remorse, to find out the truth about his death. She has discovered short-cuts were taken in terms of due process and she wants to know why. It's only natural. The only surprise is that it's taken forty years for it to happen. The truth will out, we all know that. It's only a matter of when, not if. If this was a hundred years from now it would not be our problem.'

'It is happening today, and it is very much my problem.'

'Not just yours. In France, America, the UK, all around the globe, medics, scientists and public health officials built extremely successful, lucrative careers, and lived wonderful, comfortable lives, because of what occurred on March 29th, 1987.'

'You forgot to include politicians in that list.'

'Did I? It wasn't deliberate, I assure you. Remember this, I know all the names; I know which skeletons are in which cupboards, which closets.'

'And, if it came to it, you wouldn't hesitate to unlock the doors of these cupboards and closets and let the light shine in?'

'To save at least some of my skin? Absolutely. It would be entertaining after all. Perhaps it's time for another French revolution, it's been a long time since the last one. Things have been far too cosy for far too long. The tree needs shaking.'

'My God.'

'Louis, if you can, please focus on what I am saying. All I did was pass on information, confidential, hush-hush, I had no hand in the killing. On the other hand, you...'

'Me?! I swear to God I did not want, or intend, Jean-Marie to be killed.'

'Whether you intended it, or not, you played a part. Yes?'

'A tiny part.'

'Tell me how this evening's conversation went. If you can recall any of it.'

Malherbe drained another glass of Calvados. He was drinking almost faster than he could pour. 'As I told you, she knows about her father coming here the day before his death. She was asking me about the meeting; what I remembered about it.'

'And?'

'I told her nothing. I said I could not remember anything.'

'Too drunk? Or, let me guess, you scraped out the barrel and played the dementia card.'

'What else could I do?'

'Nothing. So, why the panic?'

'She knows more than she was letting on, I'm sure of it.'

'A drunk's intuition?'

'Go screw yourself.'

'A strange request from a man desperate for help.'

'Screw you.'

'Louis, please calm down. Why did you call me? What do you want me to do?'

'I want you to help me resolve the problem.'

'What problem? I don't have a problem.'

'The Montreau problem! I've lived with it for forty-years, I'm sick of it hanging around my neck.'

'And driving you to drink. You're fortunate to have had the last forty years living in the lap of Le Vésinet luxury. Montreau

137

did not have that good fortune. In the end, all he had hanging around his neck was a noose. His daughter has been fed lies about him all her life. How do you think she feels?'

'It's time to resolve this whole mess.'

'Resolve it, how?'

'Let the truth come out.'

'History repeating itself.'

'Meaning?'

'You said exactly the same thing to me that Saturday evening after Montreau left you.'

'Yes, and I wish to God you had done what I asked. God knows I tried my best. Out of all of us, I was the one, the only one, interested in the truth. The only one urging a compromise be brokered despite being under intense pressure from all and sundry, especially from the man at the top.'

'As you said, no-one wanted, or intended, for Jean-Marie to die that Sunday afternoon. However, you know very well that there were only three solutions to the Montreau dilemma: One, let him reveal the truth to the world; two, get him by any means, legal or illegal, to accept a compromise; three, eradicate him. The first option was unacceptable to everyone, or nearly everyone, especially to the top man. Montreau knew too much about the mess in the Submarine and the even greater mess in Bethesda. He had his hypothesis and his suspicions, all he lacked was proof. On the Friday evening, after finding it, or being directed to it by a person or persons unknown, he knew for certain his hypothesis and his suspicions were correct. By the Sunday, it was clear he would not listen to reason, bribery, or threats; obvious that he was prepared to go to any lengths to expose the big lie and get the truth out. He wanted to climb on board the gravy train, pull the emergency cord hard and derail the entire thick-as-thieves, medical-science-big pharma complex.'

Malherbe took a succession of gulps of the Calvados, 'I certainly remember that. I respected him for it. Montreau had principles and backbone, unlike the rest of us. You listen to me, I cannot, I will not, be accused of murder, or of being an accessory. I know nothing about what happened after I called you, packed my things for Washington and took the taxi to Charles de Gaulle. I knew nothing more until I landed at Dulles on the Sunday evening and was collected by the top man's henchmen.'

'Henchmen? He's not a mafia don.'

'He acted like he was. He controlled everything. He's told me many, many times *The Godfather* is his favourite movie, Michael Corleone his ultimate role model. No doubt he will tell me so again at the Ritz this Friday.'

'Speaking of which, it would be a very good idea if you sobered up before then. Ask your butler to press you a clean, white shirt.'

'You won't help me?'

'Perhaps you can ask him to write your speech as well.'

'Screw you.'

Chapter Thirty-Two

As they drove up to the front of Anne-Sophie's apartment block neither of them noticed the white van heading in the opposite direction.

Her phone buzzed. *'Au Jean Bart, tomorrow 1pm, table for 3. Will try to call later. Desperate to know about HP! B x'*

'Fab. Thank you. See you. A-S x ps we've been to see Louis Malherbe. Very interesting....'

An hour later, she and Philippe were tucking into pasta and a bottle of vin rouge. Before opening the bottle, she had asked him whether she should return to his apartment and collect the medication they had left behind in the rush to go to Montreuil after lunch. He assured her he would be fine for one night and she proceeded to uncork.

'How is it?'

'The wine and pasta are both ...'

'Delicious?'

'Yes, thank you.'

'How does it compare to my mother's cooking? Be honest, I won't turf you out.'

'Both superb, I would not dream of putting one above the other.'

'Very diplomatic. Well done, good Godfather. So, tell me, why the Ritz? Why this Friday? What was this agreement you mentioned?'

'It was signed on March 31st, 1987, two days after your father was killed.'

'The same day as the fake inquest.'

'Yes. That very day, President Reagan and Prime Minister Chirac ended what the medical-science press had labelled a 'festering international scientific dispute.' They announced that scientists from the USA and France would share the credit for discovering what they had decided was the AIDS virus.'

'Malherbe from Paris...'

'And Roberto Bicchiere from Bethesda, USA. The two of them jointly wrote and signed a detailed, seven-page chronology specifying the contributions of each to the discovery.'

'Right.'

'It was trumpeted as a unique occasion.'

'How come?'

'It was the first time, certainly, in modern times, that a settlement of a scientific dispute had required such direct involvement from the highest levels of government.'

'And Friday is the closest suitable date to hold the big commemoration?'

'Yes.'

'How long have you known about this event?'

'It was announced a year ago.'

'Apart from Malherbe, who else is going to be there?'

'The great and good. As well as the not-so-great, the bad and the truly awful.'

'Where does Malherbe fit into that continuum?'

'Not great but not truly awful.'

'Not as far as we know.'

'Correct.'

'And you said the person or persons responsible for father's death will be there?'

'I am certain of it.'

Once she had finished her pasta, she looked at her laptop. 'I've brought up the guest-list. Wow! That's a big headline act.'

'Go on.'

'Antony Consolotto. *The* Antony Consolotto? America's COVID-19 czar?'

'Yes, the very same Antony Consolotto.'

'This might sound like a stupid question but why will he be there? What does he have to do with HIV and AIDS?'

'He was America's AIDS czar for almost forty years.'

'Wow! I had no idea. Antony the Great!'

'He certainly had great power. Consolotto controlled most of America's AIDS funding, the direction of research travel, which articles were printed, the titles of the papers, the abstracts and the discussions, and what happened to the heretics.'

'Heretics?'

'Anyone who deviated from the orthodoxy.'

'Orthodoxy? You make it sound like a religious cult, like early Christianity.'

'In many ways they are very similar.'

'What was this orthodoxy?'

'That AIDS was a single disease, with a single cause, a retrovirus called HIV-1.'

'How could anyone disagree with that? It's the truth, isn't it?'

'Some scientists disagreed vehemently.'

She took a sip of wine, 'My father being one of them?'

'Aboslutely.'

'Is that what Françoise and Emil meant when they said Father was "challenging"? He disagreed with Malherbe about what caused AIDS?'

'Correct.'

'What did Father say was the cause?'

'The combined, cumulative effects of persistent multi-viral, fungal and parasitical infections, leading to the overload of the immune system and its eventual burnout.'

'Right.'

After taking a sip of wine, Philippe asked Anne-Sophie who else was on the guest list.

'Peter Stacey?'

'Mr ACTUP! Poacher turned gamekeeper, one of Consolotto's closest friends. Very strange relationship.'

'Malherbe, of course. Bicchiere.'

'Surprised he can show his face. Still, he always had a brass neck.'

'Someone else you don't like?'

'He claimed all the credit for everything, including discovering the AIDS virus. He took the AIDS blood test kit patent royalties too, 100,000 dollars per annum! So, no, I do not like him. Keep going.'

'Don Bartholomew? Never heard of him.'

'Your father's bête noire, going all the way back to 1976. The original architect of the AIDS orthodoxy. Talk about salt in the wound.'

'Robin White, Jonathan Webertz, Max Estez.'

'Weasel White! The zealots! All the early deciders, I might have guessed.'

'Early deciders?'

'Led by Bartholomew, they decided, without any evidence, that AIDS was caused by a retrovirus and convinced Bicchiere and Malherbe they were right. Of course, as retrovirologists desperate to justify, maintain, and even increase their laboratories, staffing, budgets and funding, they would have said that wouldn't they? The rest of the medical-science research world, including the science media, followed them like the sheep they were and are. The CDC's Jim Cooper and Margaret Goode regarded Bartholomew as the Messiah and the three of them combined together to convince the US Health Department of the righteousness of their cause.'

'Cooper and Goode are on the list too.'

'At the top table, I bet.'

'Doesn't say.'

'Sherlock Holmes would have laughed at all of them.'

'Why?'

'Holmes told Watson that "it is a capital mistake to theorize before one has data. Insensibly one begins to twist facts to suit theories, instead of theories to suit facts." Sherlock knew that once we form a judgment, we become biased and to avoid bias takes skill, mental discipline, and constant reminders. The early deciders possessed none of those qualities.'

'They jumped straight in without looking?'

'Correct. They saw what they wanted to see. They put all their eggs in the retrovirus basket and twisted every piece of evidence and data to fit their hypothesis.'

'And what did my father think about Holmes?'

'He agreed with him one hundred per cent. Jean-Marie followed Holmesian methodology to the letter, inside and outside the laboratory. He always used to say to me: "Never mind follow the money, Philippe, you must follow the evidence."'

'Hard to disagree.'

'Who else is going to be there?'

'Michael Gottfeld.'

'Et tu, Brute!'

'Sorry?'

'When it came to AIDS, Gottfeld and your father initially sang from the same, immune system burnout, hymn sheet. Mid-race, Gottfeld switched horses and metaphorically stabbed Jean-Marie in the back. Next?'

'John Mannox.'

'Editor of Nature magazine during the 1980s, the self-styled "most important scientist in the world." Another alcoholic. Carry on, please.'

'Bernadette Hannant, Garry Shaw, Bette Kerber, Daniel Ho, Jacques Papin; who are they?'

'They provided the HIV cover story.'

'What does that mean?'

'Proteges of Bicchiere and Estez, they cobbled together a highly unlikely account of the origins of HIV-1, involving Cameroonian chimpanzees and First World War Belgian soldiers.'

'Why unlikely?'

'Belgian colonial troops went back and forth from the Congo to Belgium for nearly a hundred years. If there was ever a significant outbreak of AIDS in Belgium during the colonial epoch, no one has discovered the fact.'

'Stefan Heintz?'

'The boss of Daelig.'

'Which is what?'

'One of the biggest beasts in the Big Pharma jungle. Its anti-HIV drugs' sales continually amount to well over fifteen billion United States dollars per annum; seventy per cent of the global figure.'

'Stephen Stonehouse.'

'Naturally.'

'Béatrice! Béatrice is going! She never said! Talk about keeping her cards close to her chest.'

'She will dazzle everyone I am sure of that. Anyone else of interest?'

'Not as far as I can tell, no, I think that's it. OK, I'll wash up, you watch the news; see if we've missed any more Parcelle-related action.'

After half-an-hour of clearing up, her phone buzzed again,

*'Hi. I can't make it tomorrow. So sorry. I've been drafted in
as a last-minute substitute to go to a conference at L'Académie
Lille. Won't finish until nine-ish, meaning I won't get back until
eleven at the earliest. I may stay over in Lille and get one of the
first TGVs on Thursday morning. Stephen's still ok to see you.
Here's his number, 036333333. I've given him yours, hope you
don't mind. Sorry to let you down AGAIN. Really NOT my fault
this time. Enjoy the meal. B xx'*

*'Hi. What a shame. Just our luck. Thank you for passing my
number onto SS. I hope he won't be too bored by the time our
starters have arrived. Have a successful and productive
conference. Pop into the cathedral if you have time. It's stunning,
especially if this hideous rain actually stops and the sun comes
out. Hope to see you Thursday. Lots of love, A-S x ps hope you
make it back in time for Friday night.'*

'Friday night? xx.'

'The Ritz! xx'

*'Oh yes, that. I should be back by then but I'm not sure I want
to go. I'll come and see you Thursday morning, if you're around
that is, and not out and about carrying out a citizen's arrest on
HP! There's something, someone, I need to talk to you about.
Love, me x '*

Anne-Sophie brought Philippe up to speed about her meeting
with Stonehouse, poured herself a coffee and returned to her
laptop. She stood up immediately. 'My God! You won't believe
what's just been posted on L'Académie's web page.'

'What?'

'Why the hell is he going?'

'Tell me! Who?'

'A just announced special guest of honour!'

'Tell me!'

'Hervé Parcelle, that's who!'

'Incredible.'

'You said it, didn't you.'

'Said what?'

'My father's killer would be there; sounds like you were right.
Why in God's name is he going?'

'Perhaps he thinks at this stage of a campaign any publicity is
good publicity. I'm sure his base won't be put out seeing him rub

shoulders with the glitterati in a glorious setting. Or it could be his connection with Chirac; old Jacques was a mentor to Parcelle when he started climbing the greasy pole in the '90s. Chirac, don't forget, was co-signatory of the Washington agreement.'

She sat back down. 'What do you think I should do with our knowledge about Parcelle?'

'At this stage keep it under your hat. We know Jean-Marie was killed. We know there was some kind of conspiracy involving the police, judiciary, security and intelligence services, and the media. What we do not know yet is the motive. As soon as we find that piece of the jigsaw then we go to the authorities.'

'How will we find that out?'

'We will go through your father's notebooks tomorrow morning. There may be some clues there. Let us also see if Stonehouse has any information that can help us.'

'And if he hasn't?'

'We must keep our fingers crossed and hope it does not come to that. I am hopeful that by dinner time we should have a much clearer picture.'

'That's a positive thought to end the day on, thanks.'

Even though it was only ten o'clock, Philippe said he was exhausted, and both agreed that sleep was much needed.

As she got into bed, she noticed her phone was flashing.

'Hi. Looking forward to meeting you tomorrow. I've heard a lot about you. Stephen S.'

She wondered from whom he had 'heard a lot.' Was this 'lot' he mentioned positive or negative? Then her mind turned to the question of Parcelle. Was she really prepared to throw a massive spanner into the nation's political works at such a crucial moment? Who knew what the consequences would be if she did that? Perhaps, as Philippe suggested, it would be better if she kept a lid on things for as long as possible; better if she asked Eric to visit Parcelle privately before Friday and ask the politician directly for his explanation. One thing was for sure, Parcelle would not sleep well tonight if he knew what was known about his involvement in the crime scene.

Before she turned off her light, she sent two more texts:

'Hi, Eric. How are you? How is Hérault? I hope you're treating him well. I'm sure Céline is. Thanks to him we've sussed

out where my father was on the Saturday afternoon. *Guess where? Malherbe's gaff! Speak tomorrow.'*

'*Hi Stephen. I haven't heard much about you, apart from you don't like Béatrice to be late for work, but I'm looking forward to meeting you all the same. Anne-S.'*

Her final thought as her head hit the pillow and fell fast asleep, was that the Ritz party was only three days away, time was definitely running out. She had to hit the ground running tomorrow.

Day Three – Wednesday, 31st March, 2027

Chapter Thirty-Three

Again, the distorted voice. Nothing for forty years, now twice in twenty-four hours.

'Once more you deign to call. I am honoured.'

'I tried earlier, several times in fact; engaged each time. I thought the up-in-arms *LGBTQ+* community must have hacked into, perhaps taken down, your secure line.'

'Very funny. What is it?'

'*It* is Malherbe. He had a visit from you-know-who a few hours ago. Consequently, I fear he may have followed in the footsteps of George of Clarence and drowned himself in brandy.'

'This is interesting because?'

'He may turn.'

'If he does then, with the greatest of respect, Malherbe is your problem, not mine.'

'If he does turn, and tell all, then, with the greatest of respect, Minister of Justice and red-hot favourite to be the next President, the Montreau girl is all our problem.'

'What do you suggest?'

'Our friend in intelligence would be well advised to keep tabs on the good Professor, just in case he does decide to perform a volte-face.'

'You think it likely?'

'Very. Unlike us, Malherbe has a conscience. Drink is driving him to the edge. He may fall over at any time. If he falls, we all fall, Including you.'

'Is that a threat?'

'No, a fact. Unlike you, I know everyone and everything. Unlike Malherbe, I'm not an honourable man.'

'Anything else?'

'Yes, congratulations.'

'On what?'

'Getting an invite to the Ritz. Tickets are as rare as hen's teeth. I suppose being the red-hot favourite to be the next President has its advantages.'

After terminating the call, Parcelle muttered, 'Many, many advantages.'

Chapter Thirty-Four

Eric woke up just after six-fifteen. After struggling for ten minutes to get back to sleep, and not wanting to disturb Céline any further, he gave up and wandered downstairs into the kitchen to make a pot of coffee. He had been beaten to the punch. Sitting at the table was Hérault, who stood up immediately.

'It's OK, you don't have to move, please sit down.'

Hérault obeyed the instruction.

Mules eyed him up. 'What are you doing here at six-thirty in the morning?'

'Probably the same as you, couldn't sleep. Thought it was an opportunity to be somewhere other than my bedroom.'

'You also thought I wouldn't be around this early.'

'That as well.'

Hérault looked at Mules. 'Why did you tell me to sit down?'

'I think it's better if you're out here with me, rather than in there alone.'

'You've changed your tune; yesterday I was a scumbag.'

Mules brought the coffee to the table. 'I haven't changed my tune, at least not totally. I can keep a closer eye on you out here and you're still something of a scumbag today. You spied on Anne-Sophie's parents for the best part of three years, and you've confessed to opening the door for the killers.'

'It's history, terrible history, I can't deny it, nor can I change it. I wish I could, but I can't.'

'However, yesterday we established you had no inkling Jean-Marie was going to be murdered. Last night, Anne-Sophie told me that her father visited his boss in Le Vésinet the afternoon before he was killed. Without your input, she would never have connected those dots. Add in the fact that your recognition of Parcelle is a game-changer, and the identity of Jacques cannot stay hidden for much longer, then even I have to admit you have been invaluable to the cause. Whatever your motivation, Anne-Sophie is very grateful. If she wasn't then, believe me, you wouldn't be here.'

'I know it. I'm glad I've helped her, and the cause. That's all I can do now, help; make tiny amends for huge mistakes.'

'At the time, you did what you thought was right for you and, possibly, your country but, having said that, I don't think any of it made you happy, not even the money, nor the house.'

Hérault took a gulp of coffee and then a deep breath. 'You're right, I wasn't happy. I've never been happy: my parents hated me; I never fitted in at school; never been in a loving relationship. Classic saddo, loner, loser material. The house was great to the extent that I could shut the world out. Unfortunately, it was bought with what I knew were ill-gotten gains, blood money, as you said. So, I never felt comfortable about it.'

'You didn't steal the house from anyone. Nobody forced Scarface to give you the money. You didn't mug an old lady.'

'No, but I did invent an old lady, or at least her legacy.'

'Not the same thing.'

'I kept quiet for forty years. I skulked away in Montmarte; I should have been braver, more honest, turned myself in, faced the music, taken my medicine.'

'Even if you'd done that, you probably wouldn't have made it anywhere close to a police station. Jacques, or one of his agents, would have stopped you in your tracks. Even if you had made it, your name would have come up on a watch list. You'd have ended up being carted off to somewhere dark and nasty, never to be seen again.'

'You think?'

'I know. Anyway, you weren't the only one to keep quiet for forty years. I always had my suspicions but never acted upon them, Simon was the same. None of us is perfect, Henri, especially not me. My alcohol issues are a testament to that.'

'How's that going?'

'OK, for now. Probably because I'm excited to be involved in a case again; the heat of battle and all that. Once it's over, I'll hit the bottle again. I'm a walking, breathing, for-now living, cliché.'

'I hope not.'

'Thanks, but I wouldn't bet on it, which is only because I'm not addicted to gambling, as well as booze.'

'Thank goodness.'

'The bottom line is that you know Scarface and his methods better than any of us. I'd be cutting my big nose off to spite my ugly old face if I didn't pick your brains about him.'

Mules looked at Hérault. 'More coffee? Some crepes?'

'I don't deserve them but yes, thank you.'

'You're welcome. So, now that I've raised that unpleasant subject, is there anything else you know about Jacques? Or what happened that Sunday?'

'The only thing I can add is that I honestly don't believe murder was the intention. I heard Jacques say to one of the *Brigade* boys "Did you find it?" The response was no.'

'A search gone wrong; interrupted?'

'I think so. I only know Jacques seemed very keen on finding *it*, whatever *it* was. And gutted when it wasn't found.'

'Right.'

'What's going to happen about Parcelle?'

'That's the big question; it's down to Anne-Sophie.'

'If it was down to you?'

'I'd be paying him a visit round about now.'

'A dawn-raid?'

'Tried and tested. Never fails.'

'It's incredible to think the fate of France is literally in her hands. She has the power to turn the election on its head.'

'I'm not sure that's the uppermost thought in her head right now.'

'I guess not. Still, that's awesome power.'

'You're right, it is.'

Hérault took a mouthful of crepe, followed by another gulp of coffee. 'Strange us being here, together like this. After forty-years.'

'War makes strange bedfellows.'

'I haven't shared a kitchen table with anyone for decades, not since I was kicked out of my home at sixteen. I cannot remember ever having a decent conversation with anyone.'

Eric saw Hérault was close to tears and put a hand on his shoulder. 'It's good to have you here.'

'Thanks.'

'More coffee?'

'Please.'

Eric's phone buzzed. Anne-Sophie. He looked at the clock. Six-forty-five. His stomach sank. It was too early, it had to be trouble. He put the phone on speaker, 'Yes?'

'Eric! It's all my fault.'

'What is?'

Philippe! He's in a bad way. It's his meds.'

'What about them?'

'They're not here.'

'Hell. Where?'

'His apartment, bathroom cabinet. I should have gone for them last night. Someone needs to go to Le Marais, and I can't leave him.'

'Which leaves, me.'

'Yes.'

'We have to assume our places are being watched. It's basically a suicide mission.'

'Philippe needs his meds, otherwise...'

'I'll do it.'

Eric spun round to find Hérault looking directly at him. 'I'll go to Saint-Victor, collect the keys and Simon's address. I'll get his tablets and take them back to Anne-Sophie's. All I need is your car.'

Mules turned back to his phone, 'I don't like it. Not one bit. It's a virtual death sentence.'

'What about Philippe's death sentence? We have no choice. Without his meds, Philippe will die. Let me speak to Hérault. You go and sort your car out.'

'OK. Give me five minutes. Henri will be with you at seven-forty-five. Have the address, directions and keys ready for an immediate handover.' He passed the phone to Hérault.

'Henri?'

'Yes.'

'Thank you.'

'It's called atonement.'

'I call it courage. Be careful. Drive up to the limit, but carefully. See you soon.'

Hérault grabbed his leather jacket and headed outside where, before he got into the Saab, Mules hugged him. 'Keep your eyes peeled. Take the back roads.'

'Don't worry, I'll be fine.'

'And Henri.'

'Yes?'

'You're not a scumbag.'

'Thanks, that means a lot.'

'I want you back here by ten at the latest so we can finish off our coffee, crepes and our more than decent conversation.'

'Yes! I'll look forward to all of that.'

Chapter Thirty-Five

Atonement, guilt, excitement - whatever name was given to it did not matter to Hérault. For the first time in a long time, possibly ever, he was doing the right thing, for the right reason. He knew it was dangerous. As Mules had said to Anne-Sophie, it was almost certain suicide. That only made him feel even better about his action and the motivation behind it.

Mules had told him to take the back roads, but he did not see the point. The dark forces would have every road covered. If he was going to be picked up, it would just as likely happen on a small road as a big one. He decided it was best to go the most direct, quickest route, past the Parc Zoologique de Paris, turning right and driving parallel to the Seine, before turning left at the Pont d'Austerlitz and left again at the Rue Cuvier. As Mules had predicted, Hérault arrived at Rue Rollin at seven-forty-five precisely. Anne-Sophie was waiting for him with the keys and directions to Philippe's apartment, a flask of fresh coffee, two hot pains au chocolat wrapped in foil and a hug.

'Thanks, you've thought of everything.'

'I was well taught by my mother. However, I should be saying thanks to you. This is my mess, thank you for offering to clear it up.' She hugged him again.

'Tell Philippe I'll be back soon.'

'I will.'

'I'd better go.'

'Yes. Don't forget, drive up to the limit but be careful. See you in an hour.'

The fastest route to Rue de Sévigné saw him drive through the Place de la Bastille just after eight o'clock. A series of left turns took him past the Musée Carnavalet and he was in front of Philippe's apartment twenty minutes after leaving Saint-Victor. He did not know whether he had done the hard, or the easy part, but thought it best not to hang about thinking about it for too long. As soon as he entered the apartment, he realized it had definitely been the latter, when he saw a man dressed head-to-toe in black, including a balaclava, sitting on the sofa.

'I applaud your punctuality.'

Hérault turned round and found himself facing another man who had appeared seemingly out of thin air, wearing the same outfit as the man on the sofa.

'*Route barrée.*'

Two thoughts flashed through Hérault's brain. This time he had really run out of road, and his newly discovered belief in the existence of a benevolent, forgiving God, had lasted less than twenty-four hours.

Chapter Thirty-Six

'Voulez-Vous' was coming from her pocket. She stood up.

'Anne-Sophie Montreau?'

'Who is this?'

'Call me Jacques. Hérault did.'

'How is he? Where is he?'

'Safe. For one hour.'

'And then?'

'That's up to you.'

'Meaning?'

'Give up whatever it is you're trying to achieve and he's a free man.'

'If I don't?'

'He's a dead man.'

'But…'

'I'll call you back at nine-thirty.'

'Jacques! Wait!'

Her plea having fallen on deaf ears, she sat down and looked at Philippe. 'What should I do? Please help me.'

'I am sorry, Hérault is a dead man. As am I.'

'Philippe! For pity's sake.'

'I know you called Eric for the right reasons, but I told you not to do it; you should have let me die. It was my own fault I did not have my medication, my responsibility. Besides, if you tell Jacques you are giving up, do you think he will just leave you to live in peace in Saint-Victor, for the next forty years? No way! I told you on Monday, you are a marked woman. The only way to save yourself and get justice for your father is to expose the truth or be killed in the attempt. I am sorry, I know it is harsh, but there is no alternative. The only question you have to ask yourself is how far you will go to get the truth. What sacrifices will you make? Think of it as a game of chess.'

'My God, Hérault is no pawn, neither is Eric.'

She noticed he was trembling and took hold of his hands. 'And neither are you. Especially not you.'

He was wheezing.

'I'll call an ambulance.'

'Not yet, sit down, please. My time is truly running out. I must tell you something, something you will not like. You have to promise to hear me out, right to the end, please do not make any premature judgments.'

'But…'

'Promise.'

She sat down and took his hands in hers. 'Yes, silly old man, I promise!'

'Good. Before I start, please may I have a coffee and some toast.'

Five minutes later, duly fortified, he was ready.

'You remember Françoise and Emil mentioned that during the final week of his life, your father twice went to the Au Jean Bart, both times to meet a friend.'

'A friend who both times did not turn up.'

'Correct.'

She studied him closely. 'Oh no.'

'I was the friend.'

She took her hands away from his, clenched them and then stroked her cross. 'You're not going to tell me you betrayed my father; that you were his Judas.'

He looked at her imploringly. 'Please, you promised you would hear me out to the end.'

'Why didn't you meet him?'

'I will tell you in a moment. You also remember I told you I visited this apartment every Wednesday night.'

'To avail yourself of delicious food, wonderful wine and a free bed. Yes, I remember.'

'I did not visit that last Wednesday.'

She stood up. 'Bloody hell! You let my father down three times during his last days; more Peter than Judas. My poor mother was right to be angry with you. I'm not surprised she cut you out of our lives.' She glared at him. 'On Monday, you had me believing she had done wrong by you. No wonder it took you forty years to pluck up the courage to come and look me in the eye, and even then, you knew that by doing so you were handing me a death sentence; and now Hérault is going to be killed. So, all-in-all, thanks for nothing.'

'Anne-Sophie, please.'

She topped up her coffee and then looked into his tear-filled eyes. 'Why not?'

'Why not what?'

'Why didn't you come here on the Wednesday night?'

'The same reason I did not go to Au Jean Bart.'

'Which was?'

'I was scared.'

'Of what? Of whom? What could be more important than your best friend, and his wife who had treated you like a prince for years?'

'My editor.'

'What about your editor?'

'I was afraid of him. Rather, I was afraid of what he could do to me and your parents.'

'Which was?'

'Destroy us.'

'What do you mean? How? I don't get it.'

'Please sit down.' He enclosed her hands with his own. 'Do you recall, on Monday, I told you I loved your father? I could never have done anything to hurt him.'

'Yes.'

'I loved him, yes, but not just as a friend.'

'I'm sorry, I'm a bit muddled up. What do you…'

Then it struck her. Her mind flashed back to his sparse apartment, the lack of photos denoting any kind of relationship, and his reaction to Parcelle's 'closet' rejoinder to LeBlanc.

'You're gay?'

'Yes.'

'You loved my father physically?'

'Yes.'

'And did, did he love you that way too?'

'No.'

'Did he know you loved him?'

'Yes, I told him after too many glasses of Côtes du Rhône on the Wednesday before your parents' wedding.'

'Great timing.'

'I am renowned for it. Your mother had gone to bed and left us to finish off our third bottle. We did not normally drink so much but, well, it was a special night. Your father had been teasing me slightly, saying it would soon be my turn to get married; how he was looking forward very much to returning the favour and making the best man's speech. I told him that I would never marry. He looked at me sharply with those same brown eyes you possess and asked me what I meant. I told him I was gay and that I could never love anyone as much as I loved him.'

'This was before civil partnerships were legal?'

'Years before.'

'How did my father respond?'

'He filled up my glass and, typical Jean-Marie, he said I was Elton John, and he was Bernie Taupin.'

'Bernie Taupin?'

'Elton's, straight, writing partner. I take it you haven't seen *Rocket Man*?'

'No, should I have done?'

'Yes! For many reasons. Your father loved Elton John! He was his favourite singer, bar none. I have the DVD in my apartment. When this is all over, perhaps we can sit down and watch it together.'

She squeezed his hands. 'I'd love to.'

'Your father had no problems with my revelation. He woke up Thérèse and told her to come into the lounge and listen to what I had just told him. You see, they had no secrets from each other.'

'What was her response?'

'She just shrugged and said, "Is that all? I've known from the first time we met." Then she kissed me on the cheek and went straight back to bed. It was very funny. Your father and I did not stop laughing for a good half an hour.'

'Wonderful. So, back to your editor. What was this power he had over you?'

'The Wednesday morning of your father's last week I was called into the editor's office. Someone had told him I was gay, and that your parents and I were in a three-way relationship.'

'Do you have any idea who told him?'

'With the benefit of recently gained hindsight, I'm guessing one of Jacques' stooges, perhaps even the man himself. My boss told me that unless I promised to keep away from Jean-Marie and Thérèse, he would make sure every editor and journalist in the city knew about our sordid relationship before midday. This would be perfect timing for the evening paper print run, so, I admit it, I panicked. I was not concerned for me, only for Jean-Marie and Thérèse. He was having a difficult time at L'Académie; she was heavily pregnant. What if she suffered a miscarriage from the shock of seeing our faces on the front pages of every newspaper in Paris? Your parents had been trying for years to conceive; I could not allow them to go through more pain and anguish, so I agreed to my editor's blackmail.'

'You stayed away from my parents and the apartment, to protect them, not to betray them?'

'Yes.'

Suddenly, he began coughing. It lasted a minute. Anne-Sophie propped him up on his pillows which helped only slightly. She dialled 112 and the responder said an ambulance would be with them in five minutes. Within two, the buzzer sounded.

'Hell.'

Suddenly he grabbed her arm. 'Listen to me. Your father…'

'Yes?'

'He had been… looking for… something… for a long time…'

'What? When?'

The buzzer was sounding non-stop.

Philippe's eyes were closing.

'I think …the last week … he was close…at last.'

'Close to what?'

She thought he had slipped into unconsciousness, then,

'The books… the book.'

'Books? Book? What do you mean?'

'Ask P…'

'Who is P?! Philippe!'

His eyes were beginning to lose focus, but he continued. 'Not just for Jean-Marie…for the others …all the others.'

'Others? What others? Philippe!'

His eyes closed.

'Philippe!'

The buzzer was incessant, insistent. She ran to the door and opened it up. The medical responders came in and placed

Philippe onto a stretcher with hardly a word said. She asked if she could come with them, a suggestion that was met with a derision she did not expect. After that rebuff, she did not even think to ask which hospital they were taking him to as they disappeared down the stairs. She sat still on the sofa for five minutes, desperately trying to decide her next move.

Chapter Thirty-Seven

'Hello, boss.'

'Christ, Angela! You scared the hell out of me. How did you get here?'

'Via the garden route.'

They shook hands.

Having recovered from his shock, Eric looked at her, 'Good to see you again but, just to remind you, you're the boss now. The big boss.'

'You'll always be the boss to me. You were my commanding officer for twenty years, it's only natural I should call you that.'

'Would you like coffee?'

'Thank you.'

'Give me a moment. Sit yourself down. Céline, please can we have some coffee.'

It was nine o'clock and Anne-Sophie had just finished giving Mules the news about Jacques, Hérault and Philippe. The immediate, unexpected arrival at his back door of a former colleague, Angela Faust, accompanied by an armed officer she introduced as Daniel, was another jolt to Eric's wide wake, caffeine-overloaded system.

'Lovely house. I take it Céline deserves all the credit?'

'A house you've never visited, nor felt the need to visit, in the two decades we've known each other. Why now? Why the garden route? What's going on?'

'You tell me. Twice in the past forty-hours you've come up on my radar; that's twice too often for my liking, hence my visit to your, Céline's, lovely home.'

'What do you mean when you say radar?'

'All you need to know is that my team is listening in to certain conversations.'

'OK.'

'I'm a busy woman, so no more of your customary playing for time. What is it you're investigating that has caused a couple of cages to rattle?'

'Conspiracy, followed by cover-up, aided and abetted by everyone's favourite Chief Justice, Juliette Roulet.'

'I'm listening.'

'In 1987, a L'Académie virologist, Jean-Marie Montreau, was found hanging from his Saint-Victor apartment bedroom ceiling. Verdict, suicide.'

'You were involved?'

'As the chief investigating officer, I tried to be, but the leader of a, probably fake, *Brigade* unit, someone masquerading as Jacques, kept me at much more than arm's length from the crime scene.'

'After forty years, why the sudden interest?'

'Montreau's daughter, Anne-Sophie, came here on Monday afternoon.'

'Out of the blue?'

'Completely. She was accompanied by Philippe Simon.'

She laughed. 'Simon!'

'Why's that funny?'

'You and he hate each other.'

'When the circumstances change, you change with them.'

'Some changes are bigger than others. I would describe this as seismic.'

'Simon was Montreau's best friend, best man and godfather to the girl.'

'Small world.'

'And, reading between the lines, he's dying of cancer. He's en-route to hospital but may well be already dead.'

'Oh.'

She looked at the clock. Nine-fifteen. 'Give me a quick summary of where you are with this.'

'We've established beyond all reasonable doubt that the so-called suicide was, if not premeditated murder, at best an unlawful killing. According to the guy who let the two perpetrators into the block, Henri Hérault, the security manager, the fake *Brigade* guys were searching for something. What that something was I've no idea. Montreau came back early from a planned visit to L'Académie, presumably interrupted the intruders and got strung up for his pains. I would love to know the names of the two goons who did the deed.'

'OK, anything else?'

'Hérault was captured this morning, presumably by Jacques' men, somewhere between Saint-Victor and Le Marais. He's going to meet a grisly end.' He also glanced at the clock. 'To be truthful, I'm expecting a call from Anne-Sophie in the very near future telling me it's all over for him.'

'Right.'

'He was driving my Saab, which may help you track him down.'

'I'll try. What else?'

'Anne-Sophie's mother, Thérèse, was killed on Christmas Eve last year, after a hit and run. Can someone please give it the once-over, make sure no corners were cut in the investigation.'

'Consider it done.'

'Last thing.'

'Go on.'

'The original police dossier has mysteriously disappeared. It would be a massive help if it, just as mysteriously, reappeared.'

She looked at Daniel. 'Have you got all that?' Then she turned back to Mules and looked at him carefully. 'How's your drinking? Under control?'

'Taking it day by day, that's all I can do. This week has been the easiest week since I retired.'

'Sense of purpose, the thrill of the chase?'

'Absolutely.'

'Anything else I should know?'

'The *Brigade* unit's team leader, also Hérault's handler.'

'Jacques?'

'Yes. Had a scar under his right eye socket. I'd give up the booze for good if I could find out who he is.'

'OK, any more relevant information?'

'One last morsel, a very juicy, tasty morsel.'

'Go on.'

'The name of the Procureur who was seen entering the crime scene in the immediate aftermath of the murder and who subsequently, together with Roulet, was at the very heart of the cover-up.'

'Get on with it, I can only hold my breath for so long.'

166

'Hervé Parcelle.'

She exhaled. 'Wow.'

It was his turn to study her. 'What now?'

'At this precise moment, I've no idea. However, I do know that, once we've finished your wife's delicious coffee, you're coming with me and Daniel to my car, via the garden route.'

'Fine, first let me say my goodbyes to Céline.'

Chapter Thirty-Eight

The call from Jacques came dead on nine-thirty.

'Well?'

'Well, what?'

'What's your decision?'

'I'm not giving up.'

'Foolish girl.'

'What's your decision?'

'Hérault will be taken to a very unsafe house.' He hung up.

She called Eric again. 'Hérault is still alive, I think.'

'Thank God.'

'I'm not sure how much longer he has left.' She could hear voices. 'Who are you with? Where are you?'

'Heading into what some may describe as the lion's den.'

'What does that mean?'

'Best if I keep schtum, just in case. Any news on Philippe?'

'Not yet. I'll call the hospital straight away. Good luck with whatever you're doing and whoever you're doing it with.'

'Thanks, keep in touch. If you hear anything about Philippe and Henri, please call me.'

She sat down on the sofa and took a deep breath. Possibly for the first time in her life, she was having to deal with a difficult situation entirely by herself. No mother to protect her in her safe space, wrap her up in cotton wool, hold her hand and tell her everything was going to be all right. No Béatrice to wave her magic wand and make the bad stuff disappear. No Philippe, who was God knows where. No Eric, who was on his way to God knows where, with God knows who. Certainly, no Hérault; she did not even want to think about where in God's name he was being taken to, or, who by.

She decided to call Pitié Salpêtrière which she presumed was where the rude responders had taken Philippe. Without any of the usual 'select an option' preamble, a disengaged male voice told her Monsieur Simon was "in an emergency ward receiving the best care possible," and that "no, no visitors were allowed for at least twenty-four hours."

She texted Béatrice to bring her up to speed with the events of the morning thus far. Her friend's response was immediate,

'Very scary re Hérault. Very sorry re P. What now? B x'

What indeed? Hérault's abduction had opened her eyes to what she was truly up against. She knew she had less than sixty hours to find out who killed her father and why. To do that she had to work out what her father had, according to Philippe, been close to finding. She had a strong feeling that it, whatever it was, was the key to the whole mystery. However, at the moment, she had no clue what the key was, or where it might be. Never mind searching for a needle in a haystack, at the moment she had neither needle nor haystack.

Her pocket vibrated to 'Voulez-Vous' again.

'Damn.'

She stood up, 'Monique, hi.'

'How's your holiday going?'

'Interesting, to say the least.'

'That's good. Well, I've just had an, to say the least, interesting phone call.'

'Really?'

'Yes, really. Apparently, you've engaged in some very unethical, some might say illegal, cyber activity, concerning one of the bank's account holders.'

'Who told you that?'

'Is this the way you repay me for all that bereavement leave I gave you after Christmas, on full-pay? Everyone told me I was being far too generous.'

'I'm sorr-'

'I think we need to have a chat. Before Monday.'

'OK.'

'Call me Friday morning, at nine o'clock.'

'I will. I'm sorr-'

Her boss abruptly ended the call.

Anne-Sophie slumped back into her sofa, 'Thank you, God. As if I haven't got enough to deal with.'

She put her boss's displeasure and Friday's phone call to the back corner of her mind and focused on the here and now.

Philippe and Eric had been right, she was under surveillance, just like her parents had been. Needing something to keep her going, she brewed a fresh pot of coffee, and then focused on her needle and haystack problem.

By ten-thirty, she was no further forward in her search, but had decided it was time she started fighting fire with fire; that she may as well be hung for a sheep as a lamb. How long had she sat on the news Parcelle had been in this very room at the very moment they were cutting down her father's body? Too long. It was time to stop sitting. She knew someone who would bite her hand off to hear destructive tidings about France's next President.

She went online, found who she was looking for and sent him what she hoped was an enticing, encrypted text:

'Hello, Paul. I have an urgent and, I think, game-changing story for you concerning a recent bête noire. Please WhatsApp call / message me on this number to arrange a video call asap. Keep this to yourself. Thanks, Anne-Sophie Montreau.'

The recipient's reply was equal in speed to Béatrice at her sharpest.

'Hello, Anne-Sophie? Paul LeBlanc.'

She dialled the number.

'That was quick.'

'You said it was urgent.'

'It is. Are you OK to video call me?'

'Of course.'

'Where are you?'

'At home.'

'Before you call me can I please send you something?'

'Depends on what it is.'

'Malware protection and removal software.'

He laughed. 'I'm pretty sure I have that already.'

'It won't be as good as this.'

'Really?'

'Really. I won't talk to you unless you download it to your phone.'

'OK, OK, send it through. Make it quick, I have to go out soon. Time and an election rally wait for no-one.'

'Call me as soon as you've downloaded it, please.'

'I will.'

After sending the software she put on a thicker jumper. Perhaps it was the shock of the morning's dramatic events, perhaps it was all the driving rain but, whatever it was, she felt shivery. She hoped she was not going down with the lurgy. If she was then Stonehouse would have to take his chances. After waiting ten minutes and just as she was thinking about re-starting *'Killer in the Village'*, her video call activated.

'ASMAMS? What is this? Who are you?'

'Anne-Sophie Montreau. I'm a bank systems cyber-analyst.'

'And an anti-malware software developer.'

'In my spare time, yes.'

'Which of my several recent bêtes noires were you referring to in your call?'

'Hervé Parcelle.'

She heard his intake of breath. 'What have you got?'

After she finished her story there was another intake of breath. 'Hot stuff.'

'I thought you might be interested.'

'I am, but, obviously, before I can do anything with this, I need more than just the testimony of a former security manager, no matter how genuine he appears to be.'

'That might be difficult. I don't know who else could confirm it, only a slimeball known as Jacques. I don't know who he is, but I do know what he is and which side he's on. I very much doubt he would play ball.'

'A pity, your story's potential and saleability are blindingly obvious but without confirmation or corroboration, it's virtually worthless. There's no way my editor would run with it this close to the election. *Le Parisien* would be shut down immediately.'

'Damn. I thought you'd be biting my hand off.'

'Normally I would be, but, as I am sure you are aware, these are far from normal times, The run-up to a Presidential election is a tinder box situation.'

'As the press conference showed.'

'Precisely.'

'OK, well, if I do find someone or something which corroborates Hérault, I'll let you know.'

'OK, sorry I can't be more helpful, but…?'

'Yes?'

'There is one thing.'

'Go on.'

'Just a thought but you could always post something yourself, as a private individual, under an assumed identity if you like. I should have thought someone with your skill set should be able to construct something that is pretty much untraceable and impenetrable.'

'Wow, I never thought of that. Thanks, Paul. Genius. I'll be in touch.'

She looked at the clock. She had two hours before she was due to set off to Au Jean Bart. She poured herself more coffee, and pondered how she could make the best use of her 'skills set.' The answer came to her surprisingly quickly. She thought about her recent conversation with her boss and whether she should go ahead with something that would definitely mean she would get the sack and probably be arrested.

'Sod it, if I'm going to get hung for a sheep it may as well be a bloody big one.'

Ninety minutes later, straight after she had launched a brand-new blog, 'JusticeforJean-Marie', her phone buzzed.

'To save you a soaking I'll pick you up at 12.45 sharp. Send me your address please. See you soon. S.'

'That's very kind. Thank you! A-S. Espace Sûr, Apartment 19, 87 Rue Rollin, Saint-Victor. Sys, A-S.'

Chapter Thirty-Nine

'Can you talk?'

'I've five minutes.'

'Just to fill you in, the dominoes are definitely toppling. Hérault has been taken to less than comfortable lodgings. At some point during the next twenty-four hours, he will receive the coup de grâce traditionally dished out to traitors.'

'Why delay the inevitable?'

'I'm hoping the Montreau girl will join him and perform her own special role in the dénouement of that particular long-running drama.'

'What else?'

'Hérault will soon be joined by Simon.'

'Tell me.'

'When the Montreau girl called 112, she was connected to my boys, who had what passed for a medical emergency vehicle outside her apartment in less than two minutes.'

'1987 revisited?'

'Yes. She called Salpêtrière half an hour ago. Again, she spoke to one of the team who fobbed her off without any difficulty.'

'Excellent. What kind of state is Simon in?'

'As I said earlier, death's door is wide open. Without any medication, he'll be very lucky to make it into tomorrow, which will be a pity as I would like the girl to be involved in his finale too.'

'Perhaps give him enough medication to get him through one last night?'

'Good idea.'

'You're welcome. Mules?'

'He's still at home staring at his drinks cabinet.'

'Malherbe?'

'No cry from the heart, or anything else yet. Probably still coming to after nearly overdosing on brandy last night.'

'Why not bring Mules and Malherbe together, kill two birds with one stone?'

'Another excellent thought.'

'You're very welcome. I just wonder why I have to think of these things, not you. So, is that everything?'

'One other item; as a concerned law-abiding citizen, I contacted Montreau's boss to let her know that I believed a customer's accounts had been illegally hacked into. The boss was very stimulated by the intel. I expect Ms Montreau to have had a very uncomfortable conversation shortly after.'

'Let's hope so.'

'I'll let you get back to your rally.'

'Thank you for the update. I look forward to hearing about the next toppled domino. Hopefully, sooner rather than later.'

Chapter Forty

'Here you are, your very own PC, keyboard, username and password. Don't say I don't look after you.'

Eric had indeed walked straight into the lion's den, otherwise known as the Palais de Justice, located on the Île de la Cité. Fortunately, the building was such a hive of activity no-one noticed a hat-wearing, stick-holding, old man shuffling his way through a side entrance and down several flights of stairs into a converted basement.

'So, this is how, and where, the crème de la crème earn their corn? I imagined something a little more glamorous and hi-tech.'

'Not exactly glamourous, I agree, but it's very discreet, very under the radar, which I guess suits your purpose perfectly.'

'It does.'

'This is the photo database. Happy hunting.'

'Thanks. Two more things.'

'Yes?'

'May I have coffee please?'

'Of course.'

'And some biscuits.'

'Don't push your luck. I'm not a saint and I'm absolutely not Céline.'

'I know. No-one is.'

Chapter Forty-One

As promised, Stonehouse arrived promptly at twelve-forty-five. As she climbed into the taxi he smiled at her, 'Hello. Nice to meet you. At last.'

'Likewise.'

She hopped into the taxi, and they sped off to the Au Jean Bart.

'Apologies for the *modus transportandi* but my Aston Martin is in having its annual check-up.'

Anne-Sophie raised a questioning eyebrow at Stonehouse after the driver, on his instructions, ignored the 'Strictly No Parking or Stopping' sign, and dropped them off directly in front of the brasserie's entrance. Stonehouse grinned. It was a very pleasing boyish grin.

'I've been coming here for forty-five years, I think I've earned enough loyalty points to entitle me not to park, or get dropped off, across the road. Especially in this bloody rain, it's worse than Blighty.'

She wondered what he meant by Blighty, and how old he was. He escorted her inside where she saw Françoise and Emil propping up the bar. Their eyes virtually popped out when they saw them walk in together. Stonehouse guided her down the steps to a corner table, upon which was an ice bucket containing a 1987 bottle of *Dom Pérignon*.

'Happy belated fortieth.'

'Wow, amazing! Very thoughtful, thank you.'

'You're more than welcome. You OK?'

'Fine, except I feel totally under-dressed. I barely had time to brush my teeth, never mind my hair.'

'Béatrice told me you've been having an exciting week.'

'Is she the source of your having heard a lot about me?'

'Guilty as charged. Only the occasional morsel or two in passing, nothing scurrilous or incriminating, I can assure you. I would hate you to get the wrong end of the stick.'

Anne-Sophie enjoyed listening to his faintly ironic, middle-class, English accent.

'You like her?'

'She is very dear to my heart.'

'How come?'

'Four years ago, when I became Director of Virology, she was the first person I promoted from the ranks; in the face of, I must say, some spirited Gallic opposition.'

'What do you mean?'

'The usual carping. I was accused of tokenism, inverse sexism, all that sort of stuff. Complete codswallop, of course, Béatrice was promoted purely on professional merit.'

He looked at her, 'I don't mean to bad mouth your compatriots, but I like to think us Brits are better than that.'

After giving the waiter their orders of Souris d'Agneau and Faux-filet, and a bottle of Beaujolais Nouveau, Anne-Sophie decided to move the conversation forward. 'When did you join L'Académie?'

'Time to get down to business, eh? Let me think. I came to L'Académie to do my post-doc in retrovirology in, of all years, 1981. I was a bright-eyed, bushy-tailed whippersnapper then. Now look at me, dull-of-eye and sparse of tail, ha, ha.'

'Did you know my father?'

'Only by sight.'

'You never talked?'

'Rarely, certainly not in any great depth. We may have said 'Hello, how are you' that sort of thing. I worked exclusively in the Submarine. All I can tell you is that he seemed a decent enough sort of cove.'

'What has Béatrice told you about my exciting week?'

'That you've discovered your father was killed rather than, as you'd been told, committed suicide. That would certainly count as exciting in anyone's book, mine included. If I was writing one that is, which I'm not. Too much like hard work, or so I've been told by those who've done it.'

She had her back to the rest of the patrons, but she noticed he was continually smiling and laughing at the staff, or to other diners arriving to, or leaving, their tables.

'You seem to know everyone.'

'I should bloody well hope so! As I say I've been coming here for over forty years.'

'Which part of England are you from?'

'No flies on you. Born in Colney Heath, Hertfordshire, sixty-eight years ago. Hard to credit, I know, I look more like seventy-eight!'

She had been trying to guess his age. Her highest estimate was mid-fifties. He was very well preserved.

'Do you go back across the Channel a lot?'

'Apart from the odd conference, there's no reason to. I've no one to go back to. My English father died when I was five, a genuine suicide this time. Oops, I'm sorry, I'm not known for my tact.'

'It's OK, carry on.'

'My French mother died two decades ago. She never got over Father's death. I've no brothers or sisters, at least, none that I know about.'

'I'm sorry about your parents. Believe me, I wasn't prying.'

'I know you weren't. So, now I'm a French citizen, true red, white and blue; have been for twenty years. *Officier de La Légion d'honneur* for six. Vive La République! Here, finish off the champers.'

She was feeling squiffy and no wonder. A bottle of champagne despatched mainly by her, and it was barely one-thirty. She wished they'd hurry up with her lamb. Much longer and she'd be under the table, with or without Stonehouse.

'It's awful losing a parent so young.'

'I suppose so. However, as far as I can tell, the only difference it made to me is that I got packed off to boarding school by my mother. She couldn't cope with her grief and my whining at the same time.'

'Was 1981 when you first came to France?'

'No, that was 1978. I studied biochemistry at Hôpital Universitaire de Lille, thence to L'Académie.'

'You said you came to L'Académie "in 1981, of all years." Why did you say that?'

'1981 was the year AIDS, or GRID as it was called initially, was first recognised.'

'GRID?'

'Gay Related Immune Deficiency.'

'Why GRID?'

'The original cases were all in gay men.'

'Ah. Obvious really. When did it become AIDS?'

'It became the Acquired Immune Deficiency Syndrome in 1982.'

'Can I ask a really simple question please?'

'Definitely my favourite kind; fire away.'

'What is AIDS?'

'Basically, a person's immune system is damaged beyond repair by something they've acquired. By that I mean something they picked up, contracted, or been infected by, rather than something they were born with. Although in the case of babies born with AIDS, that distinction does not apply.'

'I see. You said immune systems are damaged. What kind of damage?'

'There is a massive reduction in the numbers of a type of white blood cell called a Helper T-cell. Imagine the immune system is an orchestra, the Helper T-cell is the conductor sending signals that direct other immune cells to fight infection.'

'T for?'

'Thymus gland, where these cells mature.'

'I've never heard of it.'

'You and ninety-nine point nine per cent of the population.'

'And the syndrome bit?'

'Once the Helper T-cells start to disappear, the immune system orchestra loses its conductor, and acts like a headless chicken, meaning the body is wide open to attack by the so-called opportunistic infections. Multiple medical conditions equal a syndrome; AIDS wasn't a single disease, it was a condition characterized by a set of multiple, associated, rather characteristic and relatively uniform patterns of infectious diseases.'

'You must think me very ignorant.'

'Not at all! A lot of people had, have, this idea that AIDS is very complex. It's actually very straightforward. Kidney transplant patients suffered from many of the same symptoms as AIDS patients, years before AIDS existed.'

She nearly spat out some of the *Dom Pérignon*.

'What?'

'It's true! In the 1960s and 1970s, these patients got super or opportunistic infections as a result of their immune systems being stood down to avoid the body rejecting the new organ; the same infections as those suffered by actual AIDS patients in the early 1980s. A good number of the transplant recipients, once they'd passed through a tipping point, died as a consequence. Despite what the CDC, NIH, NHS, WHO, L'Académie et al said, AIDS wasn't a single disease, and it wasn't new. The only new thing about 1980s AIDS was the demographics it affected.'

'Which were?'

'Sexually highly active gay males, haemophiliacs and PWIDs.'

'PWIDs?'

'People who inject drugs. In old money, intravenous drug users or IVDUs.'

'I see. I take it the CDC, L'Académie and the rest knew about these transplant patients?'

'You'd like to think so, but they don't seem to have done. If they had then they wouldn't have come out with such poorly informed piffle.'

'Such as?'

'That AIDS was contagious or infectious. You couldn't, can't, catch AIDS, or spread it around.'

'How could they not have known?'

'One of the problems with medicine back then was compartmentalization. There wasn't a great deal of fraternization between departments, faculties, or institutions; there still isn't today.'

'What about the research papers? Surely, they contained the relevant information?'

'Too long-winded, boring and, frankly, difficult. Most medics only read the abstract and the discussion sections, not the meaty bit in the middle.'

'I see.'

'There are other, less generous, explanations.'

'Which are?'

'They were too stupid to realise.'

'Oh.'

He looked at her directly, 'Or too ambitious and too ruthless to care.'

'My God.'

Speaking of meaty bits, she was now feeling very tipsy and had almost reached her tipping point. Where the hell was that lamb?

'Having said all that, I'm pretty sure that without AIDS I wouldn't be sitting here today, or rather in the Director of Virology's hot seat across the way.' He looked over her shoulder. 'Ah, here we go. Thank God, I'm bloody ravenous. Tuck in. This is my treat by the way. Cheers!'

She was too drunk to argue. 'Cheers. So, AIDS was a godsend for you?'

'Selfishly speaking, yes. Joining L'Académie in 1981 was certainly a massive stroke of luck. The amount of money being poured into HIV and AIDS research by the end of the '80s would have shamed Croesus. Still, one life lesson I've learned is not to look a gift horse in the mouth.'

'So, you were there when Malherbe discovered HIV?'

'Well, it wasn't called HIV until 1986, but yes, I was there in 1983 when the breakthrough was made. A year later, the Yanks stole the credit, literally.'

'How?'

'They took L'Académie's AIDS virus and passed it off as their own.'

'Thanks. How did they manage that?'

'It's a long story, probably too long after a bottle of Dom Pom. Suffice to say our LAV/BRU virus became their HTLV-IIIB. Literally overnight, the Yanks changed the meaning of their own retrovirus family, HTLV; 'L' for leukaemia', became 'L for lymphotropic'. Brazen.'

'LAV/BRU being the AIDS virus?'

'Yes.'

'All this helps explain the rift between Paris and Washington?'

'Correct. A rift that was never entirely healed in my book. Still, one must move on, not bear grudges.'

'You sound like someone who might still carry a grudge.'

He put down his knife and fork and looked at her. 'You're right. One of my many flaws. But look, the Yanks were just so blatant. They examined thousands of AIDS patients' samples and what did they find? The square root of sweet eff all, that's what. So, it was all down to the good old Sub. We found it, they didn't. Simple as that. However, even today Antony Consolotto drones on in his interviews about Bicchiere discovering the AIDS virus. Complete cobblers. Balderdash.'

'My father wasn't part of the Submariners, was he?'

'No, he wasn't a retrovirologist.'

'Do you know why he and Malherbe fell out? Françoise and Emil, no doubt standing right behind us and watching us like hawks, said my father held unorthodox views.'

'Sorry, I can't help you there. Béatrice told me you'd been to see Malherbe. Any joy?'

'No. He played what you English would call a very straight bat, despite his dementia.'

'Ha, ha, good old Louis. Not a bad chap but a terrible scientist and a worse teacher.'

'Meaning?'

Chapter Forty-Two

Hérault had been sitting bound and gagged on his own for what he thought must have been three hours. Then a door opened and closed within the space of fifteen seconds. He heard groaning noises, followed by words. At first, it was difficult to make out what was being said. Gradually the words became clearer,

'Silly old man.'

Chapter Forty-Three

'How was your lamb?'

'To die for.'

They froze, looked at each other, then laughed.

'Your filet?'

'Same. Dessert?'

It was three o'clock. With every passing minute, she felt more out of control. She knew it had been a long time since she last had gone out for a meal with a man, but Stonehouse was looking increasingly attractive. At this rate, she'd be having him for dessert. There was only one thing preventing her from making mental plans for later.

'Absolutely! But first I need coffee, and fast.'

'Americano?'

'Perfect. Two shots please.'

He looked up and caught the waiter's eye. In no time at all she was served with her coffee and handed a dessert menu.

'Impossible to choose. Any recommendations?'

'Let's go for all four. They're not big portions. We can share. Then some cheese for afters.'

'Are you sure?'

'Of course, let's push the boat out. It's a special occasion. Live dangerously for once.'

'OK, why not.'

'Well done! Shall I order a dessert wine?'

'I'm not sure. I think I've…'

'Come on. Be rude not to. How about a 1999 *Château Rieussec Sauternes*?'

She gave what she knew was a weird smile and steered the conversation back to the reason they were there. 'If Malherbe was such an awful scientist and teacher, how come he got a Nobel prize?'

'Another good question. First, it would have been very strange if the most important medical science discovery of the twentieth century had not been recognized. Second, it was definitely a team award for the Submarine. Louis was the lab manager, the front man, as it were. He, of course, sees it differently, but he had very little to do with the actual discovery of HIV; claiming he played a pivotal role is pushing it a tad, and that's me being very polite.'

'OK, next question. Sorry to talk shop.'

He was sitting back in his chair.

'No problem. Carry on.'

'You know how a vaccine for COVID-19 was discovered, developed and delivered in less than twelve months?'

'I know exactly what you're going to ask.'

'Tell me.'

'Why has there been no HIV vaccine after forty years?'

'Mind-reader.'

'It's a great question which gets asked a lot obviously, especially after the rapid response to COVID-19.'

'And the answer?'

'It's hard to hit a moving target.'

'Explain.'

'HIV mutates at an incredible rate.'

'More than a coronavirus?'

'Much, much more. Ah, here come our desserts and wine. Perfect. Let me order the cheese now so that it can be brought up to room temperature.'

'I have one more question to ask you about L'Académie if that's OK?'

'Of course.'

'I think Father was betrayed by an insider.'

'Really? That's hard to comprehend.'

'I know. However, that's what I believe. Do you have any idea who that insider was?'

'That's a very difficult question to answer.'

'Why?'

'It's rather like an Agatha Christie murder mystery.'

'Meaning?'

'There are a lot of suspects.'

'Was my father that unpopular?'

'Not at all! However, think about all the people who were connected in one way or another with the Submarine. All the people in L'Académie who may have thought your father was being disloyal by questioning Malherbe, his set-up and his results. That's a cast of thousands really.'

'No-one stands out?'

'I have no idea if it was the case, but if your father and Malherbe *were* at loggerheads, then perhaps a laser focus on Louis, rather than a scattergun approach, might produce better results.'

'Malherbe implied that someone apart from himself knew something. Any idea who that someone might be.'

'Not a clue. Sorry.'

'OK, thanks. I promise I won't mention L'Académie again.'

'What about outside of L'Académie?'

'Sorry?'

'Béatrice mentioned you'd made what seemed to be a very exciting discovery.'

'We have but, if you don't mind, that's not something I want to, or should, talk about here.'

'Of course. Restaurant tables have ears, and so do their occupants.'

She sipped her Americano, 'Did you have an enjoyable, family Easter weekend?'

He paused before answering as the waiter was laying their cheeseboard out on the table.

'Another conversational handbrake-turn.'

'Is that a problem?'

'Not at all, you're keeping me on my toes, I like it.'

'I hope it won't turn into a car-crash.'

'Don't worry, it won't. To answer your question, I'm afraid there was no chance of a family weekend. Not with a gap of three thousand miles between me and the family.'

'Oh.'

'My ex-wife and children live in New York. Our marriage broke up a decade ago.'

'I'm sorry, I didn't mean to stick my big, clomping, size sevens in it, again.'

'Don't be. It was all very amicable.'

'How often do you get to see your children?'

'I see the boys in the summer. They come to Paris, and I take them to the Med for a month. Happy days, but not for much longer I fear.'

'Why not?'

'They're seventeen-year-old twins, eighteen this June. I very much doubt they'll want to spend their summers hanging out with their old man after this year.'

'You never know. Who'd want to miss out on the Med? I know I wouldn't.'

'You go there often?'

'Every summer too. It's bliss.'

'Isn't it? What about this summer?'

'I haven't booked anything yet. I was already having to deal with my mother's death, now this whole father business has kicked off. It's impossible to look beyond this week.'

'So, no plans?'

'None. However, if I get out of this week in one piece, I will definitely book something.'

'Before you do anything I have a villa in Cap Ferrat which I think you'd like.'

'Gosh. That does sound like bliss. What about your boys?'

'They come and go. I usually only see them at mealtimes, or the nanosecond after the WIFI goes down, as it frequently does in the villa.'

'OK, thank you for the very generous suggestion. I'll definitely bear it in mind.'

'So, to return your question, did you have a fun Easter weekend?'

'Not especially, unless you count trying to watch an AIDS documentary as fun.'

'Ha! Absolutely not.'

He paused as the cheeses were laid out in front of them.

'As I sense we have rapidly reached the stage where we start baring ourselves emotionally, I should also say my ex-wife was my second wife.'

'Oh.'

'My first wife died in early 1981. Coincidentally, not too long before I started working at L'Académie.'

She looked at him. 'I'm sorry, again. Are you OK talking about it? You don't have to if it upsets you.'

'I'm fine, I've had forty years plus to get over it. She had a viral infection. It was very quick, less than a month from start to finish.'

'That's awful. I'm so sorry.'

'Thank you. It was a true college romance, but I was lucky.'

'How so?'

'I got a second bite of the cherry. What about you?'

'Few cherries, and even fewer bites.'

They laughed again. She could not help but notice the twinkle in his ultra-blue eyes.

Stonehouse looked at his watch. 'Well, I'll ask for the bill and a taxi to take you back to Saint-Victor.'

'I have a favour to ask.'

'Fire away.'

'Are you very busy, at work that is?'

He looked at her over the top of his half-moon spectacles. 'In general, yes but if we're talking about this afternoon, there's nothing that can't wait until tomorrow. Why?'

'I need help.'

'Go on.'

'I'm trying to find two things.'

'Which are?'

'A needle and …'

'Let me take a wild guess, a haystack.'

'You *can* read my mind.'

'I've read the odd Dan Brown or six.'

'How much do you know about what I'm up to?'

'Only what Béatrice has hinted at, and what you asked me about earlier. You're trying to find out what happened to your father.'

'Specifically, who killed him, and why. You're going to the Ritz on Friday night, aren't you?'

'Yes.'

'I was told the person responsible for my father's death will be there. That gives me just over two days to find out that person's identity.'

'Why do you think I can help you?'

'I'm not sure; instinct, alcohol, desperation. I had a team of three but now they're disappearing. I've only got one out of the three left - retired Detective Inspector, Eric Mules. I desperately need another pair of eyes, ears and hands. Especially if they belong to someone who knows L'Académie inside out. As I told you earlier, I think Father's Judas was a L'Académie mole.'

'I'll be glad to help, of course. What exactly do you have in mind? '

'My father left behind a dozen notebooks. I'm convinced the needle must be mentioned in there somewhere.'

'And the haystack too?'

'Who knows? Possibly.'

'We can look through six each. It will take half the time.'

'Would you?'

'It would be my pleasure.'

He was suddenly on his feet. 'As time is obviously short, we'd better get moving. Let me grab that bill and we can jump in the taxi.' He smiled, 'After all, we wouldn't want our driver to get a ticket.'

The ride back to Saint-Victor took only ten minutes but, as she held Stephen's left hand whilst he used his right to text, Anne-Sophie realised this was the closest she had been to a man in a long, long time. She was wondering how much closer to him she would get before the evening was out.

Chapter Forty-Four

Eric looked at the clock. Three-thirty. He had been holed up in the lion's den without success for hours. Tracking down Scarface and his two henchmen had proven to be much more difficult than he had anticipated. A thought nagged away at him which both depressed and motivated him. Unless he found the guilty men, he would have failed the Montreau family a second time.

Faust walked in with Daniel who was carrying three coffees.

'Any luck?'

'Precisely none. Where the hell are they? They have to be here somewhere.'

'I wish I knew. Where are you up to?'

'The final database.'

'Let's look together. Halve the time.'

Daniel, looking over Faust's shoulder, spoke first. 'What about him?'

'Idiot.'

'What?'

'Daniel's hallucinating. He's found the ultimate rank outsider. A thousand-to-one, correction, a million-to-one, shot.'

'Let me take a look.'

Before Eric could check to see if Daniel had hit the million-to-one bullseye, his phone buzzed. He walked outside the room. 'Yes?'

'I need you to go to Le Vésinet, please. Now.'

'Malherbe?'

'He called me.'

'And?'

'He wants to do a Hérault.'

'Result!'

'Yes! Can you please pick him up and bring him to Saint-Victor?'

'Of course. Just text me his address.'

'Will do. I'll call him back, let him know to expect you.'

'Perfect.'

'Wait, before you go.'

'Yes?'

'Watch out for the speed camera.'

'I will.'

He walked back into the room. 'Boss, I'm off. Thank you for the coffee and the biscuits.'

She looked at him. 'Old habits die hard.'

'Meaning?'

'You're obviously not going to tell me where you're going and why.'

'You're right, I'm not but, don't worry, I'll…'

'Be back.'

'Correct.'

'Eric.'

'Yes?'

'Haven't you forgotten something?'

'What?'

'You haven't got a car.'

'Damn. May I..?'

'Borrow one? Of course. On one condition.'

'Which is?'

'You tell me where you're going.'

'Ha ha.'

'It was worth a try.' Faust took a sip of her coffee, I'm afraid there might only be an old banger available.'

'Sounds like a perfect match. Thank you.'

'You're welcome.'

'Did you find my Saab?'

'Yes, outside Simon's apartment in Le Marais.'

'Of course.'

She looked at him as he headed towards the door, 'Eric.'

'Yes?'

'Take care.'

'I will, boss. You know me.'

'I do, that's why I said it.'

As soon as Eric had left, Faust turned to Daniel, who was still staring at the screen. 'You clown, don't you know who that is?'

Chapter Forty-Five

Anne-Sophie looked at Stonehouse.

'You heard all that?'

'Sort of. Sounds like good news?'

'Yes, you were right.'

'First time for everything. How?'

'Telling me to focus on your old boss.'

'You spoke to Louis?'

'Yes. He wants to tell all, in return for protection.'

'Sounds like another cause for celebration. Shall I open a bottle?'

'Probably not a good idea. I can hardly stand as it is.'

She was sitting on the sofa next to Stonehouse, looking at a text that had just arrived:

'How are things? Hope your week is going well. Would you like to meet up at some point? Or are you an 'undecided', or a 'not yet'? Michael.'

'More good news?'

'No, not this time.' She looked at him and decided once again to do what, prior to this week, she had always considered unthinkable - open up to someone she barely knew.

'OK, on Monday I was supposed to meet a chap called Michael. Thanks to my godfather I got the perfect excuse to bail out. Now I have to decide if I want to make the bailing permanent.'

'Can't help you much there I'm afraid. My experience of dates and the opposite gender has been strictly limited.'

'Right.'

'All I can suggest is the old saying, cruel to be kind. I'm sure most blokes appreciate honesty. Eventually.'

'And I appreciate the insight into male psychology.'

'Hi. My week has been very different so far. 'Not yet' is where I'm at, for the moment. A-S.'

The response came immediately. *'I appreciate your honesty, but I can't deny I'm disappointed. Very, in fact. Let me know when / if your circumstances / position change. M.'*

'Sorted. Fancy a coffee? Tea?'

'A tea sounds remarkably good, thanks. I don't suppose you have Yorkshire?'

'No, should I?'

'Best cuppa in the world!'

Leaving Stonehouse alone to make a pot of non-Yorkshire tea, she took a lukewarm, sobering-up shower. Twenty minutes later, she opened up her laptop.

'I've got something to show you.'

'I'm all eyes.'

A minute later he was looking at the blog she had posted that morning.

'It's rather, err, sparse.'

'Give me a break. I only had a couple of hours this morning. Just enough time to design it, register the domain name and upload it.'

'What might you put on it, when you have more time?'

'You remember in the restaurant you asked me about the exciting discovery I had made?'

'Yes.'

'It concerned Hervé Parcelle.'

'As in France's very probable next President?'

'The very same. He was the Procureur in charge of the so-called investigation into my father's killing. He was here in this apartment within minutes of the deed.'

'Goodness. And you want to put something on the blog about him?'

'Yes.'

'However, you're worried about repercussions.'

'You're definitely a mind reader! Absolutely. Who wouldn't be? Although I have all sorts of suspicions, what I don't have is any proof, apart from one witness statement; a witness whose character and testimony might not stand up to intense scrutiny. Any scrutiny, come to that. I lack proof and a motive. Without them, I don't have anything.'

'And you lack both needle and haystack.'

'Precisely.'

'If you track them down, you'd add detail about Parcelle to 'Justice for Jean-Marie'?'

'Absolutely, as one of my prime suspects, alongside Juliet Roulet, Malherbe and Scarface.'

'Scarface?'

'An intelligence operative known as Jacques. Very unlikely to be his real name.'

'So, do you have anything to go on in respect of locating the needle?'

'Mules told me I should focus on the last week of Father's life, especially his last weekend. If there were any clues to be found, that's where I would find them.'

He leaned forward with his cup of non-Yorkshire tea and looked at her with his piercing blue eyes. 'Let's do that.'

'OK, my big question is why that weekend? Why that Sunday? My father had been under surveillance for nearly three years without anything major happening. What triggered the sudden raid on his apartment?'

'Where are the notebooks? You said you thought the needle could be mentioned in there. There might be other clues.'

She took a slurp of tea and nearly spat it out again.

'I'm definitely bringing Yorkshire next time.'

'My God!'

'What?'

'Before Philippe became unconscious, he said my father had been looking for something for a long time and that, in the last week, he had been close to finding it.'

'Finding what?'

'I've no idea but it has to be the needle.' For about thirty seconds she sat with her hands over her face. 'Of course!'

She ran into her mother's bedroom, opened the safe and started bringing out the boxes of notebooks. Two trips later, she had them laid out on the lounge floor in front of Stonehouse; she picked up the final notebook, 1987.

'This was Father's last entry: *"At last! I have it."*' She looked at Stonehouse. 'It can't mean anything else. He wasn't close to finding the needle, he'd found it!'

'Whatever *it* was.'

'You're right, I need to calm down. I'm not any closer to discovering what the needle actually was.'

'But it's one small step in the right direction. Did Philippe say anything else that might help turn it into a giant leap?'

'Philippe mentioned a P. He said I should ask P. He also said something about the books... the book. Plural, then single. I've no idea what this meant. He also talked about 'the others' but I don't know who he was talking about.'

Seeing Stonehouse's disappointed look, she continued, 'At this point, Philippe was delirious, virtually unconscious. He could have been saying anything.'

'But at least now we've got something to go on.'

'True.'

Taking another gulp of tea, she looked, without focusing, at her father's boxes of books.

Stonehouse looked at her. 'So, we're looking for a book?'

'Yes.'

He spread his hands. 'These are books, what about one of these?'

She looked at him. 'Of course! My father's books. What was I thinking?' She kissed him on the cheek. 'Thank you.'

'You're welcome. Sometimes my doctorate in the bleeding obvious comes in useful.'

'This must be what Philippe meant. The answer has to be somewhere in the books. Not all of them, just one of them, a single book. But which one?' She looked up. Five o'clock. Just two days until the Ritz.

'Time to divide and conquer?'

She picked up 1976, but quickly thought better of it. 'It has to be later. Perhaps the time Father was put under surveillance.'

She grabbed 1984 and gave Stonehouse 1985. Despite having no real idea what she was searching for, she began racing through the contents. Nothing leapt out at them. She tried 1986, whilst Stonehouse looked at 1987. Same story, nothing. She took 1987 from Stonehouse, every instinct told her the needle had to be inside this one. She had never prayed but decided this was as good a time as any to start: *Please God, you owe me one. At least, one. Let me find something. Please.*

On March 25th, she found a clue. She read it to Stonehouse. *'P tells me might be opportunity to get the rb soon. M getting worn down because of Frankfurt and DC. May crack.'*

'Any idea what rb might stand for?'

'None whatsoever. Sorry.'

'Presumably, M equals Malherbe. Why Frankfurt?'

'If I remember correctly, Louis went there the weekend before your father's death to meet Bicchiere and thrash out their joint history of the discovery of the AIDS virus.'

'Ah yes, part of the transatlantic agreement signed in Washington, on March 31st, 1987.'

'That's it.'

'Two days after Father was killed.'

'Correct.'

She placed her right hand over her mouth and thought for a moment. 'Let's go back and see if we can see any references to rb anywhere else.'

Knowing they were looking for something, anything, with those initials, a revitalised Anne-Sophie and Stonehouse worked their way chronologically backwards through the notebooks.

After fifteen minutes he punched the air and shouted, 'Got it!'

She moved closer to him, and Stonehouse read out the all-important section from August 14th, 1983:

'I need to get my hands on M's red book. It won't be easy. It's been his bible for a decade. Personal organizer, record keeper, notebook, diary, experiments' record. Everything rolled into one. He keeps it with him at all times. Never lets it out his sight. Totally paranoid about it. Keeps it in his locked office cabinet and locks his office door too whenever he leaves it, any time of day. Possessing the red book is the key. If only I had the key...'

'It isn't one of Father's books we are looking for, but Malherbe's red book. Have you heard of it?'

'Not really. You might find this hard to believe but I rarely saw Malherbe. I worked in another part of the Sub, which is actually a lot bigger than you probably imagine. I don't remember him carrying a red book but that's not to say he didn't.'

'Whatever was in it, it was obviously important to Father. And he got his hands on it two days before he was murdered. That cannot be a coincidence. There must be a connection. There was

196

something in the red book so big it provoked a killing. I wonder what the hell it was.'

She looked at the clock, five-thirty. She calculated Mules should be arriving in Le Vésinet just about now. Which meant that Malherbe would be walking into her apartment by seven at the latest. Then, she would find out exactly why his red book had been so important to her father and why it had led to his murder. The forty-year conspiracy and cover-up would be unravelled at last.

Suddenly, her entire body was shaking.

Chapter Forty-Six

Mules indeed arrived at Le Vésinet just after five-thirty. He rang the doorbell which was answered by Malherbe's manservant wearing his customary severe expression.

'Follow me.'

Mules did as he was told and followed the manservant into what Eric surmised was the main lounge. From there, they walked through a doorway leading into a much smaller, unlit room.

'The Monsieur is in there.'

As he walked through the doorway, Mules realized he had made a massive mistake. He felt something hard hit his head and his knees buckled. In front of him was someone, presumably Malherbe, bound and gagged. There was a puddle between Malherbe's feet. A noxious smell filled the room.

Two men picked Mules up. They were wearing baseball caps. One guy was white, the other, black.

The black guy laughed. 'We hear you've been looking for us, Mules. For forty years.'

The white guy smacked him hard across the mouth. 'And now, at last, you've found us. You must be delighted.'

A man Mules instantly recognized, a scruffy-looking individual with a scar under his right eye socket, came in. He was carrying a pistol in his right hand and holding the butler's wrists with his left. 'You've been looking for me as well, Mules. It must be your lucky day. Or not.' He also smacked Mules hard across the mouth with the pistol. 'That one's for that stubborn bitch, Montreau.' Then he kneed Mules in the groin. 'And that one's just for you.' Then he turned to his helpers. 'Ready?'

'Yes.'

'Good, let's be on our way. No time for a drink, Mules. Not even a non-alcoholic one. Sorry about that. Perhaps later. Perhaps never.'

Chapter Forty-Seven

At six-thirty, whilst Stonehouse occupied himself by reading through her father's books, Anne-Sophie had called Salpêtrière for an update on Philippe. She was told there was nothing new to report but, yes, she would definitely be seeing him tomorrow. Now, it had just turned seven and she was getting agitated. Mules and Malherbe should have been seated in her lounge by now. Where the hell were they? Perhaps Malherbe had changed his mind, but Mules would surely have contacted her if that was the case.

Her phone rang. The 'Voulez-Vous' ringtone obviously amused Stonehouse.

'Thank God! Eric.'

However, it wasn't Mules. It was a 'No ID' number.

'Hello.'

'Anne-Sophie Montreau?'

'Yes, who is this?'

'Angela Faust, a former colleague of Eric Mules and currently Deputy Prefect of the Préfecture de Police. Did you contact Eric this afternoon, at about four o'clock, please?'

'Yes, I did. What's happened?'

'I've been calling him for an hour. He isn't answering.'

'Oh no.'

'Please can you tell me where he went after you spoke to him? He wouldn't tell me where he was going.'

She read out Malherbe's address.

'Thank you for that. I'll send a car to Le Vésinet now. I'll call you back as soon as I have news.'

Anne-Sophie's shaking hands told her she needed more wine. She asked Stonehouse to open a bottle of '*Dancing Queen*', one of her birthday presents from Béatrice the previous year. It reminded her she should send her friend a text update, but she decided to hang fire until Faust got back to her about Eric and Malherbe.

Stonehouse handed her a full glass. 'Something tells me you're an ABBA fan.'

'No flies on you. Yourself?'

'My tastes lean more to the classical. More Bach than Bjorn, more Beethoven than Benny.'

'Philippe would say that, musically, we're matched opposites.'

'My love of classical is most likely a reflection of my advancing years.'

She looked at him. 'You don't look your age.'

'You're very kind. Two weeks of skiing every February helps; it's excellent for the skin, as well as the muscles, just as long as you don't overdo it on the apres-ski, that can be a very slippery slope.'

'Béatrice has told me that. Many times.'

'Do you ski?'

'Not since my teens. I shattered my right knee and my confidence on a school trip. The only slippery slopes I haven't avoided recently are my dates.'

'We'll have to get you back up on the proper slopes next winter.'

'Let me guess, you have a chalet in Chamonix.'

Just as he replied with a grin and a thumbs up, her apartment buzzer sounded. She looked at the time, seven-forty-five. She prayed this would be Eric.

'Yes?'

'Angela Faust, may I come up?'

'Damn, OK.'

Faust entered with Daniel close behind her and immediately looked at Stonehouse. After gratefully accepting an offer of coffee, she updated Anne-Sophie. 'I sent a car to Le Vésinet.'

'And?'

'My officers found an empty house. There was no sign of Malherbe or Mules. A highest-level alert has been raised.'

'Any sign of a manservant?'

'No.'

Faust looked at Stonehouse again before turning back to Anne-Sophie. 'May I mention two things?'

'Of course.'

'One, please do not post anything about your father's death online.'

Anne-Sophie looked at her closely.

'And I mean *anything*. Two, I think it wise to place an armed guard on your door, immediately.'

'Of course, thank you.'

Faust stood up and looked at Stonehouse for a third time. 'I need to get on with trying to locate Eric and the others. We have to assume they've been captured. If Eric does contact you, please tell him to call me straight away. Unless I hear anything beforehand, you can take it as read that I shall come back here early tomorrow morning.'

Opening the door to let Faust and Daniel out, Anne-Sophie saw two guards already standing outside the apartment.

Faust turned to her. 'Remember, post nothing online about your father's death, especially your suspicions, or your opinions.'

Anne-Sophie returned to the sofa and sat down very close to Stonehouse. 'My God, Stephen. What am I going to do?'

'Tonight, you're going to sit tight.'

'I know one thing I must do.'

'Yes.'

'Post something online.'

'Despite Faust's warnings?'

She stood up. 'I just can't sit here and do nothing. I've lost Hérault, Philippe and Eric in less than twelve hours, and Malherbe too. I'm up against the next President, the Chief Justice and Christ knows who else. This is no game, Stephen.'

'I agree. Go ahead. Not that you need my say-so, of course.'

An hour later, having posted a few teasers about dark forces on the Jean-Marie blog, she calculated that she had done enough to promote her cause, but not enough to provoke a reaction from Faust. She topped up their glasses and looked at Stonehouse. 'So, what now?'

'We could watch that AIDS documentary you seem obsessed with.'

'Ha, ha. I guess my next step, now we think we've identified the needle, is to try and work out where the haystack is.'

'As well as the identity of P.'

'Definitely! Any thoughts on either?'

'I didn't know there was such a thing as a red book until an hour or two ago, I've absolutely no idea where it may be located.'

'What about P?'

'P is not such an unusual initial, not like X for Xander for example. There could be any number of Pauls or Paulines, Peters and Pascals.'

She looked at the clock. Nine-thirty. It would be an early start in the morning. There was nothing else she could do for her team tonight. Time to decide.

'OK. Well, that sounds like another dead end, for now. So, cutting to the chase, how would you like to stay over?'

'I'm getting a bit long in the tooth to sleep on the couch.'

'Who said anything about the couch?'

'Oh.'

'There's just one thing.'

'Which is?'

'As well as Faust, Béatrice may be coming here tomorrow morning.'

'How early?'

'Not sure, about nine.'

'OK, well, probably a good idea for me not to hang around early doors in that case.'

'Agreed.'

'And probably not a good idea to tell Béatrice I stayed over full stop. I told you she can be a bit gossipy at work.'

'OK, I won't breathe a word, if you won't.'

He started typing a text, a good luck message he said for his sons who had exams in the morning. After a minute it was good to go. All he had to do was press send but, partly thanks to the wine, and partly as a result of Anne-Sophie's attentions, he forgot all about it. Smiling, she took his hand and led him out of the lounge.

The *'Call me as soon as you get this'* text sent to her phone just after she turned off the bedroom light went unseen.

Chapter Forty-Eight

Hérault had no idea what time it was. The only break in the monotony occurred when he was led to the toilet and told to squat and release. Philippe had not said anything in hours. Hérault wondered if he was still alive. He was startled by the sudden opening of the door and what sounded like more than one person being thrown into the room.

'Get in there, arseholes.'

Hérault heard one of the newest inhabitants saying something through his gag. What was it? After a minute's intense focus, he worked it out.

'Céline…Céline… Céline.'

Chapter Forty-Nine

I hear you are having problems with the Montreau girl.
This situation must be resolved before I arrive.
T.M.

Day Four - Thursday, April 1st, 2027

Chapter Fifty

Anne-Sophie's JAZ alarm clock went off at six o'clock. She reached for Stonehouse, but he was already out of bed. She walked naked into the lounge and found him reading one of her father's notebooks.

'Did you text your boys?'

'Fiddlesticks, I forgot.'

She took '1981' out of his hands. 'See anything interesting?'

'Mmm, one or two bits and pieces.'

She grabbed his hands and pulled him back into her bedroom. 'We've got an hour, let's make the most of it.'

By eight o'clock, after tortuous showers and an unproductive phone call to Salpêtrière, they were munching toast and swigging down coffee. Anne-Sophie had already received a text.

'Hi. Hope you had an informative time with Stephen. Due into Gare du Nord at eight-thirty. Should be with you by nine-thirty. Can't wait to catch up! B x'

'Can't wait either! I'm still wondering what the 'something' or 'somebody' you mentioned on Tuesday night are... Sys, A-S xx'

By eight-thirty Stonehouse was ready to depart.

She held his hands in hers, 'Will I see you later?'

'Let's see. Probably not.'

'Oh.'

'Sorry. I've a fair bit to catch up on after taking yesterday's... err...activities. Besides, you'll have Béatrice to keep you company, and Faust.'

'That's true; if Faust comes that is. OK, well, I'll let you know if there are any developments.' She kissed him on the cheek. 'Thank you for a lovely belated birthday meal and the ..err..afters.'

'The pleasure was all mine.'

'Hardly. By the way, Béatrice said she wanted to speak to me about something, or somebody. Any idea what or who she had in mind?'

'Not a clue, sorry. I'd better go. Bye'.

'Bye.'

She had barely finished tidying up an hour later when the door buzzed. 'Hello?'

'It's me!'

'Hi! Come up.'

Anne-Sophie opened her apartment door to warn her protectors she had a visitor, a trusted visitor. Béatrice said a cheery ''Hello!'' to the guards, walked in and hugged her friend. They sat down at a kitchen table laden with fresh coffee and croissants. Béatrice picked one up and smiled, 'You'll turn into one of these before too long.'

'Probably. So, tell me about Lille.'

'You're joking! I want to hear everything about Philippe and Parcelle but,' she swigged some coffee, 'before even that, I want to know all about your meeting with my boss.'

Anne-Sophie hesitated.

'What is it? What happened?'

'Nothing.'

'Come off it. You've gone red. What is it?'

'I told you, nothing.'

'My God!'

'What?'

'You slept with him.'

'Béatrice…'

'You're a fast worker, I'll give you that.'

'Let me explain.'

Béatrice's phone buzzed. 'Damn.'

'What?'

'Speak of the devil, I have to go; Stonehouse wants me in, something urgent needs sorting.'

'You're shaking, what's wrong?'

'Nothing. I'd better go. I'll be in touch.'

Anne-Sophie decided to go after her friend. She swept past the two guards and bounded down the stairs to the entrance lobby to catch her up. Simultaneous to Anne-Sophie shouting 'Wait!', two men wearing black balaclavas burst in and barged Béatrice head-first into a wall. Picking up Anne-Sophie before she, or the two guards, could react, they pulled her down the stairs and bundled her out of the block. Throwing her into the back of a white van, they screamed, 'Move!' at the driver. A second later, Anne-Sophie had something placed over her head and wrists. In the blink of an eye, she found herself bound, gagged and terrified.

She had no idea how long the journey took but by the time the van stopped, it was obvious this was no April Fool's joke gone horribly wrong, and she was desperate for the toilet. Still bound and gagged, she was removed from the van and taken into what she guessed was a building of some sort. She made a noise, and the gag was removed.

'What?'

'I need the toilet, please.'

Whoever was minding her, laughed, 'Where do you think you are? The Ritz?'

However, after the gag was reapplied and her wrists bound together, she was manhandled to who-knew-where and her jeans and pants were taken down.

'Squat and release.'

The noise of liquid on metal was chilling but at least she had one less thing to worry about. She was led somewhere and told to sit. Badly shaken, she did as she was told. She heard the door open and close. That was the last sound she heard for what seemed like a very long time. Eventually, the door opened, and her wrists were untied.

'I've come to ask you a question. I'd love to know your opinion about a little problem I have.'

She started at the voice; she'd heard it before. When? Where?

'We have your allies here: Simon is virtually dead; Mules is OK, for now. The traitors Hérault and Malherbe are still alive, just. The question my team and I have been mulling over is, in what order do we kill them? After some discussion, I said to the others, who else to ask but their leader? She can tell us which of her pawns she wants to sacrifice first. So here I am, asking the question, who first?'

She did not respond.

'Raise your hand if you think the honour should be given to Simon. After all, he's old, very sick, in a lot of pain and, let's face it, once we stop giving him his medication, he's going to die in short order. Let him have an injection, it will very quickly put him out of his misery. You'll be doing him a favour, like putting down a sick dog, or a knackered old hack.'

She did not move.

'OK. Have it your way. Perhaps Mules is your preference? After all, if he makes it out of here, he'll only reward you by falling straight back off the wagon and most likely drink himself to death by the summer. Why waste time? Céline wouldn't thank you for it. Put your hand up for Eric.'

Again, she did not respond.

'What about Malherbe? Your father's number one enemy. Surely, he should be the first to go. He and his manservant. It's a bargain, two for the price of one.'

Still, she kept quiet.

'Ah, of course, you'd prefer Hérault, wouldn't you? Karma for him betraying your parents. At long last, some justice for Jean-Marie, as you might say, ha ha.'

She started making a noise. The speaker removed her gag. She could barely croak. 'Me. First.'

'Speak up.'

'Kill me, first.'

'Normally, I'd agree with you. Ladies first is one of my mantras and I'm all for sexual equality, but what would be the fun in that? I like to play with my food. You'll be last, don't worry. Tell you what, why don't we go for the old short-straw method? Here we are. Oh, silly me, of course, you can't see my hand. You'll just have to trust me when I say I'm holding four matchsticks. In case you're wondering, Malherbe and his manservant count as one matchstick. Reach out and take one.'

Anne-Sophie tentatively reached out her right hand.

'Well done! That's it, good girl. A bit further.'

She did as she was told, felt for the hand and dug her long nails hard into the guy's palm. Then dug them in harder. Then dug them in as hard as she could. She was rewarded with and delighted by a scream. The smack she received across the mouth gave her almost as much satisfaction. She really must have made an impression on the palm.

'How's that for karma, you animal?'

'Bitch! Gag her. Tie her up. Now! Get me a bandage, antiseptic and painkillers. Move it!' He took some deep breaths.

209

'Never two without three they say. You're lucky I don't finish you off now.'

She could hear more heavy breathing, punctuated with the odd gasp of pain. Then she heard gulping. 'Thanks. Now, go and finish off her precious godfather.'

She struggled to free herself.

'Relax. It can hardly be classed as an execution. Think of it as more of a mercy killing.'

Five minutes later she heard a door opening and footsteps.

'Done?'

'Yes, chief.'

'Good, one down, four to go. Who's next? Malherbe and the manservant? Yes, why not. Kill them both.'

There was another five-minute interval between the door opening and closing.

'Next, Hérault or Mules? Any preference, Ms Montreau?'

She did not move.

'I'll decide for you, shall I? I'm guessing you prefer Mules to Hérault, so, let's get rid of the alcoholic retired Detective Inspector first.'

She heard the footsteps of the departing assistant. She started to wretch and struggle violently. She was ungagged.

'You monster. How can you do this? Why are you doing this?'

'Patriotic duty.'

'My God! Jacques? It's you, isn't it?'

She was quickly re-gagged.

'Only Hérault left now before you get your turn. One last injection, no point prolonging his or your agony. After all he's only a rat on two legs. Do it!'

There was another five-minute gap before the door reopened and her gag removed.

'One last chance. I have an offer for you. It would be a bad move if you were stupid enough to refuse it. Fatal, in fact. The book, tell me where it is, and you live.'

Once again Anne-Sophie stayed silent.

'Oh dear, an offer you apparently *are* stupid enough to refuse. Shame. OK, I'll be back shortly, with the needle. You, I want to do myself. Say your final prayers. Put the gag back on.'

210

Once she heard the door close, she shouted, 'Damn!' into her gag. There was literally nothing she could do. Her team, Malherbe, his manservant, all dead because of her. She should have said ''No'' to Philippe at Chez Papa, told the silly old man to go back to Le Marais and leave her alone.

She thought about her parents. She had been unable to get justice for her father. She hoped fervently she would be reunited with him and her mother in the afterlife. Tears formed at the thought. Tears of joy.

As the minutes ticked away, she started thinking about Béatrice. How was she? The last she had seen of her friend was her lying sprawled on the hallway floor, unconscious. Was Béatrice going to be killed too? Perhaps she was already dead, and their last conversation had ended with Béatrice being angry and upset with her. She felt a pang the likes of which she had never experienced before.

She heard footsteps. This was it. Game over. The end. She was picked up, slung over a shoulder and carried out of the room. Then she was taken into the fresh air and thrown into a vehicle.

'It's your lucky day.'

After what felt like half an hour, she was taken, still bound and gagged, out of the vehicle. She heard it drive away. It was cold and it was pouring with rain. She was wearing a thin blouse, and her phone was back in her apartment. She was alive, but for how long?

Chapter Fifty-One

'Thank you so much.'

A blanket had taken the edge off her shivering. She discovered she had been deposited on the D190 very close to Saint-Germain Golf Club. A member trying to track down a wayward tee shot spotted her slumped against a tree and called emergency services. A police car arrived less than ten minutes later. The officer informed Anne-Sophie that most of the Paris gendarmerie had been searching for her for five hours.

'What time is it?'

'Two-thirty.'

'Hell.'

Anne-Sophie touched her cross and thought for a moment. 'Do you know Faust? I must speak to her.'

'With all due respect I don't think Deputy Prefect Faust will be interested in your kidnap and release.'

'But..'

'Believe me, she has much bigger fish to fry.'

'Please don't make the mistake of ignoring me; I'm not delusional. Faust came to my apartment last night, possibly this morning as well.'

'I'm sorry, my only instruction is to take you to Salpêtrière as quickly as possible. What happens to you after that is someone else's problem, not mine.'

With the help of a blue light and siren, it took forty-five minutes to reach the hospital, during which time Anne-Sophie tried and failed to comprehend what had just occurred. It wasn't just the murders which shook her but their clinical nature. Poor Philippe had been deadly accurate; she was facing the darkest of dark forces.

Entering Salpêtrière, the officer led her to the reception waiting room then left immediately. She really had meant it when she said Anne-Sophie was not her problem. Anne-Sophie was wondering what the hell she was going to do next when Faust walked into the waiting room. After a brief conversation, Faust left her in the waiting area and went to talk to someone in charge. Returning five minutes later, she told Anne-Sophie she was going to be taken to a private room to be checked out.

'There's no need, I'm fine, honestly.'

Faust glanced at her bruised mouth. 'Physically? I'm not so sure. Mentally, absolutely not. Probably best if we let the experts decide, yes?'

'You need to know.'

'What?'

'Mules.'

'Yes.'

'I think Eric, Philippe Simon, Henri Hérault, Louis Malherbe, and his manservant, were all murdered within the space of thirty minutes.'

'Damn it.'

'By lethal injection.'

'My God.'

'Organized by an intelligence operative calling himself Jacques.'

'OK. How did you get out?'

'I was carried out.'

'What?'

'They let me go.'

'Why?'

'No idea.'

'I see.'

Anne-Sophie held out her right hand. 'What I can tell you is that whoever Jacques is, he now has a very sore, bandaged palm, courtesy of these nails.'

She was taken by Faust to a private room with officers standing by the door. The Deputy Prefect left, promising to return shortly, but the officers stayed. After thirty minutes, which Anne-Sophie spent trying to process all that had happened since her JAZ alarm clock had sounded that morning, a doctor finally arrived. She was checked out and once nothing untoward had been discovered, and she had turned down an offer of counselling, she asked if she could leave. One of her guards made a call. Within five minutes, Faust was back in at Anne-Sophie's side.

'You have a choice.'

'Go on.'

'Either get placed into a safe house with twenty-four-seven protection or go back to your apartment and still have twenty-four-seven protection.'

'That's easy, I must go back to my apartment.'

'Will you continue your search?'

'For the truth? Of course! I can't back down. Now I have even more incentive.'

'Unwise, but it's your call.'

'It is. There's one more thing before we go.'

'Yes.'

'My friend, Béatrice Lapain, is she here?'

'I rang for the ambulance myself.'

'She's alive?'

'Yes.'

'Please can I see her?'

Fifteen minutes later, Anne-Sophie was being escorted down several long corridors to the intensive care unit. She thought with a shudder that this must have been the same part of the hospital where a dying Princess Diana was brought thirty years ago. She explained who she was to a wary medic who said she would find out what, if anything, she could tell her about Béatrice's condition. Anne-Sophie looked around and noticed a man sitting with crossed legs, reading *'Le Parisien'*. She did a double take.

'Stephen! Thank God.'

Stonehouse dropped his paper, stood up and hugged her. 'It's bloody marvellous to see you.'

'You too.'

'How are you?'

'I'll live. Unlike my friends. And… Malherbe.' She told him what she suspected had happened during the six hours between her capture and discovery.

'Where do you think you were taken?'

'I thought it was somewhere within thirty minutes of Saint-Germain Golf Club. However, Faust said I may have been driven around in circles, or back and forth, to confuse me.'

'An old Indian trick.'

'Sorry?'

214

'Never mind, it's an old British saying. Very un-PC. What else did Faust say to you?'

'Not much. What about Béatrice? How is she?'

'Sedated, but don't worry, merely precautionary. No permanent damage but they tell me she took quite a nasty blow to the head.'

'They're right.'

'You saw it?'

'Yes.'

'So, what now?'

'I'm going back to my apartment.'

'OK.'

She looked at him and held his hand. 'Will you come with me? Please.'

He kissed her hand and smiled. 'Try keeping me away.'

'Wonderful. Let's go.'

Faust was waiting for them at reception where, once again, she looked at Stonehouse longer than Anne-Sophie felt was necessary. On the way back to Saint-Victor, the Deputy Prefect told Anne-Sophie it might be a good idea if she kept her head down for a bit and let Faust work on finding out information and producing solutions. Anne-Sophie nodded and smiled. Assuming she was either too shocked or too tired to argue, Faust explained there would be a rotation of officers outside the apartment block and her door and asked Anne-Sophie if she would like an officer inside the apartment too, but she declined.

'That's the last thing I want.' She looked at Stonehouse. 'Or need.'

He squeezed her hand, which prompted yet another look from Faust.

Back at Rue Rollin, Faust sat down beside Anne-Sophie in the lounge.

'When I saw Eric yesterday morning, he asked me to look into three things.'

'Oh, yes?'

'First, he wanted to know the names of the two thugs who murdered your father.'

'And?'

'We are no further forward with that.'

215

'Great. What about the other two things?'

'He wanted me to double-check that your mother's death was one hundred per cent an accident.'

'And?'

'There's no evidence to suggest that a proper investigation was not carried out.'

'Which is not the same as saying it was not deliberate.'

'It's not, but it's the best I can do, for now.'

'The third thing?'

'He asked me to locate your father's missing case file, the police dossier.'

'Let me guess, no joy with that either.'

'No.'

'So, at the moment, your methods are getting me precisely nowhere. Thanks for nothing.'

'Under the circumstances, I'll ignore that comment.'

'You might be confident you can find information and solutions before Jacques and his killers find me, but I'm not.'

Faust stood up and beckoned Anne-Sophie to come with her to the door. 'I have to get back to my office. By office, I mean my bunker in the basement of the Palais de Justice.'

'Do you regularly see Parcelle?'

'Yes, why?'

'If you see him later, please send him my regards. Tell him I hope he sleeps well tonight.'

Faust looked at her sharply, a look which Anne-Sophie returned with interest.

'I'll be in touch. Please don't do anything reckless. Something, anything, which will jeopardize, or slow down my inquiry.'

'I won't. Promise.'

'You can believe me or not, but we are on the same side.'

'I know.'

'One last thing.'

'Yes?'

'Why didn't you call me last night?'

Chapter Fifty-Two

'Four dominoes down, one still standing.'

'Meaning?'

'Mules, Simon, Hérault, Malherbe, and his butler. All despatched.'

'And the girl?'

'Reprieved.'

'Because?'

'Of a last-minute intervention.'

'From?'

'Our mutual friend.'

'Why?'

'He said it wasn't open for discussion.'

'Really. OK, keep in touch.'

'I will.'

Chapter Fifty-Three

'Tell me where it is, and you live.'

That was the offer Jacques had made to her. An offer which he no doubt would have withdrawn the moment she told him anything. Of course, although she thought she knew *what* it was, she had no idea *where* it was, so she could not have made a deal even if she had wanted to.

Whilst Stonehouse contemplated her father's notebooks once again, she brewed a fresh pot of coffee, and pondered her haystack problem. Ten minutes later, when she sat down and snuggled into him, she was no further forward. A small crumb of comfort was that her father's murderers had not located the red book in 1987 and they had not managed to locate it in the intervening forty years. On the other hand, she only had just over twenty-four hours, not forty years, to find the needle, the haystack, a motive, the mastermind *and* present all of the evidence to Faust before the Ritz party started. No pressure! She *had* to find the red book. Unfortunately, it was still, as far as she was concerned, a million miles away.

Stonehouse took her hand and looked at her. He had a thoughtful expression on his face. 'Think logically. Where would your father hide something important? There can't have been too many places. If he obtained the red book on the Friday evening and he was, I'm sorry to remind you, killed on the Sunday evening, then he only had the book in his possession for a maximum of forty-eight hours. You know from Hérault, rest in peace, that Jean-Marie was out of the apartment for most of Saturday. He went into L'Académie in the morning and then visited Malherbe, also RIP, in the afternoon. You've told me that, according to Hérault, your father left the apartment on the Sunday morning to go back to L'Académie and returned by midday. So, whatever he did with the red book, he did it sometime between Friday evening and Sunday lunchtime. Another thing to consider is Malherbe's reaction when he discovered the red book was missing, which he must have done when he made his regular as clockwork Saturday morning trip into work. Unless, for some strange reason, he was in cahoots with your father, one can only guess he was absolutely fuming. Was that why Jean-Marie had to go to Le Vésinet on Saturday afternoon? To be hauled over the coals by Malherbe and be grilled about his precious red book which had gone AWOL?'

'Sounds very plausible.'

'If that was the case, it further narrows down your father's already narrow window of opportunity. Jean-Marie knew Malherbe would have turned L'Académie upside down to find the book. So, whatever he did with it, he must have done it on the Friday night or Saturday morning; early Saturday morning.'

'Right.'

'Any ideas?'

'Not really.'

He gripped her hands and his blue eyes locked on hers. 'Think, Anne-Sophie, think.'

'Hérault never mentioned Father going anywhere on the Friday night. However, he also said he had been tied up that night because of newcomers moving their stuff in. There's every chance Father slipped out unnoticed at some point. The haystack had to be somewhere Father knew well; somewhere he wouldn't have to hunt around too long for the right location, and it had to be somewhere within half an hour's walking distance of the apartment. Where the hell would that be?'

He stood up. 'My nickname in the lab is Professor Logical.'

She looked at him expectantly.

'Have you got a map of the city handy? I have a feeling visualisation will help us crack the mystery of the haystack.'

She rummaged around in a pine chest of drawers and after a minute dug out a 1977 map of Paris.

'Here we go.' She opened up the map and laid it out on the lounge table. As soon as she started studying it, the answer came to her. She put her right palm against her forehead. 'Of course! Where else would he take something important, but somewhere important to him.'

He gripped her hands even tighter than he had before. His blue eyes were now ablaze. 'Tell me.'

'The Luxembourg Garden! It's so obvious. Mother and Philippe both said the Luxembourg Garden was father's favourite place in the entirety of Paris. Hérault said the same thing. It was the one place where Father felt truly at ease; where he went when he had something to celebrate. It's only twenty minutes' walk from the apartment. On the Sunday afternoon, my parents went to the Garden. Perhaps it was only then that Father hid the book. It ticks all the boxes! I'm literally kicking myself for not thinking of it sooner.'

'Well, don't kick yourself too hard, we still have a lot of work to do, possibly miles to cover. The Garden is a big place, sixty acres. We have to somehow narrow it down to an area we can search quickly, bearing in mind we will have the added distraction of armed guards looking over our shoulders and breathing down our necks.'

She hugged him and smiled, then sipped her coffee. Despite the intense grief and shock she felt at the loss of her team, and the damage done to Béatrice, she knew that all her emotions had to be placed on the back burner until this entire business had been resolved once and for all.

She sat down beside Stonehouse again. 'Mother said to me many times that Father loved to sit beside a statue in the Garden.'

Stonehouse started getting up from the sofa. 'OK, let's move.'

'Unfortunately, my mother also told me there are exactly one-hundred-and-six of them. There's no chance we can look at every single one in the limited time we have.'

He slumped back down. 'Sugar lumps.'

She sat with the back of her right hand once more hovering over her mouth. 'Let's look through Father's notebooks, see if there are any mentions of a statue.'

'Good idea. You take 1980 to 1984, I'll take the rest.'

'But first, there's something I need.'

'Yes?'

'A kiss. Just a little one. To keep me going.'

'Oh, go on then. Twist my bendy arm.'

After that interlude and after another ten minutes of searching for any reference to a statue, Stonehouse spoke first. 'Any luck?'

'I may have something. Give me a minute.'

Several times the letters SOL had appeared in the notebooks in connection with visits to the Garden, but she did not have a clue what the letters stood for. She brought up a map of the Garden on her computer. Beginning at the end of the Garden closest to Saint-Victor, she started scanning for anything that resembled SOL. Nothing. Slowly making her way westward she had no joy and was on the verge of giving up when she saw it and screamed, 'That's it! Yes! Look. Again, it's so blindingly obvious. It all fits, even the New York connection.'

Stonehouse looked at the screen, put his arm around her, and grinned. 'Everything's obvious, with the benefit of hindsight.'

She went immediately to talk to the guard outside her bedroom door to ask permission to leave the apartment and the block. At first, the guard replied with an emphatic, non-negotiable, 'Non.' However, Anne-Sophie's incessant, insistent badgering wore her down. The guard contacted Faust who, upon receiving the call and a brief explanation of the context, immediately asked to speak to Anne-Sophie.

'You want to go for a drive and a walk?! Have you got a death wish?'

'It's not just a random walk. I need to find something.'

'What?'

'The thing that can provide you with the proof my father was murdered and blow up the conspiracy behind it.'

Five minutes later, a worn-down Faust admitted defeat. She granted permission for Anne-Sophie to leave the apartment, on strict condition that she and Stonehouse were to be driven to and from the Garden by the guards, who would also accompany them on their search.

Convinced she had discovered the haystack she shouted to the guards, 'Come one, we're off!'

It took only two minutes to drive to the Rue Guynemer and park up. Five minutes later she was gazing in utter dismay at the Statue of Liberty. It was on a plinth surrounded by a square hedge. If her father *had* hidden the red book in its vicinity, then it would be an impossible task to find it without drawing attention from the half-a-dozen citizens who were standing in front of the statue, huddled together under their umbrellas; citizens who undoubtedly would not hesitate to ask her guards what they thought they were playing at, allowing someone to root around one of the world's most recognizable symbols. The rain had never felt heavier than it did at this moment.

Stonehouse saw her dismay and hugged her. 'What do you want to do?'

Anne-Sophie could not think of another location that ticked the same number of boxes as the statue. If the red book wasn't here, it wasn't in the Garden. If it wasn't in the Garden, it could be anywhere. Or nowhere.

'This is hopeless. Get them to take us home, please.'

In the car, she wrapped Stonehouse's arms around her and closed her eyes.

Back in her apartment, Anne-Sophie looked at the clock, six o'clock. Twenty-five hours until the Ritz opened its doors. 'That's it, I'm done. They've won.'

'You can't give up yet. There's still plenty of time.'

'I've been thinking.'

'Go on.'

'You know what's even more depressing than not finding the book?'

'No, tell me.'

'That my father did not hide the book at all.'

'What?'

'He destroyed it.'

Chapter Fifty-Four

'OK, Parcelle, apart from my father's, let's see what other skeletons you've got in your cupboard.'

Having made up her mind that sitting around doing nothing was an unacceptable option, she decided to do something that would definitely get her sacked, arrested and imprisoned. At seven o'clock, twenty-four hours before the Ritz party was due to begin, Anne-Sophie crossed the Rubicon and hacked into the phone of France's Minister of Justice. As a gentle preamble, she set his alarm to go off every thirty minutes beginning at midnight.

'Sleep well, Parcelle.'

Next, she accessed his texts and emails. It did not take long to discover France's red-hot favourite to be the next president was engaged in a very unpresidential exchange of texts with a woman he called his 'femme sexy.'

'Oh my God. Read these.'

A little more digging revealed the 'femme sexy' to be none other than Marie de Confort, a thirty-five-year-old political reporter for *24 France*.

'It's the woman who asked him the final questions at the press conference. No wonder he said, *"My pleasure"*. Look at these!'

If the dozens of photos De Confort had sent Parcelle in the previous six months were an eye-opener, even more revealing was the video footage of the two of them naked in bed together.

'And this!'

'Goodness. He has been busy. And surprisingly inventive, especially with La Hulotte chocolate mousse. Never mind President-elect, perhaps he should be rebranded the President-erect.'

'What do you think I should do with them?'

'I'm afraid I have no idea.'

'I have, a really good one.'

She put her phone on speaker and punched in a number. 'Paul? Anne-Sophie Montreau.'

'Yes?'

'I have some extremely interesting texts, photos and videos concerning a certain politician which I'm sure you and your readers would find them riveting.'

'Extremely interesting texts, photos and videos obtained how and where?'

'Does that matter?'

'Unfortunately, yes, the 'how's' and 'where's' do matter, very much. I'm guessing the politician didn't just hand his phone over and tell you to do what you will with them?'

'No.'

'In that case, at this exact moment, I'm going to have to decline. As I explained to you yesterday, my paper cannot afford to take any risks this close to the election. The last thing I want is to have a court order, or some kind of injunction, slapped on my editor's desk. Notwithstanding the fact I'd be sacked.'

'Would other papers, media outlets, *24 France* for example, say the same?'

'You'd have to ask them, but I rather think they might. It's all about timing, Anne-Sophie. You need to strike at precisely the right moment. I'm sorry, I have another call I need to take. Bye.'

She looked at Stonehouse, feeling, if possible, even more crestfallen than she had in the Garden. 'For goodness sake, I feel like a Pigalle sex worker who can't give it away.'

'There's always your Jean-Marie blog.'

'What do you mean?'

'Put something on there. Not necessarily whole photos, full texts or videos. Definitely no names, no pack drill.'

'What?'

'Another Briticism, sorry. Post some kind of teaser and one or two clever people might even start connecting the dots.'

Anne-Sophie used all her photoshopping wizardry to produce headless photos and, half an hour later, with Stonehouse's help concerning some of the wording, the teaser was complete and posted. Posted not only on the blog, but on the other Presidential candidates' social media sites, and every media outlet on the planet. All from an untraceable IP address.

What next? She stroked her cross, 'Of course! If it was OK to do it to Hérault, it's definitely OK to do it to Parcelle.'

'OK to do what?'

Very quickly, Anne-Sophie was soon having a good look at Parcelle's bank accounts. It didn't take her long to hit her second jackpot.

'Well, well. I'm not sure his base would be quite so happy with Hervé if they got wind of this.'

'What have you found?'

'A two months old, presumably very secret, offshore bank account, containing twenty-five million Euros.'

'That's a hell of a lot of chocolate mousse.'

'Isn't it.'

'How offshore?'

'The Cook Islands. So offshore, I've no idea where it is.'

'Somewhere in the Pacific, between Australia and the United States.'

'That's a giant haystack.'

'Martin Ruane.'

'Who?'

'AKA Giant Haystacks.'

'What are you talking about?'

'Back in my day, he was the most famous wrestler in Britain.'

'I'll take your word for it.'

'I'm presuming Parcelle hasn't won the lottery so where did his Euro millions come from?'

'I'm trying to trace its origins, ah, here we go. An account in the name of Mornec Bros. Surprise, surprise, also offshore. The Caymans this time. Let me see who the Mornecs are. My goodness.'

'What?'

'Listen to this. The Mornec Brothers gang, also called "the M" or "the Montreuil gang", is a Gitanes criminal group from the region of Paris. It is the most influential gang in the French capital. They control many criminal activities, such as prostitution, drug dealing and illegal slot machines in Paris. They also have good connections with the Corsican mafia and the Maghrebian gangs. They made their money from hold-ups in night-clubs, illegal slot machines and prostitution bars. The Mornec brothers have invested heavily in building speculation in Paris and - get this - they also own a luxury villa on the French Riviera. Hey, you could be neighbours!'

'I thought I was the droll one.'

'Talk about ill-gotten gains. Parcelle was given twenty-five million Euros by the meanest gang in Paris at the start of the election campaign. This is pure dynamite.'

'Who'd have thought it, a French politician up to his eyeballs in merde.'

'I know! It should be the end for him, but you know what, I won't even bother telling Paul LeBlanc about it because, frankly, there's absolutely no point. He'll only wring his hands and mutter something about bad timing. However, I'll tell you something for nothing, this is bad timing for Parcelle.'

'What are you going to do?'

'Long-term? I'm not sure. Immediate term, I'm going to relieve Parcelle of his fortune.'

'As Tommy Cooper used to say, just like that.'

'I won't ask who Tommy Cooper is but, yes, just like that.'

Wide-eyed, Stonehouse watched Anne-Sophie quickly and calmly relieve the Minister of Justice of his Euro millions, then freeze him out of his own offshore account.

'Where's it all gone?'

'Never you mind.' She beamed, 'Parcelle's millions are history, and hopefully so is his campaign. Who's next?'

She looked again at the list of guests due to attend the party at the Ritz and decided to trigger the alarms on all their phones as well, including Antony Consolotto's. Then she switched her attention to the French and international intelligence agencies that she felt were involved in the conspiracy to kill her father. She was going to turn them into the institutional and technological equivalent of bound and gagged terrified citizens awaiting lethal injection. Into those organizations' systems, she introduced worms. These were a much superior attack mechanism to viruses because, as she told a mystified Stonehouse,

'Worms do not need a host system or user action to spread.'

'Sorry, it's all Dutch to me. Double Dutch at that.'

She explained to him that not only would the worms begin munching their way through apps and folders in the hosts' main systems, but they would also spread to phones or devices linked to these systems by Bluetooth.

'Sounds like, bottom line, they can do a lot of damage.'

'They can. A lot of damage, very quickly.'

After another hour's intense activity, she again pressed send.

'Right, you lot, let's see how you like it.'

On a roll, and feeling that might was most definitely right, Anne-Sophie uploaded thousands of secret service documents to a different flash drive; documents which, if released, would signal the death knell of the entire global intelligence network.

Yes, this was about justice for her father, but it was also about taking revenge. Revenge for her father, for Hérault, Eric, Malherbe and, most of all, Philippe. Revenge for herself and her mother, for the lives they could have had but which were taken away from them the moment her father was killed. Revenge for the assault on Béatrice. Revenge was as good a motive as any. Never mind all that turning the other cheek rubbish. In the right circumstances, an eye for an eye was very effective and very satisfying.

She briefly considered infecting the medical and science institutions that many of the Ritz guests worked for or led but decided that the potential harm she might cause to patients was a line she would not cross. For now.

She turned to an open-mouthed Stonehouse. 'I feel so much better than I did an hour ago.'

Her jeans vibrated to 'Voulez-Vous.'

'Angela.'

'What did I tell you?'

'Sorry?'

'I said, don't do anything reckless. My team tells me someone from Saint-Victor is hacking into some very important individuals' devices, as well as institutional accounts, including those belonging to intelligence agencies.'

'And?'

'Don't insult *my* intelligence by denying you're responsible. I know what you do. I know what you're trying to do. Either call a halt or I get my guards to arrest you and your accessory.'

'Accessory?'

'Stonehouse.'

'I'll call a halt when you start making some arrests of the people who killed my parents, and my friends.'

'Anne-Sophie, listen to me. I know you feel you're in the right. Perhaps, morally, you are. However, you're not helping yourself. Two wrongs don't make a right. Plus, you're making my job so much harder. I'm telling you, stop the attacks.'

'And I'm telling you, Angela, make some arrests.'

'Listen to me.'

'No, you listen to me. I'm more than happy for you to arrest me; for your guards to take me in. I want the world to hear my story, my family's story, Eric's story. Journalists like LeBlanc may not be interested but I'm sure the rest of the world is.'

'You won't call off the attacks?'

'No.'

'On your head be it.'

The line went dead. She smiled at him.

'I have to say you don't look fazed by that phone call.'

'Au contraire, this is the most fun I've had in a long time. Apart from last night of course.' She looked up, eight o'clock. Her smile disappeared. 'However, all this fun isn't helping us discover the location of the haystack. It's time to get my brain moving up a gear.'

He looked at her quizzically.

She made up a pot of fresh coffee, the fuel she required to make her final push of another extraordinary, shocking day.

Chapter Fifty-Five

'The books...the book...ask P.'

After exhausting all logic chains, and nearly herself, the final avenue left for Anne-Sophie to explore was Philippe's very last words. She looked at Stonehouse, 'It's simple; to find the book we have to ask P. Therefore, we must work out who P is.'

'And where he, or she, is.'

'That as well.'

'Putting my Professor Logical hat back on and narrowing it down, P was someone who knew your father and, I'm betting, worked with him. How else would P have known about Malherbe's red book? Let's go back to the books and see if we can find a few P's.'

After half an hour, one first name, Patrice, had cropped up several times after 1982 but never with a surname attached. Anne-Sophie turned to the internet. There were five Patrices listed as having worked for L'Académie in the 1980s. It took fifteen minutes to track down their numbers and another ten minutes and five phone calls for her to shout, 'Bingo!'

She grinned at Stonehouse who had missed the vital telephone conversation due to an urgent call of nature. 'Sorry, it's my age, and the coffee.'

'Do you remember a Patrice Morison?'

'Doesn't ring any bells, sorry.'

'I'm going to visit him.'

'What? Now?'

'Of course. No time to lose.'

'Where is he?'

'The social and economic polar opposite of Saint-Cloud and Le Vésinet.'

'There are plenty of those in Paris. Which one in particular?'

'Pointoise.'

'You'll be thankful for a guard if you're going there.'

'Will you come with me?'

'It's very tempting but I think I'll pass on a night out in Pointoise, thank you.'

She looked at the time. 'An hour each way means I probably won't be back until at least eleven. Feel free to go to bed.'

'I'll be very happy reading your father's books, as long as you don't mind.'

'Not at all. You never know, you might find the haystack. If you do, text me!'

'Of course.'

'Great stuff. OK, the sooner I go, the sooner I get back.' She kissed him on the lips. 'Bye for now. Be good.'

After receiving the go-ahead from a fuming Faust, who insisted Anne-Sophie could not go out without at least one of her guards, she left the apartment and headed up onto the A15. She reached Pointoise at nine-thirty. Finding the block where Patrice was living took fifteen minutes more, and his basement flat another two. She rang the buzzer.

'Patrice? Hello! Lovely to meet you.'

He looked at her, then at the guard. 'Anne-Sophie, I presume. Likewise. Come in.'

'Thank you.'

Unshaven and unkempt, dressed in a track suit, Patrice did not look like a man who took care of himself or his tiny, one-bedroom apartment. Piled-up, soggy cardboard boxes filled most of the floor space. The flat was cold, and she was not shocked to notice damp and pockets of mould covering most of the walls and skirting boards.

'I'm sorry to impose myself on you without giving you much of a warning. Is there a place close by I can treat you to a bite to eat?'

'There is. But there's no need.'

'Come on, show me. It's the least I can do after interrupting your Thursday evening. My treat.'

'OK, thank you. Let me spruce myself up a bit.'

She wasn't shocked either when she heard him coughing relentlessly in the bathroom. However, he looked a different person when he emerged after ten minutes. He had shaved and put on a pair of trousers and a clean, white shirt.

Thankfully, in light of the incessant rain, it was only a five-minute walk to La Bonne Graye. That was long enough for her to notice his wheezing and heavy breathing, but he appeared to pick up a little once he was inside the warmth of the bistro. That improvement gathered even more pace when they began tucking into a beef casserole, which he washed down with a glass of Côtes du Rhône red. The guard sitting at the table next to them was having the same, but that wasn't Anne-Sophie's treat. She smiled, 'I don't know about you, but I'm ready for this.'

'More than ready.' He looked to his right. 'As is your companion.'

She laughed, then turned serious. 'I know it's none of my business, but I can see it's not good for your health living in that flat.'

'You're right, it's not.'

Anne-Sophie frowned but Patrice smiled, put down his knife and fork, and held her hand, 'Good for my health. Quite the opposite.'

She squeezed his hand in return.

'So, tell me, Anne-Sophie, why did you ring me? Why the sudden need to visit me, out of the blue, after forty years?'

She told him about her search for her father's killers, the deaths of her mother, her allies and Malherbe, as well as her hunt for the red book.

'Back then, in March '87, did you believe my father hanged himself?'

'Nobody believed that; certainly, nobody who knew Jean-Marie well.'

'And you did?'

'Very well. In January 1982, I was an unemployed epidemiologist from Toulouse looking for a job. I literally walked into L'Académie, asked for one and got one. I was assigned to the Submarine and given the specific responsibility of monitoring the growing number of African AIDS cases in Paris. Because I am black everyone assumed I was the cleaner, the janitor, or such like. Jean-Marie looked out for me from day one and thereafter for the next five years. He was a massive help to me and my family.'

'Even though he didn't work in the Submarine himself?'

'That's the person he was, kind, caring, even got me a trial for Pointoise rugby club. I was quick, had good hands and wasn't afraid to get stuck in; in short, a natural number seven. I only got the opportunity because of Jean-Marie. Your father was a wonderful man.'

She took his hand again. 'I'm very glad to hear that. So, why, if nobody believed it was suicide, did no-one say anything to the police? Or to journalists, like Philippe?'

'Fear.'

'Of what?'

'Everyone was told in no uncertain terms not to talk about Jean-Marie to the police, the press, anybody.'

'Told by whom?'

'The big cheeses; Malherbe's superiors.'

'Deraingeur?'

'He was certainly a big cheese, yes.'

'And if someone did talk?'

'They didn't last long at L'Académie. I was proof of that.'

'What happened?'

'I got kicked out not long after your father died.'

'Why?'

'The cheeses suspected, with good reason, that I'd colluded with your father to help him get his hands on Malherbe's red book.'

'You helped him?'

'Of course! He'd helped me. I owed him everything.'

'But helping my father cost you your job?'

'More than my job.'

'What happened?'

'Someone made sure I didn't work in a Paris medical research unit again. Unfortunately, I had a sick wife and an even sicker child, so I couldn't leave Paris or look further afield. Then, to cap it all, I got sick too, had to give up everything, including my rugby. I haven't worked for thirty years. Now I live in a mouldy, draughty, cold apartment; my rent's about to go up, I've got nothing much to live on and I can barely breathe. It's not a great combination.' He looked down at his plate, 'I doubt I will live to see another Christmas.'

'Who was that someone?'

'I'm not sure but I had, have, my suspicions.'

'What happened to your wife? Your child?'

'My daughter died in 1988, three months after we moved into the flat, pneumonia; it wasn't the healthiest of places even then.'

'And your wife?'

'Laure committed suicide six months later.' He smiled grimly. 'A genuine suicide this time.'

With tears trickling down her cheeks, Anne-Sophie took both his hands. 'Why did she do it?'

'Grief for our daughter, Emily, grief for my reduced status and grief for my depression.'

She hid her face in her hands. Her father, Philippe, Eric, Henri, Malherbe, his manservant, Laure, Emily, and Patrice; all victims of an insane conspiracy. How many more victims was she going to find? What about 'the others' that Philippe had mentioned? She had no idea who they were, nor how many. She stroked her cross and pondered her next move. After some moments, she made up her mind.

'We have a lot to talk about but there's not enough time now. I want you to come back with me to Saint-Victor tonight.'

He looked at her. 'That's very kind, thank you. But why?'

'I need your help to track down the red book.'

'Of course, I would do anything for the daughter of Jean-Marie Montreau, but I'm not sure how much help I can give.'

'You knew my father, you worked in L'Académie and you like getting stuck in. You're going to be a great help; I just know it.'

Anne-Sophie, Patrice and the guard walked back to his flat where they collected a case full of clothes, as well as a couple of the soggy cardboard boxes which Patrice assured her contained relevant information. Then they drove back to Rue Rollin.

In the rush, she had forgotten to text Stonehouse with an update, or to say she was on her way back to the apartment, and he did not look best pleased to see Patrice walking behind her into the apartment. She also noticed that Patrice's face hardened when he saw Stonehouse, but she put it down to a rekindling of unhappy memories. Having shown Patrice how best to navigate the shower, and saying goodnight after he was safely ensconced in his bedroom, she returned to the lounge.

Stonehouse stood up and took hold of her hands. 'Let's go to bed.'

'I'm too full of caffeine and adrenaline to have any chance of falling asleep.'

'Who said anything about sleeping?'

'Before we turn in, I need to get something off my chest.'

'By all means. Don't mind me.'

'Stephen…'

He sat back down. 'This sounds serious, fire away.'

'Have you been keeping anything from me? About your past, your family?'

'Why do you ask?'

'The way Faust keeps looking at you. The way Patrice looked at you. Also, the feeling this is all going too well.'

He held her hands and looked into her eyes. 'I can assure you there are no skeletons in my cupboard, and I don't own a closet.'

She laughed. 'I believe you. Thank you for not getting upset or angry with me for asking.'

'I'm only surprised you thought I would.'

'As you've been honest with me, it's only fair I should reciprocate.'

'What do you mean?'

'Béatrice knows you stayed over last night.'

'How?'

'She asked me how our meeting had gone. I blushed.'

'Oh well, can't be helped.'

'She seemed to be upset about it.'

'Strange creatures, women; emotional, hard to read. I gave up trying ages ago.' He pulled her off the sofa. 'Come on, I want to show you my impression of the President-erect.'

'Ha ha. Unfortunately, I don't have any chocolate mousse in the fridge.'

'Shame.'

'And I'm not in the mood for any…ahem…action. Not after today, sorry.'

'I completely understand. I'd be disappointed in you if you were.'

As she took off her jeans, the pocket buzzed.

'Call off the attacks.'

'Make some arrests.
'Do it.'
'I'll sleep on it.'
'I am not your enemy.'
'Prove it.'

Chapter Fifty-Six

I am at Dulles, boarding.
I trust you will have good news for me when I land. TM

Day Five. Friday, April 2nd, 2027

Chapter Fifty-Seven

'What is it? Can't sleep?'

'For God's sake, do something about that bitch.'

Never before had he, nor, he suspected, anyone else, ever heard Parcelle sound ruffled, never mind out-of-control. 'As I said, our mutual friend says we are to leave her alone.'

'Screw him. And her. And you! Why the hell didn't you finish her off when you had the chance?'

'I just told you.'

'Next time a gift horse puts her head in your mouth, do me a favour, bite it off.'

'It could be worse.'

'How?'

'The Montreau girl could get her hands on the photos and texts Juliette sent you.'

'Screw you.'

The call being terminated, the recipient allowed himself a rare grin. It had not been often in the past forty years he had gained an advantage over Parcelle. This was truly a moment to savour; one he would like to tell his grandchildren about. Except he could not tell them because he did not have any; because he'd had no children; all because of...

Chapter Fifty-Eight

She lay in a state of suspended animation. Is this what Plato meant by meeting your 'other half'? Had she found her very own Robert Langdon? Stonehouse even had the same blue eyes as Dan Brown's hero. She knew she was getting far ahead of herself, but she had never felt anything like this before. It was scary how compatible they were. They had the shared experience of losing their fathers at an early age and she could not deny that his knowing Jean-Marie, and working in the same institution as him, were added attractions. Now that Philippe was gone, she was desperate to cling onto anyone who had the slightest connection to her father.

How would Béatrice respond if she knew the full story of what had occurred between her boss and Anne-Sophie? Béatrice! She had thought of her friend constantly throughout a sleepless night, but however much she was desperate to visit her, Anne-Sophie knew her only priority today was to locate the red book. Once she found it, the explanation for the killings would be revealed and the identities of the guilty people uncovered. Hopefully, then, she would be able to make peace with her oldest friend.

Anne-Sophie looked at her phone, six-thirty, and for a final time wrapped her right arm around her lover. She headed off to the bathroom to resume her daily struggle with the shower and fantasize about her and Stonehouse's happy future together. Fifteen minutes later, she returned to an empty bed. After getting dressed, she walked into an equally empty lounge and kitchen; empty apart from a note:

'Hello. Sorry, had to dash off. Going to check in on Béatrice before work. See you later, S. x.'

She made herself a pot of coffee and popped some bread into the toaster. Sitting down, she tried her best to resist the urge to feel any anger or bitterness at Stonehouse's unexpected departure. Béatrice would no doubt tell her once again it was karma, that what goes around, comes around. She had let down numerous men over the past twenty years. Do unto others…

She looked at her phone:

'This is serious. I am serious. Call off the attacks or else I will arrest you. Myself.'

'OK. I'll stop them. But I'm serious too. If you haven't made any progress by the end of today, as in actually arrested someone other than me and Stonehouse, I will resume the attacks, on an even greater scale. As I said yesterday, I will be very happy for you to arrest me. I can't wait to have my day in court, to see the whites of Parcelle's eyes and watch him squirm.'

As Patrice did not appear for another hour, Anne-Sophie at last had time to watch *Killer in the Village* from beginning to end. When he did emerge from his bedroom, she noticed he glanced briefly around the lounge and the kitchen.

'Don't worry, he's gone.'

'I wasn't worried.'

'But I could tell last night you weren't exactly overjoyed to see him; or, I have to admit, vice-versa.'

'Not exactly, no.'

'May I ask why?'

'Let me just say he was not the most supportive colleague after your father's death, when the witch-hunt started.'

'I'm sorry about that.'

'Don't be, it's not your fault. You're not responsible for what happened forty years ago.'

'Breakfast?'

'Yes, please. That would be wonderful.'

'Sit yourself down on the sofa.'

She made up a pot of tea and, reasoning he needed more than a slice of toast to set him up for the day, prepared scrambled eggs and sausages. After five minutes she looked across at him, his eyes were closed.

'Didn't you sleep well?'

'Wonderfully, thank you. Do you mind if I ask how your shower was this morning?'

'Amazingly good for once. Why? Oh, did you do something to it last night?'

'Only a tweak.'

'Well, whatever the tweak was it worked wonders. Thank you!'

'It was the same tweak I made just over forty years ago.'

She stared at him wide-eyed.

He smiled and then nodded across at her frozen TV screen. 'That's exactly what Jean-Marie was.'

'What do you mean?'

'A detective hunting for a killer, searching for the truth about the cause of AIDS.'

'I see. Did he find it?'

'He told me he had, yes.'

'I take it you mean HIV?'

'Oh no, definitely not that.'

'Really? What then?'

'Jean-Marie had his own theory.'

'Which was?'

'It's in one of my cardboard boxes.'

'Intriguing.'

'I'll show it to you when we have more time.'

'Shrink it down for me, into one sentence.'

'AIDS had nothing to do with HIV.'

'Interesting, Philippe told me the same thing.'

Once Patrice started tucking in, she got down to the immediate matter in hand. 'You agree my father was murdered?'

'What else?'

'I've worked out the *how*, but I've struggled to work out the *why* and, apart from Parcelle and the mysterious Jacques, the *who*. I did suspect Malherbe but, as he has suffered a similar fate to my father, I think I can safely say it wasn't him.'

'Cui bono.'

'What?'

'Who benefits? The police always say there's a high probability that those responsible for a certain event are the ones who stand to gain the most from it.'

'OK but who stood to gain from my father's death? How could anyone gain from the death of a virologist?'

'I'm surprised you ask that question after the pandemic. Anybody who criticized the official line about the origins of COVID-19 was ridiculed. AIDS was the COVID-19 of its day, perceived and portrayed as an existential threat to humankind and your father disagreed with the official explanation of its cause.'

'You're right, of course.'

'Ultimately, Jean-Marie was a threat. Already we've started to work out why he was a threat. Now we have to focus on who he was a threat to. Once we do that then you can start putting together a list of suspects.'

'Philippe told me that, in terms of suspects, the Ritz party guest list was as good a place to start as any.'

She heard 'Voulez-Vous'. It wasn't one of her contacts and she did not recognize the number.

'Hello?'

'Anne-Sophie Montreau?'

'Who's this?'

'Marie de Confort.'

Anne-Sophie stood up. 'What the hell do you want?'

'I wanted to let you know I am writing a new post for my *24 France* blog which I will upload in less than thirty minutes.'

'Why is that interesting to me?'

'Because it will explain why anyone who takes any notice of your pathetic 'JusticeforJean-Marie' blog page clearly needs their head examining as much as you do.'

'What carrot has Parcelle dangled in front of you? Apart from the obvious, which isn't really a carrot at all, judging by the photos. Has he offered you 'Special Advisor Communication and Strategy'? Or will you have to make do with a weekly slot in the Élysée Palace master bedroom admiring the ceiling whilst he pumps you with his presidential edict?'

'I suggest you devote more time thinking about your own future, instead of mine. Then you might make something of yourself, rather than continue to drown in your self-created, self-centred, perpetual cesspool of mediocrity.'

'Publish what you like. I'll publish what I like, including uncropped photos and unedited videos of you screwing the odds-on favourite to be France's next president. Hopefully, these new insights into Parcelle's character and body might be enough to turn the tide in favour of Mathilde Honneur.'

The line went dead. She sat down on the sofa. Patrice was looking at her with raised eyebrows.

'That was a very rattled, unofficial member of Parcelle's campaign team. So, where were we? Oh yes, you were, I hope, about to explain to me in more detail, why my father was a threat, and to whom.' She looked at the wall clock, ten o'clock. 'It will have to be the abbreviated version. Time is running out to find the red book.'

'I'll keep it as brief as I can.'

Even the shortened version took an hour, after which Anne-Sophie made fresh coffee. She sat down and, not for the first time during this unbelievable week, put her head in her hands.

'So, that's why you think my father was killed. He had gotten his hands on the red book which confirmed his theory about what caused AIDS, or rather, his theory about what didn't. The proof he needed to expose his opponents who had lied about HIV being the cause.'

'Correct.'

'It's not true though, is it.'

'What isn't?'

'About HIV not being the cause of AIDS?'

'Why not?'

'Surely, it's impossible to get away with something like that for forty years?'

'Is it? If we had time I would tell you about Thalidomide, Tuskegee and Pellagra.'

'Unfortunately, we haven't. They'll have to wait.'

'OK.'

'And you're absolutely certain the red book contains the proof?'

'It has to. Malherbe wrote down everything important in there. If it isn't there, it isn't anywhere.'

'So, the big question is, where do you think Father hid the book?'

'The most obvious place imaginable.'

'So obvious I haven't got a clue.'

'Voulez-vous' sounded again.

'For God's sake.'

This time it was her boss. Anne-Sophie decided to ignore her. She ignored her again when the call was repeated less than thirty seconds later; and she also ignored the text which followed.

'If you still value your job at the bank, call me back. Immediately.'

'Sorry about that. So, which very obvious place are you talking about?'

'The Submarine.'

It was a good job she was sitting down but even then, her legs felt wobbly.

'What? No way. Why there?'

'Obviously, it's only a guess, albeit an educated one. You know after what I've told you about the experiments in 1983 that Jean-Marie was obsessed with what was going on there. He considered it to be a covenstead, rather than a citadel of science. Knowing your father and the way he was like I did I think the Submarine could well be the place.'

'What do you mean, the way he was?'

'Beneath the surface, Jean-Marie had a wicked sense of humour. He would have thought it a great joke to hide the book right under his enemies' noses. He was good at completing crosswords and solving puzzles. Perhaps he liked setting puzzles too.'

She thought it through. The Submarine was within thirty minutes of the apartment; Hérault had said her father had gone to and from L'Académie constantly during his last weekend. It absolutely would be the last place his enemies would look.

'Hiding it in plain sight.'

'Well, not quite plain sight, your father didn't make it easy for his enemies, after all it hasn't turned up in forty-years. It won't be easy for you either, I am sure of that.'

She sat back, breathed in, and exhaled slowly.

'True.'

'Just because we think it is there, won't make it any easier to find. There are four genetic engineering units, as well as half a dozen small labs, to look through, plus, a converted laundry cupboard. It will take a while to search them all.'

'My father had access to the Submarine?'

'Yes. By '87 that part of the Sub was redundant. A new lab was built in 1984 thanks to the new money for AIDS research. The security at the more-or-less forgotten old labs was non-existent. Your father could have just walked straight in.'

'And now, is it still accessible?'

'That I don't know. I haven't been inside the building for nearly four decades.'

'Of course not, I'm sorry. Is there a particular place within the Submarine you would start looking at first?'

'Believe it or not, the converted laundry cupboard, Room C-101. It's where all the important 1983 AIDS virus experiments were carried out and where I spent a lot of my time. Yes, that would be my first port of call.'

She looked again at the clock, mid-day; seven hours until showtime. 'Would you like lunch?'

'Well…'

'How about an omelette? Something simple; ham, cheese, mushrooms, and salad.'

'It sounds anything but simple, but it does sound delicious, thank you.' Patrice saw immediately that tears had started forming in her eyes. 'What is it? What did I say?'

'Philippe called anything on his plate, or in his wine glass, delicious. Usually after he'd just told me how peckish he was. I'm sorry, I can't believe what has happened this week.'

'Don't apologize, I can't even begin to understand how much stress you've been under.'

'Thank you, but I know I can't be distracted. Time is running out, as Philippe also often used to say.'

After they finished their lunch, despite Anne-Sophie's protests, Patrice washed and dried the dishes. She thanked him, then said,

'Right, I should go. Wait here, please. Help yourself to, well, anything. Wish me luck. I'll see you when I get back.'

'Are you meeting Stonehouse?'

'Yes, he can get me into L'Académie, into C-101.'

'Of course. Good luck.'

She pecked him on the cheek and gave him a spare key, 'Just in case.' She headed off down the stairs, virtually pulling one of her guards, who was at the same time desperately trying to contact Faust, after her.

This was it, all or nothing.

Once the door closed, Patrice whispered to the walls,

'Be careful, Anne-Sophie, be very careful. Please.'

Chapter Fifty-Nine

This was his moment. He and he alone would decide. For too long he had followed others. Well, no longer. He was in charge, not Parcelle, nor their mutual friend. It was time to complete the trinity. He would resolve the Montreau problem once and for all, by doing it his way, no-one else's.

Chapter Sixty

Before she and the guard exited the apartment block, Anne-Sophie collected her mail which she stuffed into her shoulder bag. Once she was sitting in the police car, she texted Stonehouse:

'Hi. Hope you've good news re Béatrice. Can you meet me at Au Jean Bart please? 15 mins. #Haystack A-S xx.'

'I'll be there! x No new news re B, sorry x'

Entering Au Jean Bart, she was amused to see Françoise and Emil sitting in their usual spot and, also as usual, dressed identically. However, before she had an opportunity to speak to them, Stonehouse walked in. After a hug, he led her to the opposite end of the bar, much to the couple's obvious frustration.

'I want you to take me to the Submarine, please. Now.'

'Why?'

'That's the haystack. Or at least Patrice thinks so.'

'My word! Cunning. Right, let's get going.'

It was two o'clock when they arrived at what Stonehouse told Anne-Sophie was the back entrance to L'Académie. He turned to her guard,

'Journey's end, old girl. Strictly L'Académie employees and honoured guests only. It gives me no pleasure to say it, but you aren't an employee or a guest, and, looking at your jacket, it appears you have no honours.'

The guard looked at Anne-Sophie, who shrugged her shoulders and mouthed 'Sorry.' Whilst the guard frantically took out her phone, Stonehouse pressed his electronic lanyard against the entrance portal and stood aside to let Anne-Sophie through, 'Ladies first.'

From the outside, she had had no clue about the scale of L'Académie. Stonehouse told her its staff enjoyed the luxury of a five-hectare campus, which housed thirty-nine buildings, twenty-three of which were used for scientific research; several of these buildings were categorized as historical monuments.

Altogether, L'Académie had a total of forty-eight-thousand square metres of laboratory space.

'Impressive. However, I'm only interested in one building and probably less than one-hundred square metres of lab space, Room C-101.'

'Of course.'

Within five minutes Stonehouse was guiding her in the direction of the high-security P3 lab nicknamed the Submarine. Even if the rest of the campus had undergone a revamp in recent years, the same could not be said of this area. To Anne-Sophie, it looked very run down and shabby.

Once again it seemed Stonehouse had read her mind. 'This part of the building has not been in use for many, many years.'

'Replaced by bigger, better, brighter facilities.'

'Much more expensive facilities, yes.'

They walked for twenty minutes before finally reaching a remote, deserted part of the building.

'Right. This is it. The Submarine.'

'Thank goodness. Where's C-101?'

'This way.'

Five minutes later they were standing outside the door.

'How long do you think it's been since it was last opened up?'

'No idea, a decade. Two, possibly three.'

No matter how long it had been, entering C-101 was easy enough thanks to Stonehouse's passkeys. Obviously, the more difficult task was going to be locating the red book, if it was there at all.

'Why did Morison think it might be in here?'

'Patrice told me my father loved crosswords and puzzles. Plus, he apparently had a wicked sense of humour. Hiding the red book here would tick those boxes.'

'Sounds logical. Well, what do you think of C-101?'

'It does actually feel like a converted laundry room.'

'Before the AIDS virus good times rolled, space and money were both tight. After the virus was discovered, money and space were no object. The L'Académie bean counters gave us as much of both as we wanted after 1983.'

She could not believe the cramped conditions and asked him how safe it had been to carry out complex scientific experiments in these circumstances.

'Not very, contamination was a constant hazard. Nowhere was one hundred per cent safe against that particular eventuality in the eighties. It's not much better today, even in these state-of-the-art times.'

'Contamination's a bad thing, isn't it?'

'Contamination is the dirty laundry, pun intended, no one in research wants to talk about but it couldn't be more important. Although contamination can have serious and widespread negative impacts, such as rendering a sample unsuitable for testing, or yielding incorrect results and data, contamination events are generally not tracked or reported.'

'So, a lot of lab research could be bad science, invalid?'

'Unfortunately, yes.'

Although she knew the book was not going to be hidden somewhere obvious, Anne-Sophie could not resist trying the cupboards, cabinets and drawers, just in case. She was right, no joy. As Patrice had said, her father had not made it simple or easy for his enemies and it wasn't going to be simple or easy for her either. She looked around the lab and then got down on her knees.

'Let's try the floor. See if any of these tiles are loose.'

It was not long before Stonehouse exclaimed,

'This one here! It's got a crack along the side of it. Let me see if there is a chisel somewhere. There should be. Ah, here we go.'

He eased the tile up and an eager Anne-Sophie looked underneath. 'Nothing.' She looked at the wall clock, three o'clock; four hours. She scanned the tiles, desperately hoping to find another with a crack running alongside it. Finally, in the far back corner, she found one.

'Stephen, over here. Bring the chisel, please.'

After five minutes of chipping away and easing the chisel in and out, he told her the tile was ready to be lifted. This was it. All or nothing.

As he lifted up the tile, she got down on her knees.

'What can you see?'

'Nothing much. Wood, a piece of cupboard door, or something.' She passed the wood to Stonehouse. 'Apart from that, zilch. Anywhere else we can try?'

'No, I think that's our lot.'

'Damn it.'

As she reached the door, she turned around to give the room one last scan. She looked at the sink again. There was a cupboard underneath she had not tried. Getting down once more on her haunches, she saw it was filled with cleaning fluids, washing bowls, brushes and rubber gloves. She quickly cleared out the junk and had a closer look.

'Put your phone torch on, please? Thanks. There's some sort of trap door. Might be the water valve. Hell, it's metal, weighs a ton.' She had to lie down flat on her stomach to access and lift it.

'Prop it up!'

She reached inside and felt around, but there was nothing. It was game over. 'Damn it!' She stood up, very frustrated and very sweaty. She felt bitter tears forming.

'The book's obviously not here. We'd better go and look in some of the other labs.'

As she reached the door, something to her left caught her eye, another door. 'What's that?'

'The little boys' or girls' room.'

'What does that mean?'

'The bathroom.'

She stopped dead in her tracks. Then smiled. 'Oh, Dad! You didn't, did you?'

'Sorry?'

'Have you ever seen *The Godfather*?'

'No, and before you ask, I haven't seen *Star Wars* either. Give me Hitchcock any day. Why *The Godfather*?'

'I'll explain later.'

She ran to the door. The toilet was an ancient affair, with a wooden boxed cistern above. 'Yes! Talk about cunning. As Tessio might have said, "it's perfect".'

She felt around the gap between the box and the back wall. Her fingers touched plastic. She gripped and pulled. Her hand emerged holding a Leclerc shopping bag which contained something that felt distinctly book-shaped.

All or nothing.

She glanced at Stonehouse who looked as tense as she was feeling.

'You had better do the honours.'

'What?

'Take a peek.'

She slowly unwrapped the shopping bag and looked inside.

'Oh my God.'

'Is it?'

She pulled out an object wrapped in plastic, many layers of plastic.

'A riddle wrapped in a mystery, inside an enigma.'

'Sorry?'

'Winston Spencer Churchill's description of the Russians.'

'OK, here goes.' Slowly, she unwrapped the plastic layers and took the object out of the bag.

All or nothing.

Chapter Sixty-One

'Let's get out of here.' No sooner had the words left Anne-Sophie's lips than two stocky individuals, one black, one white, both carrying pistols, burst into C-101. She and Stonehouse were thrown roughly to the floor and swiftly bound and gagged. Then they were picked up and shoved through the door where they were met by half a dozen police officers, also armed. Standing behind them was a familiar blonde-haired figure.

'Drop the guns. Kneel down. Release your captives.'

The two assailants did as they were told without demur.

Once she'd been unbound, Anne-Sophie immediately walked across and slapped her assailants. 'That's for my father.' She slapped them again, even harder. 'And that's for my friends.'

Faust pulled her away. 'Calm down.'

'I am calm. Extremely.' She looked at the Deputy Prefect. 'How did you know we were in trouble?'

Faust told Daniel to take the two captives away, then tightly gripped Anne-Sophie's right wrist.

'I told you I wasn't your enemy, but can you say the same in return?'

'What do you mean?'

'The attacks haven't stopped.'

'Damn! I'm sorry, really sorry. I meant to, honestly. I'll do it as soon as I get back to my laptop, I promise.'

'You've already broken one promise.'

'I won't break this one. Promise.'

Faust released her grip.

'Where did the thugs come from?'

'From Rue des Volontaires. The back way.'

'So, how *did* you know we were in danger?'

It was only whilst being blue-lighted back to Saint-Victor that the Deputy Prefect, despite her anger, and after being reassured again by Anne-Sophie that she really had meant to stop the attacks that morning, told her who they had to thank for their escape.

'It was the guy sitting next to you.'

Anne-Sophie looked at Patrice who had a big smile on his face. She clasped his right hand in hers then turned back to Faust who continued, 'He spent an hour outside the entrance to L'Académie pleading with my officer to contact me.'

Anne-Sophie looked again at Patrice. 'Because?'

'I had a bad feeling.'

'I'm glad you had it. We're glad you had it, aren't we, Stephen?'

Stonehouse momentarily interrupted his texting, 'Abso-bloody-lutely! Couldn't be gladder.'

Anne-Sophie tapped Faust on the shoulder. 'Why did it take an hour?'

'Because I couldn't be contacted.'

'Why not?'

'Because I was dealing with the fall-out from your attacks. My team's phones have all but melted.'

'I'm sorry.'

'I did tell you that you were making my job harder than it needed to be. The attacks almost cost you and Stonehouse your lives, which some might have said was karma.'

'They might. Is there any news about Béatrice?'

'Nothing I'm afraid, she's still in a coma.'

'Hell.'

Immediately upon entering the apartment, and under Faust's hawk-like eyes, Anne-Sophie set to work undoing Thursday night's handiwork; most of it. After an hour, having completed her task to Faust's satisfaction, she took hold of Stonehouse's hand and looked at the Deputy Prefect.

'We need to take - thanks again to Patrice - quick, fabulous showers. Then, hopefully, we will at last find out, courtesy of the red book, why my father was killed.'

'And possibly by whom.'

'Yes. Could I ask a cheeky favour, please?'

'Sure.'

'Could you make a …'

'Pot of coffee.'

'Thank you, and...'

'Heat up some pains au chocolat.'

'Yes, please! And Patrice would you please…'

'Start looking through the red book?'

'Thank you! This Plato mind-reading thing could catch on.'

When she and Stonehouse emerged thirty minutes later, Anne-Sophie could tell from Patrice's glum face that all was not well.

'What is it?'

'I can't find anything that stands out as a smoking gun.'

'Damn it.'

'There are lots of experiments, formulae and the like, but no obvious stand outs in terms of admissions of guilt; nothing that is going to worry the Ritz party goers or identify the mastermind behind any plot to kill Jean-Marie.'

Anne-Sophie sat down and slumped on the sofa. Stonehouse put his arm around her shoulder. 'Let me double-check the book, just in case.'

Patrice stood up and took a step towards him.

'Just in case the black guy has missed something? You think I don't know what I'm doing? Don't think I've forgotten what you did to me at L'Académie.'

Anne-Sophie stepped in between them, 'Patrice!'

'Easy old boy, just making sure, for Anne-Sophie's sake. After all, she's the most important person in the room, the reason why we're all here. Perhaps we should stick to the here and now, not go back over ancient ground.'

Whilst the others munched on their croissants, Stonehouse pored over the book. After ten minutes he took off his glasses and looked at Anne-Sophie, 'Do you want the good news, or the bad news?'

'Bad first.'

'There is no smoking gun.'

'Damn. What's the good news?'

'Patrice was right. As I knew he would be.'

Anne-Sophie looked at a frustrated Faust. 'What can we do?'

'Without a smoking gun, there isn't a lot we, I, can do. It's over.' Faust looked at her phone. 'No!'

'What?'

'The car carrying the two thugs from the Submarine…'

'What about it?'

'Rammed on the Pont Saint-Michel. There've been shots. All the occupants...'

'Yes?'

'Are dead.'

'My God.'

'Including Daniel. I need to go. I'm sorry.'

Faust ran to the door. For what seemed like the hundredth time that week, Anne-Sophie buried her head in her hands. Once again Stonehouse wrapped his arm around her. 'I'm awfully sorry.'

'More deaths because of me and for what? A wild goose chase.' After five minutes, she lifted her head and turned to Stonehouse, 'Thanks for being here for me.'

'There's no-where else I'd rather be. No-one else I'd rather be with.'

She looked at the time, seven o'clock. 'Stephen!'

'What is it?'

'The Ritz.'

'What about it?'

'You need to go. It's your big night.'

'I'm hardly in the mood for a celebration.'

'You'll have to get in the mood.'

'And I'm not exactly dressed for the occasion. Any occasion.'

'What do you need?'

'Invite says black tie.'

'So, tux, tie and a pressed white shirt should see you cutting the mustard?'

'Seems about right.'

She stroked her cross. 'Mother kept some of Father's clothes. Let me see if there's anything suitable. Give me five minutes.'

It took ten for her to reappear carrying a jacket and shirt.

'What about these?'

He looked doubtfully at the jacket.

'Try it on. There you go, perfect. Fits like a glove. What do you think, Patrice?'

'Like a glove.'

She looked at Stonehouse. 'You can borrow them.'

'Thank you.'

'On one condition.'

'Which is?'

'You take me with you.'

'Sorry?'

'If you can be Jean-Marie Montreau for the night, there's no reason why I can't be Béatrice. She's nothing if not very practical. Annoyingly so, sometimes. She wouldn't want her invite to go to waste. Plus...'

'Yes?'

'I want to meet the person responsible for my father's death.'

'What?'

'I told you; Philippe said that person or persons would be at the Ritz. I just want to be in the same room as him, her, they or them. I want that person to see me, to know I'm not afraid of them. I want to see the whites of their eyes, make them feel uncomfortable, make their rear ends sweat.'

'But-'

'But what? Don't you want me there? Not good enough for you, is that it? You don't have to tell me I'm not as smart as Béatrice, or as sexy. I've known that for decades. However, if nothing else, I can wear the pendant and earrings she bought me for my birthday, as a sort of tribute.'

'Great.'

'I can look half decent when I scrub up, you know.'

'I'm sure you can. What about the shirt?'

'What about it?'

'It needs a press.'

'Give me fifteen minutes. By seven-thirty, you'll have a pressed shirt, I'll be scrubbed up and then we can both go to the ball. Deal?'

'But..'

'Deal?'

Chapter Sixty-Two

Parcelle was adjusting his black tie when the phone buzzed.

'What's going on?'

'Plenty.'

'I really haven't got time to talk.'

'Getting ready for the Ritz?'

'Yes.'

'I'll be there in two hours.'

'Why do I have the sinking feeling you've screwed up; again.'

'Two hours.'

Chapter Sixty-Three

It was eight-thirty before a taxi dropped the two of them off at the entrance to the Ritz foyer. The delay occurred because Stonehouse had insisted on making a detour to pick up cufflinks from his apartment on the Rue Dutot because, 'I feel naked without them.'

They asked to be taken to the Salon Louis XV, which according to their guide was 'a spectacular confection of exquisite, gilded woodwork, long mirrors and crystal chandeliers.'

The hyperbole cut no ice with Anne-Sophie who whispered to her straight-faced companion, 'Like I give a monkey's about any of that.'

After quaffing a glass of 'rich, complex and ethereal' *Champagne Barons de Rothschild Réserve Ritz* in less than ten seconds, she and Stonehouse were shown to their seats. She, finding herself sitting next to Antony Consolotto and, presumably, Peter Stacey, surmised that they were at the top table. Confirmation of this came when she saw Hervé Parcelle and Juliette Roulet seated directly opposite her. She sank a second glass of champagne in equally short order, barely noticing the 'elegant golden colour, fine aromas of white fruits and light accents of brioche.'

She called across the table to Roulet. 'Hello Juliette! I can't tell you how marvellous it is to see you again, and so soon. Hervé! We meet at last. Had to make do with the older model I see. Could Marie not make it tonight? Will she be waiting for you later on at the Palais, lying back on your desk, ready for you to give her even more chocolatey pleasure.'

'Anne-Sophie, please.'

'You talk to Antony, Stephen, I'll talk to my new friend Hervé, and his old mistress. That's right, Juliette, not that it was rocket science exactly, but yes, I finally worked out how you made it to the top. By keeping quiet about the Procureur in public, whilst screwing his brains out in private. Good work. How does it feel to be replaced by a younger, faster, far less wrinkly model? Turns out there are some things that even money cannot buy, or Botox hide. If I was you, which, thank God, I'm not, I'd be asking for my money back from the plastic surgeon.'

For some reason, Parcelle seemed more interested in looking at Stonehouse than he was in listening to her. So, after downing her third glass of *Barons* in less than five minutes, she got up and walked around the table to speak to the favourite to be France's next president. She crouched down between him and Roulet, her mouth very close to his ear, her hand gripping his tightly,

'Hello, Hervé. Well, this is nice, isn't it? Finally, an opportunity for us to chew the fat, one-to-one. How did you sleep last night? Any interruptions, apart from Marie trying to stoke your fires. Another night in with just you, her and several cartons of La Hulotte was it?'

She turned to Roulet. 'Do you like my necklace and earrings? *Elsa Peretti* don't you know? Probably not as much as you like La Hulotte smeared on you by old Hervé. Or is whipped cream, behind closed doors with the curtains drawn, more the fashion in Saint-Cloud? Sit down, you old bag, and drink another glass of fizz. I'd make the most of it if I was you. You won't get another opportunity like this for a long time, if ever, not if I get my way.'

She turned back to Parcelle, her mouth, if possible, even closer to his ear. 'Were you this close to my father in March 1987? His feet at any rate. Did you help cut his body down? Sit still and don't move. You aren't going anywhere. Where's that fizz? That's better. Lucky for you that Mules and Hérault are dead, isn't it? Cui bono and all that. Now, listen to me. I'm not going to let this go. Even if you make it to the Élysée, I'll be with you twenty-four seven, virtually, making sure things don't run as smoothly as they should. Little things, like your phone alarm going off every half an hour, will be the least of your worries. Imagine what I could do the night before you're due to have a chat with the President of China, or America.'

'Anne-Sophie.'

'What?'

'Why don't you come back and sit down.'

'In a second! Hervé, have you tried accessing your offshore account recently? The one with the twenty-five million Euros?

259

Take my advice, don't bother. What do you think the Mornecs will say when they find out you've lost all their money? Oi, what is it?'

Stonehouse had come across and firmly taken hold of her arm. 'Come on, the food is about to arrive.'

'Oh, thank God, I'm beyond myself.'

Even in her drunken state, she had to admit the various courses tasted divine. Unsurprisingly, the combination of champagne, delicious food, the traumatic events of the past few days and lack of sleep, caught up with her. Putting her head down to rest her eyes for a couple of minutes, she was soon fast asleep.

Bizarrely, she was woken by the strains of 'Happy Birthday.'

'What's happening?'

'It's Bicchiere's ninetieth birthday.'

'Bully for him. Have I missed much?'

'Not really, a lot of boring, self-congratulatory speeches about HIV and AIDS; advances in drug treatments, the latest vaccine updates. Plus ça change! There's also been some chatter about mobile phone alarms going off through the night.'

'Funny that.'

'Isn't it? Well, now you've woken up, I think it's time for us to go. I've got a few things I should be getting on with tomorrow, things which require me to have a decent amount of sleep and an early start.'

Still drowsy, she squeezed his hand and was about to ask him what those things were, when she turned to look at Parcelle and Roulet, who had been joined by a third party. Suddenly, she was wide awake and very sober. Even though he was sitting with his back towards her, she was absolutely certain she was looking at someone she had met recently, very recently.

'Excuse me, Stephen, I need to go use the facilities.'

'Sorry?'

'I'm bursting.'

'Ah, OK, don't be long. I've ordered an Uber, it'll be here in ten minutes.'

She managed to stop herself from running out of the salon but once she was outside, she sprinted to the toilets, reaching for her phone as she ran. She dialled as soon as she got inside a cubicle.

'Angela? You and your team need to come to the Ritz. Now! The Salon Louis XV. I'm sitting opposite Parcelle and Roulet. How long? OK. Quickly!'

Exiting the cubicle, she ran straight into the back of Roulet, who had obviously heard every word of the phone call and was walking to the door. Anne-Sophie grabbed the Chief Justice around the back of the neck and shoved her into the just-vacated cubicle. Snatching Roulet's phone out of her hand, she dropped it into the toilet bowl and flushed. She then pushed Roulet's head down into the bowl and flushed again.

'I hope I haven't damaged your listening skills, or dislodged any of your Botox, because I want you to listen very carefully. Got that?'

'Yes!'

'Good. Don't even think about leaving here for at least fifteen minutes. If you do, I promise I will kill you. Understand? Do you understand?!'

Roulet's extremely anguished noise of affirmation was enough to satisfy Anne-Sophie. She flushed the Chief Justice's head again, and sprinted back to the entrance to the Salon, before slowing down to walk back to her chair.

Stonehouse leaned across.

'You OK?'

'Yes, fine. Just felt a bit wobbly when I sat down in the loo. Must be the *Barons.*'

The person she had recognized was now sitting in Roulet's seat and entirely focused on an agitated-looking Parcelle, who regularly glanced across at Stonehouse.

After a minute Stonehouse looked at his phone and stood up. 'Let's go. The Uber's here.'

'Give me two minutes, I'm feeling wobbly again. I don't want to be sick in the cab. That would make it a very expensive ride.'

Stonehouse took hold of her arm and pulled. 'I can afford it. Come on.'

She shook his hand away from her arm. 'Two minutes I said! What's your big rush. Tomorrow's Saturday. Sit down, relax, talk to your good friend, Tony. Have another drink, do anything, just shut up.'

Stonehouse said nothing, but his eyes flashed.

Come on Angela, come on. Where the hell are you? Oh, thank God.

Faust and a dozen officers ran into the salon. She looked at Anne-Sophie who nodded towards the man sitting next to Parcelle; a man with a bandaged hand and a scar under his right eye. Anne-Sophie started walking around the table to introduce herself to him, but she was beaten to the punch by Faust who grabbed Jacques by the scruff of his neck and pushed his head down sharply onto the table.

'That's for Eric.' She repeated the action, 'And that's for Daniel.'

Anne-Sophie somehow resisted the temptation to tell Faust to calm down and watched the Deputy Prefect seize Jacques' hands and handcuff them behind his back.

'Director-General, I am arresting you in connection with the murders of Jean-Marie Montreau, Philippe Simon, Henri Hérault, Louis Malherbe, Michel LeClair, Lieutenant Daniel Beaucourt and Detective Inspector Eric Mules.'

Chapter Sixty-Four

You have disappointed me.
You have two hours to end this psychodrama.
If by then you haven't succeeded, you're on your own.
TM

Chapter Sixty-Five

After Parcelle, Roulet and Jacques had been escorted out of the Salon by Faust and her officers, Stonehouse was still in a hurry to leave.

'Come on, let's go.'

In the Uber he asked Anne-Sophie if she would like a nightcap at his apartment.

'Yes, as long as we go to see Béatrice first.'

'Isn't it rather late?'

'I feel guilty that I haven't been to see her. Don't you?'

'We can go first thing in the morning.'

'But..'

'If there is any change, I'll be the first to know.'

'What do you mean?'

'I'm down as next of kin.'

'What?'

'As I'm her boss, and her parents are both getting on a bit, she thought it was a good idea.'

'Right.'

'Don't worry, she's in good hands. The best.'

'I know.'

'So, nightcap?'

'OK, if by nightcap you mean coffee.'

He put his arm around her, looked directly into her eyes and smiled.

'It can mean anything you want it to.'

His apartment block was situated three hundred and fifty metres from L'Académie and the apartment itself was on the first floor. Anne-Sophie, who had earlier remained in the taxi when Stonehouse had collected his cufflinks, was impressed. It had a large lounge which opened onto a balcony with a spectacular, unobstructed view of the lit-up Eiffel Tower. The open-plan kitchen, with its high-spec appliances, and the brand-new bathroom with walk-in shower, put her own wreck of an apartment to shame. Two large bedrooms and the refined decorations completed the overall impression that this was an apartment belonging to someone who had hit the heights of their profession.

'It looks very elegant. Just like its owner, wearing my father's tux.'

'It'll do.'

'How does this compare to your villa in the Med? Or the Chamonix chalet?'

'Similar to the chalet in that they are both products of the nineties. Very different to my Cap Ferrat villa. That's an older property, still a bit of a tip, but right beside the beach, which is always a plus.'

'It must be.'

'And it's got a tennis court, admittedly ancient, but usable.'

'Fabulous.'

'You did say coffee, didn't you?'

'Yes please.'

He came over with the pot and some heated milk and, sitting down next to her on the sofa, took her hands in his, kissed them and put his arm around her.

'Well, that was a spectacular way to end the evening. Are you all right?'

'Fine, thanks. I can't believe Jacques had the balls to turn up like that. What was he thinking?'

'He obviously didn't know you were going to be there.'

'You'd think Parcelle might have tipped him off after we'd walked in.'

'Either he had no idea Jacques was going to make an appearance, or he had no way of contacting him; or he wanted to drop him in it.'

'Why?'

'No idea. However, I think we'll find Jacques's arrival was in some way connected to what happened at the Pont Saint-Michel.'

'Wow, I hadn't thought of that.'

'Faust obviously had.'

'That's why she's the Deputy Prefect, and I'm not.'

'Yes.'

'I can't wait to find out who Jacques actually is, what he is the Director-General of.'

'I don't know about that, but he is the final piece of your jigsaw.'

'What do you mean?'

'The final piece of the Montreau murder mystery.'

'Not quite.'

'No?'

'I still don't know who the L'Académie mole was.'

'That's true. I forgot about that. Another needle in a haystack scenario.'

'Yes. Do you know who he is?'

'The mole?'

'No, Jacques.'

'Never seen him before.'

'Have you ever met Parcelle?'

'Not knowingly. Why?'

'He kept looking at you. Just like Faust did.'

'Typical politician. Shifty.'

'Ex-politician, I hope. I reckon he'll be getting a grilling from Faust right now, as will Jacques and Roulet. I guarantee they'll all have some dirt on each other. Their rear ends will be very sweaty that's for sure.'

'Most definitely.'

'I wonder what each of them knows about Father's murder? Seems to me Parcelle and Roulet would know more about the aftermath and the cover up than the build-up and the act itself. Of course, Jacques knows everything about yesterday's killings, and the names of the thugs who strung my father up, but that doesn't help me get to the bottom of the conspiracy. Unless any of them knows the identity of the L'Académie mole, or they tell Faust where I can find another piece of physical evidence, then, I've literally, very unfortunate pun intended, reached a dead end, run out of road.'

She turned to him and was irritated to see he was paying more attention to his phone than he was to her.

'What do you think?'

'About what?'

'You weren't listening, were you?'

'Sorry.'

'What were you looking at?'

'Where?'

'On your phone.'

'My calendar.'

'Full?'

'Not especially.'

'What about tomorrow?'

'What do you mean?'

'You said you had things to do tomorrow.'

'Did I?'

'Yes, three times. That's why we had to leave the Ritz so quickly.'

'Oh yes.'

She unwrapped herself from his arm and looked at him. 'What things?'

'What do you mean?'

'What are the things you have to do tomorrow?'

'Why?'

'Only asking, just making polite conversation. You're obviously not interested in solving my father's murder anymore, so I'm asking you what you're up to tomorrow.'

'Just a few things. Nothing earth-shattering.'

'So why the need to leave early? Especially as tomorrow's Saturday. Surely this was a great networking opportunity for you. A chance to rub shoulders with international colleagues. I mean, come on, how often do you get to sit next to the legendary Antony Consolotto?'

'Don't.'

'Don't what?''

'Lecture me.'

'I wasn't.'

'Or dare to presume to tell me what I am, and what I'm not, interested in.'

'I'm sorry.'

'It's not as if you took full advantage of the "opportunity", is it? The only contact you had with the "legendary" Consolotto was drooling on his shoulder, whilst snoring your head off.'

'I'm sorry I fell asleep, and for the drooling.'

'It wasn't just that.'

'What else was it?'

'The way you acted towards Parcelle and Roulet.'

'What about it?'

'It was a disgrace. This was a special occasion at the Ritz, and you acted like a drunken Parisian fishwife in July 1789.'

'You know why I behaved like that, don't you?'

'Because you quaffed far too much champagne, far too quickly and got far too drunk.'

'Technically, yes. The underlying reason, as I hope you know, was my anger and revulsion towards that particularly loathsome couple.'

He looked at her.

'There's a time and a place, and the Ritz, tonight, was neither.'

She finished off her coffee. 'I'm sorry I embarrassed you. I thought you of all people would understand. Tonight was exactly the right time, and the Ritz exactly the right place, because they were the only time and place. When will I next get a similar opportunity? 2067?'

She stood up. 'I knew deep down you didn't want me to go tonight. I'm sorry I showed you up in front of the world's medical science crème de la crème. I know you would have much preferred Béatrice to be there instead of me.'

She looked at her phone. 'Damn.'

'What?'

'My phone's died, and I have no charger. Can I borrow yours please?'

'No, it's at L'Académie.'

'You only have one?'

'Yes.'

'OK, we're both tired, a good night's sleep will do us the world of good. I think I'd better walk home. The fresh air will clear my head after the *Barons*.' She picked up her shoulder bag.

'But.'

'It's probably best if I leave now, before we have a blazing row.'

He stood up.

'Sorry, that isn't happening.'

'What the hell do you mean?'

He stroked her cheek. 'I can't let you go when you're so upset. Let me make you a milky coffee. Then we'll talk about much more pleasant things; summer in the Med, winter in the Alps.'

She looked at him for five seconds, then sat back down and smiled. 'OK, but only if you're sure. Those do sound very pleasant, especially the bit about summer in the Med, thanks.'

Whilst Stonehouse went into the kitchen to prepare a pot of coffee, Anne-Sophie had a rummage around in her shoulder bag. She pulled out the mail she had collected on her way out of the apartment that morning. As Stonehouse would be five minutes, she decided to look at it and see if she'd missed anything important since Monday. She discarded the junk mail straight away. Of the remaining four envelopes, two were bills and one was a letter from Monique. It contained a written warning about her conduct that week, which Anne-Sophie crunched up and put back into her bag.

The fourth envelope was A4 size, brown, and had a Le Vésinet postmark. She stared at it. Le Vésinet? What? Who? Malherbe, it had to be. She did not know anyone else who lived there. When had he sent it? Why had he sent it? What had he sent?

Chapter Sixty-Six

'What have you got there?'

Heart racing, she had opened the brown envelope; inside was a white envelope and another, much smaller, brown one. She had put the latter into the inner compartment of her bag. For thirty seconds, she had stared at the white envelope and pondered whether to open it. Then, aware of the silence, she had looked up. Her heart rate had increased by another fifty-per-cent. Stonehouse was standing at the kitchen door, motionless, watching her.

'I was just checking my mail.'

'I can see that. Who's that from?'

'I don't know. I haven't read it.'

'Who do you think it's from?'

'No idea.'

He walked over, picked up the A4 envelope and slapped her.

'Stephen!'

'No idea? Really? Why lie to me?'

'I don't know. I'm sorry.'

'Don't ever lie to me again.'

'I won't.'

'Or try to deceive me.'

'OK.'

'Promise.'

She looked at him. His eyes were ice blue, but the Robert Langdon comparisons ended there and then. 'I promise.'

'Good. Now open the envelope and read it to me.'

'But-'

'Don't screw with me. Don't question me. Read it. All of it.'

'I will, I'm sorry.'

After Anne-Sophie finished, Stonehouse held out his hand. 'Let me double check it, just in case.'

'In case of what?'

'You've lied to me, again. God help you if you have.'

'I haven't lied to you.'

'Do I have to ask again? Hand it over.'

She looked at him again, then handed over the letter. He spent five minutes perusing the contents, after which he smiled, crumpled it up and tossed it in the bin.

'What did you do that for?'

'I doubt I'll read it again. You certainly won't.'

Her mind was racing nearly as fast as her heart. Why had Stephen been so concerned about a letter from Malherbe? Concerned enough to slap her. After reading the letter why had his expression rapidly shifted through the gears of puzzlement, confusion and finally relief? Why would she not be reading it again?

'Is it true?'

'Is what true?'

'What Malherbe said in the letter.'

'Which bit?'

'That HIV wasn't the cause of AIDS?'

'One hundred per cent true.'

'Both Philippe and Patrice told me that's what my father believed.'

'What did you say to Morison?'

'I told him it was impossible. For forty years the planet has been told by the CDC, WHO, UNAIDS, L'Académie, everyone, that AIDS is caused by the deadly virus, HIV-1.'

'How did Morison respond?'

'He told me it was entirely possible. Is it?'

'Absolutely, the 'HIV causes AIDS' narrative is a big lie. Perhaps the biggest ever in medical-science and that's not a short list. However, as 9/11 showed, if you tell a big enough lie and repeat it often enough, most people will believe it. The 'HIV causes AIDS' scam is positive proof that you can get away with virtually anything if the right people are behind it.'

'And the right people were behind it?'

'Of course. The NIH, the CDC, White House. And that was just the Yanks.'

'Why did these people and institutions do it? Why did you go along with it?'

'Greed, personal aggrandizement, renown, prizes, fast cars, faster women; whatever floated your boat.'

'If HIV isn't a deadly virus, isn't the cause of AIDS, then all the HIV testing, the drugs, PReP, all of it, is a waste of time.' Suddenly, a penny dropped. 'Millions of adults, children and babies, the 'others' as Philippe called them, have been taking, or been forced to take, unnecessary, poisonous drugs.'

'By Jove, you've got it! You're obviously not as sharp as your beloved father but you got there in the end. However, much as I would love to talk for the rest of the night about the ramifications of the 'HIV causes AIDS' myth, I need to crack on. I'll finish off making your coffee and I think I'll brew up a pot of Yorkshire. It always helps me think more clearly as the clock nears the witching hour.'

She needed to think too, and fast. Malherbe's letter stated her father had proof HIV didn't cause AIDS. However, nothing in the red book confirmed this. So, where was the proof? It could literally be anywhere in the world. Or could it? Suddenly, it was obvious. Again, blindingly so. Malherbe *had* sent her the proof; the smaller envelope she'd put into the inside compartment of her shoulder bag contained the proof. It had to. Involuntarily, she reached into the bag and started tugging at the zip. Immediately, she realized she had made another mistake. A huge mistake. Stonehouse was standing over her, with an unpleasant smile playing on his lips.

'Don't mind me. I thought I saw you slip something inside your bag earlier. Carry on.'

She pulled her hand away.

'It's OK. I was just looking for some lip gloss. They feel a bit dry.'

He slapped her again. Harder than before.

'What the hell!'

'What did I say to you about lying?'

'I wasn't.'

That provoked another, even harder, slap.

'Stephen! Stop it.'

She stood up. He shoved her back onto the sofa and grinned. 'Anne-Sophie, please. We've both read Malherbe's letter. It says your father got his hands on the proof he needed. The red book doesn't have proof of anything. So, where is it? We both think it's inside your bag. So, stop screwing me around, unzip your bag and let's see if we're correct.'

When she hesitated, he raised his hand. 'Do I have to hit you again?'

She complied, pulled out the envelope and handed it to him. He tore it open, read through the sheets of paper and smiled. 'Do you want the good news or the bad news?'

She shrugged.

'The good news is that we were correct; it is the proof your father craved, and that I desired; it is the smoking gun. Or, more accurately, the actually on-fire gun. I knew Malherbe had it somewhere.' He laughed, 'I bloody knew it.'

He looked at her. 'Well, well, perhaps it's true. Great minds do think alike. Which is something I never thought I'd say about the two of us. Compared to Béatrice your mind is as dull as dishwater and as empty as a brand-new dishwasher. However, after this I may have to recalibrate. Perhaps we are destined to be together. Perhaps, after all, you are truly my other half.'

He looked at her and sneered. 'I'm joking. However, almost despite myself, I have been wondering if, perhaps, you might make an adequate, third Mrs Stonehouse. Unfortunately, and this is the bad news, because of this smoking gun, and what happened earlier tonight, that can never be.'

'What do you mean?'

'To coin a cliche, you and other people know too much.'

'I don't understand.'

'Only one of us can survive and it's not going to be you.'

'Why?'

'Sorry, no time for explanations. Things to do, people to see, places to go. You know how it is.'

He looked at her again. 'Perhaps you don't.'

'Stephen, please.'

'Have it your way. You obviously want an explanation and, despite the fact I am on a very tight schedule, I will, unlike last night, give you one. I suppose it's the least I can do. They say confession is good for the soul and therefore the next few minutes will be very good for mine. Not that I'll have much of a soul left after tonight.'

He sat down.

'OK, here goes, confession time. For forty years the name Montreau has been a curse. I would never have guessed it would haunt me for so long. Look at me, even now I'm wearing the clothes of the one person I've truly despised and hated. Even now, I'm looking into the eyes of his daughter, who I screwed every which way two nights ago. As a wise man once said, it's a funny old world, innit?'

'Wise man?'

'Phil Collins, Philadelphia, July 1985. However, I've only myself to blame. I should have kept a much closer eye on Montreau that Friday evening. I knew he'd taken the red book, but I didn't know where he'd hidden it, until today. For forty years I tried everything to get Malherbe to tell me where the book and the sheets of paper were. I was convinced they must be together somewhere. For once in my life, I was wrong, but I did get one thing right. As soon as Jean-Marie exited Malherbe's office and L'Académie that Friday night, I contacted the person you call Jacques. The person I know to be Alain Saint-Maxim.'

'All this time you've known who Jacques was?'

'Of course.'

'You said you'd never seen him before.'

'I hadn't, our only contact before tonight was via the telephone.'

'Who is he?'

'Director-General of the *DGSI*, the biggest of France's Intelligence Services' big cheeses.'

'My God. Eric was correct.'

'Good for him.'

'And you? You were the L'Académie mole who betrayed my father?'

'L'Académie's answer to Bill Haydon? That's unfair. Unlike dear old Bill I was working in the interests of my country - albeit adopted - not against them.'

'Unfair? You betrayed my father, Patrice, and God knows who else.'

'French national interest and, much more importantly, the honour of L'Académie, were at stake. Without HIV, L'Académie was finished. The Yank vultures were circling. For no other reason than his own pathetic theories about AIDS, your father was prepared to defecate from the top of the Eiffel Tower onto L'Académie, and his own colleagues who were working fifteen-hour days. Jean-Marie was no martyr, just a sore loser who couldn't accept defeat; a dead weight holding L'Académie and scientific progress back.'

'And then, all thanks to you, he was just dead.'

'All thanks to Saint-Maxim, you mean. In this Darwinian world only the most adaptable survive. Jean-Marie refused to adapt to the new reality, ergo he couldn't survive.'

'You were the most adaptable beast in the jungle, the greatest survivor of them all.'

'Darwin wouldn't disagree and who am I to argue with good old Charles? Whilst Montreau's career crashed and burned spectacularly, my own rose like a meteor. In three glorious years I was transformed from obscure, back-stage, tenured researcher, to unit head, then professor. Invitations to conferences, new facilities, research grants, new post-docs, prizes and honours flowed in. Talk about aggrandizement; the sky was no limit, I could also see the stars, infinite like my ego. Your father's meddling put all that into jeopardy. He refused to conform, see sense, succumb to financial inducements, or accept a transfer to sunnier climes; therefore, he had to go.'

'All so logical.'

'Hence my nickname.'

'You put Saint-Maxim onto my father in April 1984.'

'Correct.'

'Why then?'

'In April 1984 it was purely business. Jean-Marie had set up his pathetic *AIDS Truth Group* in response to the false announcement from the Yanks that they had discovered its cause. As I told Alain, your father was hell bent on destroying everything that we in the Submarine, the epicentre and pinnacle of French scientific progress, were trying to achieve.'

'And before April 1984?'

Chapter Sixty-Seven

'Before April 1984, it was personal. Extremely.'

He saw her uncomprehending eyes.

'Your father killed my wife, my first wife. Not directly or deliberately maybe, but as good as. I took her to see him in the early spring of 1981 on the recommendation of someone whose judgement I respected. She'd had a blood transfusion after a late-term miscarriage in the summer of 1980 and had been feeling unwell for months. I say unwell, she'd been seriously sick with fatigue, fevers, diarrhoea, weight loss and bloody awful night sweats. Montreau told us there were any number of explanations as to why she was feeling rough, but that it looked to him an awful lot like a cytomegalovirus, aka CMV, infection. CMV was his specialism.'

'I've watched something about CMV recently.'

'Harmless most of the time but, in the wrong circumstances, deadly. As many kidney transplant patients, and all of the first AIDS patients, found out.'

'Oh yes, that's it, it was mentioned in *Killer in the Village*.'

'Probably. Well, if CMV was his specialism, I would have hated to see him trying to get to grips with stuff he didn't know much about. He recommended that she go to Salpêtrière, as it had some of the best doctors in France. They would sort her out, but he insisted there was no rush, no need to panic. A month later she was on a ventilator. Another week, she was in a deep coma. A week after that, she was dead. I don't know about your father's wicked sense of humour, but he was certainly wicked.'

'My God. I'm sorry.'

'Sorry? Is that all you can say? I was sorry too when I gave my consent to her life support machine being switched off. Imagine having to feel, as I have done for forty-six years, that you've killed the love of your life. Imagine carrying all that guilt and shame around with you every single day. All of it down to that bloody useless father of yours who immediately scuttled off to America. Then, after he came crawling back, he had the brass neck to tell Malherbe and the rest of us that our AIDS research was a stinking heap of merde. What a shyster! Now you understand why I was so desperate to get a job at L'Académie. It meant I could keep a very close eye on Jean-Marie Montreau and if ever opportunity knocked to do him a bad turn, I was Johnny-on-the-spot.'

'What about your wife?'

'Which one?'

'Your second one.'

'What about her?'

'How much did, does, she know about any of this?'

'Nothing. She brought up Stephanie and the boys, managed the house and looked after the dinner parties.'

'Stephanie?'

'My daughter.'

'You never mentioned her.'

'Didn't I?'

'No, you didn't. How old is she?'

'Five years older than the boys.'

'Don't you see her when you see the twins?'

'I haven't seen her in, what, half a dozen years.'

'Why not?'

His phone buzzed.

'Béatrice!'

'Dream on. She should have shuffled off her mortal coil hours ago.'

'What?'

'You mean you haven't twigged that either, even now?'

'Twigged what?'

'Béatrice was my useful idiot. I promoted her for a reason, two, actually, neither of which had anything to do with her scientific ability. One, so I could screw her as often as I liked to, which I liked to, a lot. Two, very much more importantly, I used her to keep extremely close tabs on you. That's how I first got wind you'd been transformed after forty years of living like someone in a vegetative state, into a woman on a mission. Poor Béatrice was caught in a terrible bind. Either betray her best friend or say no to the Director with whom she was infatuated, and upon whom her very well-paid job and future career depended. Expensive presents, like that Swiss watch she loves, sorry, loved, to flaunt so much, didn't harm the cause either. Even so, I still felt it prudent to send her to Lille on Wednesday as an insurance policy; just in case she was tempted to do a Hérault, or a Malherbe.'

With this revelation, Anne-Sophie's head started spinning. That week, all the time she was telling Béatrice what was going on, her friend had been passing the information directly and immediately onto her *cinq à sept*. That explained Béatrice's mysterious, 'nothing much happened' weekends; the sudden, last-minute, rearranging of arrangements; her wearing of a cardigan in a very warm kitchen, in order, as Anne-Sophie now knew with certainty, to cover up bruises inflicted by this animal; the fearful look in her eyes when receiving a text; the setting off in the wrong direction after their birthday meal; Françoise and Emil's cryptic comments in Au Jean Bart about levers and ladders; Béatrice's angry response when she realized Anne-Sophie and Stonehouse had slept together. Poor, poor Béatrice.

'She's dead?'

'Should be.'

'Because of you?'

'Yes.'

'You were the someone she wanted to talk to me about. She wasn't angry with me, she was worried about me. She wanted to warn me, about you.' She leapt at him, 'You evil monster!' He shoved her back onto the sofa.

'I had no choice. Once you told me she knew about the two of us I had to act. Fortunately, the *DGSI* has a long reach, even as far as the intensive care unit of Salpêtrière, as its predecessor demonstrated in August 1997, and even if its Director General is currently being grilled by the sensationally sexy Faust.'

'The *DGSI* has killed her?'

'I bloody well hope so! They've had the best part of two days, and surely even the French, in this Communist democracy of theirs, can't be that inefficient. There was enough sodium thiopental, pancuronium bromide and potassium chloride left over from yesterday to do the remaining two jobs.'

'Two?'

'You two come as a pair. Can't have one without the other. As I've proved this week.'

'I was your other useful idiot?'

'Of course. Another very useful idiot. Another very screwable, useful idiot too. Especially after a couple of glasses of *Dancing Queen*, which was unsurprisingly so much classier than the sanitized Swedish pop pap it was named after. OK, I will concede, you're not as good as the try-anything-in-the-sack-once Béatrice, but it does a man good to ring the changes. Keeps the interest, and everything else, up.'

'You sick psycho.'

He slapped her hard. Twice. 'You should show a little more gratitude.'

'What do you mean?'

'You've had an extra day on the planet thanks to me.'

'I don't understand.'

'Well, there's a shock. Did it not once cross your tiny brain to question why you'd been given special, last-minute, treatment in Saint-Germain?'

'Of course, but I was too busy trying to find the needle and haystack.'

'And leading me to both, thanks very much. It was me who contacted Alain and obtained your release. You weren't meant to be there at all, but twice I stupidly forgot to send the text which would have called off the attack dogs yesterday morning. Obtaining your release was all very last-minute dot com and caused me no end of hassle and aggro. However, it gave me a double win. Béatrice was removed from the picture and you, as I hoped and anticipated, finally led me to the red book. Securing the smoking gun has been a massive bonus, the cherry on the icing on my cake. As my mother used to drum into me, ''there's no such thing as wasted work, Stephen''. If it's any consolation, after you're long gone, you can rest assured that I will be forever grateful for your invaluable assistance in helping me to tie up these forty-year-old loose ends. In fact, I give you my word of honour that I will drink a toast proclaiming my undying gratitude to you every April 2nd.'

She felt sick. It was as if she had never heard of due diligence.

He looked at the clock.

'Time is running out; I'd better get moving. In the words of the Scottish play, '*If it were done when 'tis done, then 'twere well it were done quickly.*' It's a shame, it really is. I would have gladly sailed off into the Med sunset with you this summer, had my wicked way with you again and again, and afterwards let you live your life in peace. All would have been well. However...'

'However?'

'That all changed tonight.'

'Why? How?'

'God almighty! It's a recurring theme with you, isn't it? I find it hard to believe none of your teachers wrote 'must think harder' on your reports. I'll try to explain it in words of fewer than two syllables. Up until this evening I knew all about Alain Saint-Maxim and Hervé Parcelle and I really do mean *all* about them, especially after last night's photos and videos of Parcelle and his latest floozy. And, as has been said for centuries, all knowledge is power.'

'Knowledge itself is power.'

'Sorry?'

'Francis Bacon.'

'Really? Anyhow, I knew that, for both of them, dealing with your father was also as much personal, as it was business. It's OK, I know you don't understand, so I'll explain. Parcelle never forgot it was your father who cost him the election to the Rotary Club's Executive Committee in 1977.'

'And Saint-Maxim?'

'Apparently Jean-Marie stole his girlfriend three years later.'

'My God.'

'When you boil it down, all three of us were motivated by personal hatred of Montreau and a deep-seated desire to take revenge. So what? In my book, revenge is as good a motive as any. Don't you agree?'

'Yes.'

'Good. Now, where was I? Oh yes, I knew all about the other two protagonists, but they knew nothing about me. Not until tonight and not until you insisted upon scrubbing up and sticking on the *Elsa Peretti* jewellery that I helped Béatrice choose in Geneva.'

'I...'

'Don't understand? I know you don't. Think about it. Why do you think I was reluctant to say yes to you coming to the Ritz? Why do you think I delayed our entry an hour by coming here first? Even if that detour did help me in another respect, which I'll come to very shortly. Why do you think I was so keen to get away at the earliest possible opportunity?'

Chapter Sixty-Eight

He looked at her blank expression.

'My God. Talk about going from hero to zero. In the space of thirty minutes, you've gone from useful idiot to just plain idiot. Let me explain. For forty years I kept my identity hidden from Parcelle and Saint-Maxim. How they didn't work it out I have no idea. I know Saint-Maxim isn't the sharpest tool in the box, as his hare-brained scheme to have us abducted from L'Académie, and the débâcle at Pont Saint-Michel this evening, proved. Still, even his lack of wit must have a limit.

'On the other hand, I knew from the moment you made your fatal suggestion to go to the Ritz, there was an excellent chance that, immediately I walked into the Salon with you by my side, the penny would drop with Parcelle. He is a very sharp tool, possibly the sharpest in France. In many ways, if you take out his role in a four-decade long murder conspiracy, the serial adultery, his anti-LGBTQ+ agenda and the offshore twenty-five million Euros acquired from the meanest gang of criminals in the capital, it's a tragedy for France he may not become her President. Anyway, I was correct in my assumption. You were spot on when you said he couldn't stop looking at me. I could see the wheels turning inside his brain. Once Saint-Maxim arrived, the game was up. Whilst you were making yourself intimately acquainted with Consolotto's shoulder, Alain came across, shook my hand and greeted me with, "Our mutual friend, I presume." Trust a Frenchman to get his Victorian Brits jumbled up. Their arrest, together with that of Roulet, whilst welcome in many respects, means I am in very choppy, very dark and very deep waters.'

'Why?'

'I've no doubt that, right now, Parcelle and Saint-Maxim, will be pinning all the blame on me to Faust, and with good reason. As you now know, it was me who gave your father's name to Alain in the first place. Me, who told Alain the red book had gone missing. Me, who said your father was on the verge of blowing apart a multi-million-franc international agreement due to be signed in just four days' time. Me, who recommended your father's killers, Richard Casquet and Camille Desmoullers, to Alain. Me, who tracked your father to and from L'Académie like a ravenous bloodhound that whole bloody tedious weekend. Me, who told Saint-Maxim to recruit Parcelle by dangling the carrot of a fast-track up the legal and political ladders. Me, who kept the person at the apex of America's public health institutions up to speed with the latest developments. The same person who will be saving my bacon, Francis or otherwise, in the next hour.

The only thing none of them knew about is the one piece of physical evidence connecting me with your father and his death, the smoking gun. Now, thanks to Malherbe's denouement and your imminent appointment with your maker, no-one will ever know about it.'

He again glanced at the clock. 'OK, time to rock'n'roll, as Bach never said.'

He tossed the sheets of paper onto the floor and produced a Beretta M9 out of her father's tuxedo inner pocket.

'Half an hour ago, you had an opportunity to attempt an escape. However, you were so entranced by the thought of a romantic summer holiday in the Med you sat straight back down again. Foolish girl. Béatrice would not have made that mistake, besotted as she is; was, I mean, ha ha.'

Pointing the pistol towards her forehead, he placed a L'Académie satchel bag in front of her. 'Open it up, that's it. Take out the tape and scissors. No, don't even think about any funny business. Cut two strips; put one strip over your mouth. Good. Pass the second strip to me. Now turn around. Put your hands behind your back. That's it. Very good.'

He wrapped the tape tightly around her wrists. 'Turn back around. Good girl, well done on obeying orders. I do love a compliant woman, it's extremely sexy. Shame we didn't get to the bondage stage but there's only so much you can do in one night. C'est la vie.'

Still pointing the pistol at her head, he dragged her into the kitchen and commanded her to sit down. 'So, all in all, you've only got yourself to blame. By forcing me to take you to the Ritz you effectively signed your own death warrant. That must be a bitter pill to swallow for you. If you could swallow at this moment that is, which you can't. Right, what's next. Oh yes. I told you I'd made good use of the cufflink detour. To paraphrase Valerie Singleton, here's one I prepared earlier.'

He took a hypodermic syringe out of the kitchen's massive American fridge freezer and placed it carefully on the marble dining table. 'If it's any consolation which, on reflection and in the circumstances, it probably won't be, I can't dispose of your body like I did your father's. To give them their due, Alain and the boys got Jean-Marie to L'Académie really bloody rapidement. He was put through the Submarine mincer quicker than you could say HIV. You know that grave you've been dutifully attending for the past forty-years? It's emptier than Parcelle's Cook Island bank account, ha ha. I've no idea if a body was placed inside the coffin, but if one was, it categorically wasn't your precious father's. His was all fed to the guard dogs. Rest assured they didn't leave a morsel. My revenge was complete, as well as sweet. Very, very sweet. Now, stand up!'

Her refusal to budge was rewarded with another slap, which fortunately hardly registered, she was feeling so numb.

'As I need to speed things up, I'm giving you a double dose of sodium thiopental. As long as you don't struggle, it'll be over very quickly. Struggling will only prolong your agony.'

She clenched her fists tightly. To think, just four days ago her biggest source of anxiety was going on a birthday date with a really sweet, empathetic bloke. Stonehouse wasn't wrong; she was a useless idiot. Totally useless.

A moment of silence was shattered by a ringtone, the climax of the Prélude to Bach's 'Cello Suite No. 1 in G Major'. Anne-Sophie started. She had heard the music recently, but she could not recall when.

Without lowering his pistol, Stonehouse answered his phone.

'TM! I'm sorry about the horror show at the Ritz. Thanks, that's very magnanimous of you. Yes, in the words of Basil Fawlty, I'm doing it now. The limousine? Very good. Is there room for a body in the boot? Excellent. What? Someone will come up and collect it? Even better. Is my diplomatic clearance ready? Superb. Great, I'm almost good to go. I'll be at Charles De Gaule in an hour. I'll call the limo when I'm done with her. Bye.'

He grinned at her.

'Recognize the Bach? You should do. It nearly upset the apple cart on Monday night. Anyway, I'm very pleased to report that it looks like my bacon is going to be well and truly saved.'

Stretching for the syringe, he relaxed his grip on her ever so slightly. This was her last chance. She struggled to her feet and head-butted him flush on the nose. Whilst he sank to his knees and copious amounts of blood started flowing into his mouth, she saw a Stanley knife beside the toaster. Somehow, she managed to manoeuvre it so that she sliced through the tape on her wrists. After that it was a relatively straight-forward matter to rip the tape off her mouth. It hurt, but she'd had far more painful electrolysis, *'Damn!'* Stonehouse was back on his feet. Now he had the syringe in his right hand and the pistol in his left.

'Where were we before you rudely interrupted me? Oh yes, I was about to kill you.' He advanced towards her. 'Get down on your knees. That's it, well done, again. Shame it's a very different scenario to Wednesday night. That's one thing I will miss about you, one area where you scored higher than Béatrice. You have a very naughty mouth. Never mind. Plenty more fish in the sea.'

'Is that what you said when your wife stopped you from seeing Stephanie?'

He slapped her again.

'Was that the reason for your marriage break-up? Molesting your own daughter. You pig.'

'Ah, so you are capable of putting two and two together after all. Better late than never, I suppose. However, now, for you, it really is too late. You'll never get to meet my second wife, Stephanie, the boys or, in fact, anyone else, ever again. Mine will be the last face you'll see. How lovely for you.'

He placed the Beretta M9 against her temple, grabbed her arm and pointed the needle towards it. Then he snarled at his smart speaker,

'Play Bach. Very loudly. Good, that's better. No one can hear your whining now. Advantage, Stonehouse.'

Chapter Sixty-Nine

With the syringe less than a centimetre away from Anne-Sophie's skin, multiple random thoughts flashed through her brain. She thought of the suffering inflicted upon Béatrice and Stephanie. She thought of Philippe and Eric, of the help they had given her, and would have given her this week, and in the future. She thought of Hérault, the villain turned hero who had sacrificed his life for her and Philippe. She thought of Malherbe's letter and the smoking gun. She thought of Philippe's 'others', the millions affected by what her father obviously believed was a huge medical-science scandal, conspiracy and cover up. She thought of Patrice and his dead loved ones. She thought of her father, who, until less than five days ago, she had spent her whole life rejecting. The father she now loved more than her words could ever express. She thought of Parcelle, Roulet, Saint-Maxim and the maniac who was poised to extinguish her life. She thought of their absolute power and their absolute corruption. She thought about the identity of the mysterious TM who had contacted Stonehouse just as he had been on the cusp of delivering the coup de grâce.

However, more important than all of those other thoughts combined, was the final one. She thought of the self-defence lessons her mother had bought her as an eighteenth-birthday present, as another form of protection. A thought which impelled her to get to her feet, twist her body and launch a swift, powerful kick directly into Stonehouse's groin. As he sank in agony to his knees, she kicked him in the mouth, compelling him to drop the pistol and the syringe. In less than a second, the pistol was touching the side of a whimpering Stonehouse's head, and the tip of the syringe was scraping his neck.

'Game, set and match, Montreau. Tell me I'm wrong but I've got a funny feeling you're now regretting calling me a useless idiot, lying to me, using me and Béatrice for your sexual gratification, and slapping me half-a-dozen times in the last thirty minutes.'

This was it. Her moment of ultimate revenge for her parents, allies and the others. Revenge for Stephanie and Béatrice. Her Béatrice. Anne-Sophie was calm, as calm as she had been the whole week, her entire life. She had never felt such peace, such contentment. Justice would never feel, or ever be, so poetic. She was set to deliver the coup de grâce but then noticed the papers lying at Stonehouse's fingertips and stopped.

'Pick the sheets up. Pass them to me. Good. Now keep still. Very still.'

She rested the sheets on the back of Stonehouse's head and read them.

'Friday March 27th,
Laboratoire de Retrovirologie Moleculaire, L'Académie
Confidential
Dear Louis.

We have, as Churchill would have described it, a gathering storm.

First, the bad news. Recently, you asked me to analyse archival samples established here at L'Académie in January 1983 and in Bicchiere's lab in September that same year, to settle once and for all the true provenance of the virus now known as HIV-1. These analyses have shown that a viral contamination of virus 'LAV BRU' (renamed HIV-1 in 1986) by virus 'IDAV LAI' occurred on August 3rd, 1983. The contaminated LAV BRU/LAI culture ('M2T-/B') was sent to Bethesda in September 1983. It was relabelled in April 1984 by Bicchiere as 'HTLV-IIIB', and passed off by him and the American government as his own discovery. Bicchiere alleged that 'M2T-/B' was mixed with nine other samples in a pooled experiment, but our tests show that none of the ten samples in the pool look remotely like 'M2T-/B', or 'HTLV-IIIB'. Those tests conclude that the origin of 'HIV-1' is virus 'LAI'.

Second, the even worse news. Further analysis indicates that, as well the viral BRU/LAI contamination, there was also a prior bacterial contamination of LAI caused by the undetected presence of mycoplasma. As we know only too well, mycoplasmas can produce a virtually unlimited variety of effects in the cultures they infect and, in the worst cases, all experiments might be influenced by the infections and artefacts that are produced. I believe that this contamination totally transformed the BRU virus culture, made it highly infectious, a different pathogen entirely.

Of course, anyone with half a scientific brain could have worked all this out four years ago. Unfortunately, you have not been blessed with even that and you were too busy pressing ahead with landing the 'Big Fish', the Nobel Prize, to give your attention to what was going on at the coal face. Like Bicchiere, you were gripped by Stockholm fever, and nothing could loosen it.

The original 'LAV BRU' virus, discovered January 1983, could only be kept alive by numerous infusions of, and reinfections with, fresh blood from a Spanish tourist of unknown provenance, and umbilical cord tissue obtained from a maternity hospital. This retrovirus produced barely a ripple of reverse transcriptase activity and could not be grown in different T-cell lines, no matter what was tried.

Suddenly, in the second half of the year, 'LAV BRU' was producing huge amounts of reverse transcriptase activity, could be grown in T and B cell lines, and was being used to produce AIDS testing kits in large quantities. It was bloody obvious either this was a different virus, or contamination had occurred, or both.

We knew right from the onset that the unusual virulence of the LAI virus marked it out as different to BRU. Straight away, unlike BRU, LAI generated large amounts of reverse transcriptase, it grew very well immediately, we had ten litres of LAI-origin fluid by the end of August 1983, and, as a result, we were able to get the Western Blots and ELISAs.

We speculated whether LAI possessed some important genetic difference to BRU, now we know the difference was caused by the mycoplasma contamination. The reference strains of HIV-1 used by virtually every AIDS research laboratory on the globe are derived from the double contaminant 'M2T-/B'. If good scientific practice is followed, then they, and all AIDS blood test kits, should be destroyed immediately, and all AIDS virus research declared null and void.

Third, the worse news of all – there is no back-up plan. Bicchiere, despite his claims of having a hundred isolates, *actually has precisely zero. As for L'Académie, 'LAV BRU was a dud, the 'seminal' 1983 BRU paper can be thrown into the nearest bin, and we haven't got anything remotely like LAI in our locker.*

What's to be done? If any of this emerges then our enemies across the Atlantic will have a field day. They will quite rightly ask whether L'Académie would have been more gainfully employed these past three years testing its own materials and cleaning out its own stables, instead of self-righteously accusing Bethesda of jiggery-pokery. If this comes out before Tuesday, you can bet your bottom franc that even the pathetic surrender agreement will be whisked off the table quicker than you can say merde. You can also rest assured that if our enemy within, the traitor Montreau, gets his hands on this information, he will stop at nothing to ensure it is widely propagated. It goes without saying this cannot happen.'

In a call late last night TM told me his one-hundred-percent focus is on presenting HIV-1 as public enemy number one. There cannot be any more distractions. However, Montreau's obsession about the cause of AIDS has been and continues to be a huge distraction. TM ended the call by telling me that, as there is no knowing what stunt Montreau might try to pull, the problem must be resolved before the agreement is signed in Washington next week. In his words, 'HIV heresy must be crushed.'

As we know, Montreau has been right all along about the origin of AIDS. AIDS is an infectious disease syndrome which is the product of immune system overload, with multiple contributory factors, very similar to the syndromes suffered by transplant patients for a decade or more. If Montreau gets his hands on these test results, we will be in the deepest shit imaginable. By 'we', I mean scientists, public health officials, the pharmaceutical companies, the media and the politicians. Major federal budget allocations, AIDS public health policies, media amplification of fear, catastrophic predictions of heterosexual transmission of the disease, prophecies of a worldwide pandemic, doom-laden adverts, CDC and WHO statistical reports, the zealotry of gay activist groups such as ACTUP, are all driven by the dogma that AIDS is a new contagious disease, caused by a new and deadly virus, transmitted within the general

289

population by sexual intercourse and contaminated blood products. All the people who convinced the public of this will be, to put it bluntly, screwed.

More pertinently, this laboratory, and many other scientific research institutions around the globe, including the NIH, CDC and Chesterfield Laboratories, will most likely be shut down. TM has already been warned by the Office of the Secretary of Health and Social Services that, if the truth emerges, the public will start asking some very serious questions, such as: 'If this isn't the AIDS virus, how do we know the blood supply is safe?' 'How do we know anything about transmission?' 'How could you all be so stupid?' 'Why should we ever believe you again?' 'Isn't it high time the swamp was cleaned?' 'Shouldn't Montreau be put in charge of AIDS research globally?'

The public will be seeking blood, contaminated or not, and, frankly, it is not beyond the realms of possibility that some of the most famous scientific researchers in the world, including yourself, could end up on trial and put, eventually, behind bars. The press boys will be writing endless articles, no doubt wittily concluding, without any hint of irony, that it is incredible what contamination can do to a culture.

As I said, a storm is gathering. To avert it, Louis, for seven more days, or at least until the agreement is signed and sealed, you must keep off the booze and keep your precious red book under lock and key. It must be kept well away from the prying eyes and hands of Montreau, and his negro collaborator. If you can manage that then, by the time you return from Washington, the Montreau problem will be dead and buried. Or, more accurately, swallowed by the dogs patrolling L'Académie's compound.

Enjoy your trip!

SS.'

A stunned Anne-Sophie laid down the papers and breathed deeply. At last, she understood everything. Why her father had been killed and why it had happened that Sunday. Why Eric, Philippe, Henri and Malherbe had been killed. Why Béatrice had been killed. Why she had almost been killed. Patrice was right, because her father knew with absolute certainty that the 'HIV causes AIDS' orthodoxy was a house of cards instigated by a double incidence of contamination in Paris and theft by the Americans, he had been a massive threat to the multi-billion dollar, pan-global, 'HIV causes AIDS' industry. A threat that had to be removed. A life that had to be extinguished. Without compunction.

Now Stonehouse's life was to be taken without compunction. An eye for an eye, no question. The only question left for her to answer was which weapon she would use to provide the killer blow, the pistol, or the syringe. Just as Stonehouse whispered a barely audible apology, the decision was abruptly taken out of her hands. With no warning, she was bumped into from behind, another pair of hands was placed on top of hers, and she jerked forward. Involuntarily, the pistol discharged God knows how many rounds into Stonehouse's sweating temple. Simultaneously, the syringe embedded itself deep into his throbbing carotid artery. For a second everything went red.

'My God, what's happened?'

Anne-Sophie dropped the weapons, spun around and hugged her best friend more tightly than she had ever hugged anyone in her entire life. Then she walked into the kitchen and wiped Stonehouse's blood and brains off her face with an expensive-feeling tea towel. She returned to the lounge, handed Béatrice an equally expensive-feeling, tea towel and then hugged her again, even tighter.

'He told me you were dead.'

'He absolutely is.'

'How did you get here?'

'Give me a second.' Béatrice turned her head. 'Play Bach quietly, please.' She turned back to Anne-Sophie. 'That's better, I can hear myself think. I've had enough of that particular composer to last me a lifetime.'

'So, you're not into classical music after all?'

'A little bit, but definitely not Bach. Not now. Not ever.'

'Tell me what happened at the hospital.'

'A miracle!'

'What?'

'I woke up about two hours ago and told the doctors I felt one hundred per cent OK. Of course, they didn't believe me, but once they'd run their tests and could find no reason to keep me in, I was free to go. I came straight here to collect as much of my stuff as I could and take it to my apartment. When no one answered the buzzer, presumably because no one could hear it, I used my keys to get in and, voila! I found you poised to execute my boss and ex-lover.'

'Ex?'

'I take it there's a reason why you wanted to kill him?'

'Many.'

'One of them is probably the same reason why I wanted to get out of his apartment and the relationship.'

'He was the somebody, and your relationship with him was the something, that you said you wanted to talk to me about yesterday?'

'Yes.'

Anne-Sophie kissed her friend's clean forehead and then stepped back. 'I'm sorry at this particular moment to take a leaf out of your book and be so practical but I'm in desperate need of a phone charger. You haven't got one by any chance, have you?'

Béatrice rummaged in her bag, 'Several, take this.'

Whilst Anne-Sophie waited for her phone's resurrection, she made a pot of coffee but her desire for a croissant was frustrated by their complete absence in the cupboards, or the fridge freezer.

'Typical Rosbif.'

She brought the coffee to the table and sat down. She put her arm around Béatrice, and the tension seemed to flow out of her friend's body.

'Thanks for the coffee, and the arm. Now, what the hell are we going to do?'

'What do you mean?'

'What are we going to do about our problem? Him. What do we say to the police about him?'

'I'm not sure I get you, sorry.'

'How do we explain what happened?'

'I'll tell the truth.'

'But we'll ...'

'I'll tell the truth.'

'But..'

'That's it. The whole truth and nothing but the truth.'

'But..'

292

'I've spent five days unravelling a forty-year lie. I can't suddenly turn around and start lying myself.'

'Anne-Sophie-'

'As soon as my phone has sufficient charge, I will call the Deputy Prefect of Paris.'

'But..'

'One thing.'

'Yes?'

'Leave me to do the talking.'

'But..'

'All of it. Understand?'

'Yes.'

'Promise?'

'Yes, I promise.'

'Good.'

As soon as her phone was sufficiently charged, Anne-Sophie called Faust. 'Angela. You need to come to 125, Rue Dutot, first floor, *Le Creuset*. There's been a domestic incident. One fatality. You'll need to bring a crime scene investigation team. Preferably not a *Brigade* unit, real or fake. Also, and this *is* urgent, there is a plane heading for the States which is due to fly out from Charles de Gaule in the next hour. It could be a private jet, charter job. Stonehouse *was* meant to be on the flight, but he is no longer capable of travelling. Or doing anything, really. However, the man ultimately responsible for my father's killing will be on that flight; you must either prevent him from getting on it or prevent it from taking off. That man was also at the Ritz tonight. Got all that? Good. OK, see you soon.'

Anne-Sophie walked across the lounge, carefully picked up the sheets of paper splattered with Stonehouse's blood and brain matter and sat back down beside her friend. They put their arms around each other and read the sheets together.

'I think that's what a jury would call admissible evidence, Ms Lapain.'

'I agree, Ms Montreau.'

They embraced again for what seemed to both of them to be a long time. So close did they feel to each other that not even the sound of the apartment's buzzer spoiled the moment.

Béatrice gripped Anne-Sophie's hand and looked at her. 'I'm so sorry for what I did to you. To your mother. To everyone. This is all my fault.'

'Hardly. I'm sorry for what I did to you in respect of Stonehouse, even if I had no clue I was doing it.'

'No.'

'However, none of that matters now.'

'Really?'

'It's over.'

'Sure?'

'Absolutely. I blame myself. I should have seen the signs earlier; much, much earlier. Would have done if I hadn't been so blinded by self-pity and self-obsession. Looking back, it was so bloody obvious. As bloody as those sheets of paper.'

'Everything's obvious with the benefit of hindsight, isn't it?'

'It is.'

'I have a question.'

'Fire away.'

'If I hadn't jumped on your back, would you have killed him?'

Anne-Sophie looked at her. 'What do you think?'

Before Béatrice could respond, Faust, accompanied by a dozen officers entered the apartment. They were followed by Patrice who looked down at what was left of Stonehouse's head.

'Good riddance to bad rubbish.'

'You really didn't like him, did you?'

'No, I really didn't.'

'Why?'

'Your father always told me Stonehouse was a two-faced weasel who had lied to everyone about his wife's death in 1981. He was Malherbe's puppet master, the rat who engineered my departure from L'Académie and brought about the death of my wife and child.'

'You might have told me sooner.'

'You seemed very wrapped up in him. I'm not sure you would have listened.'

'What about you, Angela? Were you aware Stonehouse was a dangerous psychopath? You certainly stared at him a lot.'

'When I first saw him on Wednesday evening, I knew I recognized him from somewhere, but, until two hours ago, I could not remember where. Then in a flash, it came to me. He was on an American sex offenders' database; a consequence of crimes committed against his daughter.'

'Against Stephanie? What crimes?'

'He was accused of pimping Stephanie out to a paedophile ring.'

'Convicted?'

'No but placed on the database nonetheless.'

Anne-Sophie gripped Béatrice's hand. 'No-one at L'Académie knew?'

'No, his offences were committed in New York. The Americans did not need to share that information with his employer. Aside from us, no one on this side of the Atlantic knew about, or had access to, the database.'

'Ironic, considering he always bad-mouthed the 'Yanks'.'

Faust sat down opposite Anne-Sophie and Béatrice. She looked at them and then Stonehouse's body. 'What happened?'

Béatrice opened her mouth, but Anne-Sophie gently nudged her, then looked directly at Faust. 'Before I answer, I have a question for you.'

'I'm not sure that's quite how it works but go on.'

'Why didn't you stop my cyber-attacks against Parcelle et al?'

'What do you mean?'

'You knew what I was doing. I assume you could have stopped me at any time, but you didn't. Why?'

'Why do you think?'

'Because you were onto Parcelle and were more than happy to let me do your dirty work. I was your useful idiot, your human and cyber shield.'

'You tell me what happened here.'

'Stonehouse was going to kill me, using either the pistol, the syringe, or both. I turned things around and beat him to the punch. Well, to the syringe and pistol. He was hoisted with his own petards.'

'*You* killed him?'

'Yes.'

Faust looked at Béatrice and then at Anne-Sophie. 'One hundred per cent *you*?'

'As a very evil man said earlier this evening, abso-bloody-lutely.'

'I'm going to have to arrest you.'

'Of course. There will be no cover-up, not this time.'

'Sure?'

'I'm not sure that's how it works but, yes, I'm sure.'

Anne-Sophie stood up, embraced Béatrice tightly and then did the same to Patrice. She held out her hands to the Deputy Prefect. 'This is where you cuff me and take me in.'

Faust looked at her and smiled faintly, 'That's definitely not how it works.'

After instructing Béatrice to take excellent care of Patrice, Anne-Sophie handed Faust a very crumpled piece of paper, several sheets of bloody paper, and a phone. 'These are for you.'

'What are they?'

'Your smoking guns. My defence.'

'The phone?'

'Stonehouse's. Make sure you redial the last received call ASAP. You might hear an airport announcer in the background.'

Faust passed it to one of the officers.

'Do it.'

She turned back to Anne-Sophie, 'Are you ready?'

Anne-Sophie looked at Béatrice. 'No, but I have no choice.'

Faust led Anne-Sophie out of the apartment block and then stopped. 'Goodness me. Incredible.'

'What?'

'It's finally stopped raining.'

'Wonders will never cease.'

Anne-Sophie had turned round to look back inside the block. Faust looked at her, 'You're not ready, are you. What is it, the twenty-five million Euros?'

'Ha, I knew I was right about you! No, it's not about that. Please can you give me a minute?'

'Of course. Take your time.'

She ran up the stairs and found her oldest and best friend, in tears, standing at the door. They embraced, kissed tenderly, then said in unison.

'I've just realised something.'

'Me too.'